An Olive Branch for Sante

Antonio Casella

Yellow Teapot Books
AUSTRALIA

Cover picture by kind permission of Spencer Woodard,
© Anthropogen Photos http://anthropogen.com

This novel was written with the assistance of a Murdoch University Research and Development grant. My grateful thanks to Murdoch University and to Professor Vijay Mishra for his very competent supervision. Many thanks also to Guido Bulla, Van Ikin, and Gaetano Rando for their kind comments, and to Rosanne Dingli, June Houston, and Libby Thompson for proof-reading the manuscript and giving me their valuable advice. An extract from this novel was published in the literary magazine *Westerly*. My thanks to *Westerly* editors Delys Bird and Dennis Haskell.

To June Houston

Casella's first novel was *Southfalia*. His body of work includes the novels *The Sensualist, Men and Fathers*, and *An Olive Branch for Sante*, and the plays *The Ghost of Rino Tassone*, and *To Catch a Bride*.

Research: *The Italian Diaspora in Australia, Exile and the Writer, Style in Patrick White's 'The Aunt's Story'*.

Also by Antonio Casella

Southfalia
The Sensualist
Man Fragmenting

Mention of Sicily stirred the waters of memory in Sara-Jane. Long submerged images rose to the surface like flotsam: Nonnu's unlaced boots, his knobbly knees beneath blue canvas shorts, Nonna's thin face with eye sockets like spectacle rims, a swing hanging from an olive tree, the shadowy outline of that other woman, the one with the wiry black hair and the terse face. These images threatened to hold her mind captive, so she pressed them down to the depths.

Never mind all that stuff now, memories are self-indulgent, a sign of weakness, a wasteful sentimentality. Memories, good or bad, can hold your life to ransom. The bad ones turn you into a victim, the good ones lead to a wasting disease called nostalgia. That is, life lived in the past, an illusion of living, life as a mirage. No thanks, not for her. Give her the present, any day.

To the present, then. The levigate touch of the bar of Dove inside her hand did the trick. She ran it over her breasts, let the water wash off the suds. She wanted to go on this assignment because it would be good for her career. That was it.

She didn't want to sound too keen though, or Bob Woldridge, Rattlesnake Bob, the editor of *Escapes*, would use it to get his way. Although, what else he might want from her she couldn't imagine, given that she was right now washing herself clean of body fluids, his and hers, while he snored off the effort with a snooze.

Draped in a white towel, Sara-Jane stepped on the bath mat from where she could see his back curled in a semi-foetal position.

'Bob.' She called through the bathroom door. 'It's

nearly two-thirty.'

'Shit!' He kicked off the sheets and gathered his things off the floor. He slipped on jocks, cupping his hand over the precious bulk of his manhood and let it drop into the bulging pouch.

'Aren't you going to have a wash?'

'No time. Anyhow, I like the smell of a woman on me. Gives me that extra charge.'

A woman. Not her in particular. Fine, it suited her. Sara-Jane: twenty-four year-old and ambitious, bedding her forty-three year-old married editor, a man carrying the sort of baggage that ensured he would not become one for her. She felt secure in knowing his demands would go no further than the four walls of a bedroom. And of course, there was more than one use for the bedroom. To glean useful information, for example.

'Why Sicily?'

"Cause the Boss has gone cuckoo in his old age, that's why. He is off to Sicily on some religious pilgrimage and wants a journalist to go with him to do a feature.'

'Could be interesting.'

'It's crap. *Escapes* is a travel magazine, not a rag for religious nuts.'

'Have you got someone in mind?'

'What do you mean?'

'To go to Sicily.'

'Not yet.'

'I speak Italian.'

'Yeah?'

It hardly registered. Despite the perfunctory response, his attention had drifted to his foot trying to find a way into a trouser leg. She allowed the conversation to ease to neutral chatter; watched him as he buttoned up his body shirt over his chest, on which hung a thick gold chain in a curly mat of salt-and-pepper body hair. She waited until they were in the car before she broached the subject again.

'I don't mind doing it.' She knew it would get his attention.

'What?'

'Go to Sicily.'

This time Bob looked straight at her. Although she tried to sound casual his ear sharpened at the intensity in her voice as she pronounced 'Sicily'. She could sense him waver between dismissal and acquiescence. It was all in the timing. She should have pursued it when he first mentioned it, as they left the office, then he would have been more amenable. Now her power was diminished, squirted out with the flow of his orgasm.

'Nah, we'll send a man.'

'Why a man?'

'Those Sicilians are notorious bum-pinchers. Hardly the sort of place for a young blonde.' He meant to sound protective, fatherly. It didn't quite come off, considering that, as he talked, his eyes massaged the contours of her breasts through her top.

As the car came to a stop at the lights he turned to her. 'That was good stuff.'

She waited for the inevitable smirk and patronising wink; instead, a serious change descended on his face. The bottom lip curled nervously, it reminded her of the British Prime Minister, Gordon Brown.

'How old are you, Janey?'

Janey was his term of endearment, but it had become a diminutive designed to keep her in her place. One day, when things changed between them … For now she let it pass. 'You know how old I am.'

'Twenty-five next birthday, right?'

She didn't bother confirming it. She was mad at him

for trying to make her seem older.

'The thing is, Janey, I need you here.'

'Nonsense, Rachael can do my job.'

He considered her with a side glance. His head, whose baldness was blurred by a number-two haircut, sank between his shoulders. His uncharacteristic nervousness she found disconcerting.

'I mean, I need you.'

She suppressed a nervous giggle. What was that about? They had an understanding, an arrangement that suited them both. He was married with two children – or was it three? Was he now thinking of a trade-in for a new model? If so, he could count her out.

'How are your kids?' She said the words dispassionately, and for good measure added, 'must be hard on your wife, bringing up kids when you're … so busy. Personally, I wouldn't want the responsibility.'

'They're not kids anymore. The oldest is nearly eighteen …' In the tunnel, he proceeded to tell her their marriage had no more spark left, how they had drifted apart, and other such phrases men used to justify leaving their wives.

Sara-Jane listened, allowing him the perfunctory 'hm…hm', even nodding agreement, to keep him sweet. But as the car came out of the tunnel, she had taken two decisions: she would go up and see Franzetti herself; and this would be the last time she would bed Bob. Pity about the latter, though. Bob had been good value, despite his propensity for admiring his own pectorals in the mirror. Pity he'd gone and spoilt it by going serious on her. This Bob she found decidedly unattractive. She much preferred Bob the bastard, the predator. At least there she felt safe knowing the limits. Now the situation threatened to move into a space she had no wish to enter.

Bob kept silent until the car pulled into the underground car park, but he must have been thinking hard, and now he wanted her to do likewise. 'You think about it, Sara. We have now been together … what? … three years? Just about. They've been good years. I'm ready to move up a notch, to something more substantial. We could make a good team, you and me. I can feel it. Think about it.'

'These underground car parks smell like a gas chamber.' She sprang open the car door, nearly hitting the new Lancer in the next bay. 'I need to go up for some fresh air.'

Exasperation made him churlish. 'What's this shit about Sicily, anyhow? Why would you want to go to a place like that?'

*

Before going up, Sara-Jane tied her blonde hair demurely on the back of her head, toned down her lipstick by wiping her lips with a Wet One, and closed the cleavage on her cross-over blouse by pinning the collar with a fake pearl brooch.

The oval shape of his real oak desk encased Clem Franzetti's long frame, which rose above the level of the desk, suggesting some unseen, iceberg-sized power below the surface. His face had the expression of someone eating a slice of lemon. Mr Franzetti was not your typical boss. There was no sure-fire confidence about him. He seemed a little tentative, ambivalent. Such ambivalence found expression in his physical delineations. He had a long nose, whose safety-pin nostrils flared like air pumps as he breathed, but his eyes were relatively small and close together, while his eyebrows arched across his forehead. His square chin jutted out, suggesting a pugnacious nature, but a dimple softened the impression. On the phone he had the booming voice of a heavily built man; in fact, he was thin and long-limbed, and his stomach slid inwards from his ribs.

Sara-Jane waited for permission to speak. He placed an elbow on the curved arm of his chair and the other hand over his wrist, then nodded, looking not at her, but at some shadow beyond her.

She feigned a decorous degree of nervousness. 'As you know, Mr Franzetti, next month is the anniversary of the death of Mary MacKillop.' It would please him that she should know such detail about Australia's only saint. 'What I had in mind ...' She brought out her portfolio of notes and sketches on a design for a feature.

Mr Franzetti hardly reacted.

Sara-Jane took his silence for approval. 'Should I go ahead with it?'

'It looks promising. Just remember, Jane, with material of a religious nature, you'll need to run the piece past me before it goes to print.'

'Yes of course, Mr Franzetti ...' It was a good time to make her move. 'There is another matter I wanted to consult you about. The assignment on the Tindari shrine, I'd be very keen to do it myself. None of the staff speaks Italian.'

'And you do?'

'Yes, quite fluently.' And here she hoped he wouldn't put her to the test.

Mr Franzetti, unlike Bob, seemed impressed, although she only had a slight tilting of the eyebrow to confirm it.

'You see,' she lied sweetly, 'my grandparents are from there, on my mother's side. Naturally, I've always had an interest in that part of the world.'

Franzetti's eyes journeyed forth out of some distant region and came to rest upon her, perhaps for the first time since she had known him. 'I see, how very interesting.' He got out of his chair, moved to the front of the desk and circled once around her, without taking his eyes off her, as if trying to catch the right angle.

'Well, can I go?'

'What?' He recovered from his reverie. 'Yes, of course, I didn't mean to detain you.'

Sara-Jane wondered whether she should persist. Normally she wouldn't dare, but somehow she sensed she had acquired power in the last few moments. 'I mean, can I go to Sicily?'

A pause. But he wasn't thinking about her question. Clearly something else was occupying his mind. She had never been so close to him before. Predictably his aura was diminished by proximity. He looked unkempt, absent. Maybe Bob was right in saying he had gone strange since the death of his wife and son. The impression was not helped by the fact that a faint smell of mustiness came off him.

Finally, he tilted his head, presented his left cheek. 'Sicily eh? Did you say your folks are from Sicily?'

'Grandparents.' She corrected him. Even a lie needed to be consistent.

'That's … very interesting. My mother was born there.'

A bridge, as if by magic, opened between them.

'Hm. Has Bob said I'll be travelling to Sicily also?'

'You're going on a pilgrimage, I believe.'

Franzetti's eyebrows did another tilt. 'That's the official line, however there's more to it than that … the thing is I don't want this to go any further than yourself … I mean, even Bob is not privy to the whole story … you see, I'll be going to a clinic … to get some tests. No, there's nothing wrong with me, strong as an elephant – as you can see by the size of my proboscis.' The old man indulged in a rare chuckle. 'But at my age, you can't be too careful …'

She did not ask why he had to go all the way to Sicily to get tested.

*

Sara-Jane had lied to her boss; technically, but not in substance. Even though they were not her genetic grandparents, Nonnu and Nonna La Rocca were the only grandparents she'd ever known.

Now that she was going to Sicily she allowed herself to peer into the dusty frame of her past and saw the picture of an old man in a blue and white check flannel shirt coming in from the garden in cracked leather boots. He took them off in the laundry and shuffled about the house, calling in a wheezy voice. 'Sara, Sara… *unni si?*'

And little Sara-Jane would hide under the table – always under the table – while Nonna put a finger on her lips and called out. '*Nun c'e chiu' Sara. Si nni iu. Nun c'e.*'

Then Nonnu started looking all over the kitchen, in the cupboards, inside the old fridge with squeaky hinges, behind the door, where he rattled the broom and the mop in mock frustration, under the embroidered tablecloth … and all the while declaiming in Sicilian, '*Unne' dda figghia? Ma unne'? Scumpariu.*'

Finally, unable to suppress a fit of giggles, Sara-Jane's blond head bobbed up from under the table. '*Cca sugnu!*'

And she would fly into his arms, 'Here I am!' burying her face into his warm flannel shirt, taking in the smells of fresh earth, citrus blossom and olive brine.

Nonna was ever busy in the kitchen, in the laundry, in the spare room, where she had an old sewing machine and made her flouncy little frocks with a clover-leaf collar, which she embroidered with figures of animals. On the back veranda she sat on the wooden chair that smelled of linseed oil, plaited her blonde hair and tied it with red ribbons, which Sara-Jane liked to undo and let dangle over her eyes. On the late afternoons she cooked her pasta in the kind of sauce she had not eaten since.

'She won't eat anything else,' she mock-complained to Pina, from next door, but in reality was proud her cooking was such a hit with the child.

Sarina was even closer to Nonnu because, being retired, he was always there and when Nonna was at work he looked after her. Nonnu never told her off. When they went to the shops he let her sit in the parcel basket and wheeled her around. The only time she heard him growl was when pink galahs came and picked at the soft-shelled almonds of his tree outside the kitchen, and he rushed out shouting as he poked a cane in the air.

'*Via, via porcu diavolo! Vi sparu nta testa!*' His Adam's apple trilled inside his throat and his face went as pink as the parrot's feathers.

Once, she remembered, when she came home from kindergarten, Nonnu was waiting for her in the drive. He took her by the hand and led her through the house to the back, talking to her in a mixture of Sicilian and a few words of English that he knew.

'Looka, Sarina, *veni, ti fazzu vidiri nna cosa bedda.*'

On the edge of the back veranda, where a massive passion-fruit vine clambered up a trellis, Nonnu lifted her up and sat her on his shoulder, then pointed to a little bird's nest woven in the vine.

It took a while for Sara to locate two tiny eggs, looking like white eyes in the nest. Sara gasped with delight. For weeks, while the birds were nesting, Nonnu barricaded the back door. To get in the house from the garden they had to go through the garage and use the front door. A visit to the nest became a daily ritual for her and Nonnu.

Sometimes Nonna would yell at her husband in Sicilian. 'Ignazio, let that poor bird be, or it will leave the eggs. *Si peggiu d'un carusu.'*

One day, when Sara came home, Nonnu was particularly excited. He took her to visit the nest and instead of two eggs there were two tiny pink heads, with yellow-rimmed beaks. As they sensed movement in the foliage they stretched their necks and opened their beaks wide: two helpless beaks, clamouring for the right to a life.

These memories were her real childhood, before the rest of it; before her mother reappeared when she was just seven, with her latest boyfriend, to reclaim her. She never saw her Sicilian grandparents again.

What followed was a six-year ordeal of wandering around the east coast, moving from town to town, from man to man. And the smells were stale and the memories nebulous. The food often came in wrappers, in tins, and her mother's breath had the constant sickening stench of alcohol and tobacco. Finally the memories of Nonnu and Nonna were blurred in the murky chaos of her life with Mother.

*

There was a pattern in the way her mother, Sheryl Giffen, related to men. She always fell for domineering, violent ones. Afraid of being abandoned, she gave herself to a new man, gave in to his demands, changed herself to his ways and became vulnerable to threats and blackmail, until the effort exhausted her.

The longer the relationship endured, the more intense grew her fear that the man would leave her sooner or later. In reality it was she who grew weary, or rather, she tired of bending to her partner's will.

Then, when Sara-Jane was thirteen, her life took yet another turbulent turn. Sheryl's latest boyfriend was Savier, a much younger man, who had arrived in Australia as a refugee from East Timor. To be fair, he was the best of a bad bunch of boyfriends. At least he wasn't violent, nor, as far she knew, did he have a criminal record, or do drugs. The problem was that he had a sweetheart back in Dili, to whom he intended to return, when things had normalized there.

This revelation should have warned Sheryl off him. Instead she became besotted. When the time came for him to go back, she felt betrayed and abandoned, even though she was aware of the situation right from the beginning. The night before his departure they went on a river cruise down to Fremantle. On the boat, she drank more than usual, a bad sign, as alcohol made her mawkish.

There was salsa dancing on deck, to the rhythm of a Latino band called Havana Nights. Sheryl started to argue with Savier, swearing and abusing him. So Savier left her on deck and went down. When they got to Barrack Street jetty, half an hour later, he went looking for her. Her body was found in the Swan River the next morning.

*

Sara-Jane's next-of-kin was her natural father, whom she had never met, or at least did not remember meeting. Her mother referred to him simply as 'the bastard'.

He was, as it turned out, Detective Sergeant Russell Toohey, a burly, red-faced man, with a walrus moustache and potbelly to match. This Sergeant Toohey did not have the money to support his daughter, but he had contacts. Someone from the local Rotary Club came to the rescue and awarded the child a one-year scholarship at an exclusive boarding school, with the proviso that if she applied herself it would be extended.

This was the break Sara-Jane needed. In the manicured gardens of Saint Cecilia, she mapped her future. In that closed, claustrophobic, snobbish environment, where she spent five years of her life, Sara-Jane observed, learned, thought. She came to realize that even though you begin your life inside another person, the surest way to a life of misery is to depend on other people for your happiness. This simple realization allowed her to leapfrog ahead of the others. She saw adults as unreliable, deceptive. The only one you could rely upon was yourself.

On Fridays, when the parents of other boarders rolled up at school in their Mercedes, Volvos and BMWs to collect their daughters for the weekend, Sara sat at the window of the dormitory and consoled herself with the thought that aloneness is also freedom. It depended on how you took it and what you did with it. So she would go to her desk and get stuck into her books. While the others played dutiful daughters, sisters, or best friends, she could get on with what really counted: her studies. She felt superior in her independence. When the daughters were dropped off by their parents, tending bored cheeks to be pecked, she could see the insecurities in their expressions and a kind of stupidity in their guise. She read somewhere that the most pampered domestic animals are often the most stupid. Yes, it was equally true of humans.

She realized too that your power over others is directly proportional to your usefulness. Success in essence meant making people feel you had, or could get, what they wanted. So, she would take what she wanted from others and give to those who were of use to her. She was comfortable with that deal.

At Saint Cecilia's Ladies College she didn't make real

friends, just survival alliances. She didn't play any sport, but she did join the debating team. Her life was hers to make. She was determined to avoid the mistakes of her mother and fall prey to men. She would not fall in love, she didn't believe in it. Falling in love was merely a pretext for the weak to justify idiotic behaviour or to get what they wanted by stealth. It was an excuse to control another human being, or a need to be controlled. Falling in love was a cop-out for those unwilling to take responsibility for their own life. Falling in love had nothing to do with loving, assuming that such a thing really existed.

Her mother kept falling in love. Well, what further proof did she need that the whole love thing was nothing more than emotional self-indulgence? Seventeen year-old Sara-Jane knew the truth. Her mother, for all her obsession with 'falling in love' or 'being in love', in reality had never loved anyone, not the abusive men she collected, not her only daughter, and certainly not herself.

*

A life contained in a box. An old Lindemans cardboard wine cask, the mauve now faded to sepia over the eleven years since it came to her in this very box, was sealed with masking tape. At the time she didn't even want to open it. Whatever remained of her mother, of a life that had more pathos than tragedy, she didn't want to know. She avoided anything that reminded her of her mother's weakness, her sentimentality, her manipulative personality, her used-up life.

Now that she was going to Sicily she wanted to shed light on a dim childhood connection, which time was threatening to sentimentalize. No, this was not nostalgia.

Her feet were firmly grounded in the present. She owed a debt to that kind couple from her early childhood who had given her love and security. It had allowed her to survive and grow strong through the tough years.

Now sometimes she found it difficult to believe that those early memories were real. Perhaps she had made it all up. Had Nonnu and Nonna really existed? Was it possible her life was constructed on the clouds of an imagined reality? This possibility, absurd though it was, gnawed at her. Sometimes she woke up and thought she heard Nonnu's steps shuffling into her tidy, manageable, busy present. But when she looked up into his face, she couldn't tell whether the smile on the weatherworn face was friendly, amused or mocking. Secrets and confusion can devour you slowly.

So it was time to act. Time to bring that dusty box out of the drawer, open its secrets, look the demons in the face and strip them of any power they still possessed.

The box did not disappoint. Or rather it confirmed that her mother's life was as empty as she expected. A few worthless trinkets of jewellery: silver and gold-plated earrings, fake mother-of-pearl pendant, a quartz watch of an unreadable origin, a pair of matching crystals, a silk cerise scarf with black and white yin and yang symbols, and several rings with suspect sapphire and opal stones.

The one that caught Sara's eye was a simple gold friendship ring. She held it up to the light and read its inscription: *With love, Sara. 18.6.1979.* A lock of blond hair was encased in a glass locket with wooden frames, labelled *Sara-Jane, 1981.* So there was a time when her mother did not think wholly of herself.

And then, an envelope, yellowed by time and – judging by the torn state of its edges – opened by nervous fingers. Inside she found the photo of what looked like a couple and their child.

The woman, she knew, must have been her mother's friend, Sara. The one whose name she had inherited; the same one who kept wafting in and out of her earliest memories, sometimes as a witch, sometimes as an angel, but mostly just at the far end of the memory lens. She stood by, watching her husband help the child take his first steps. What struck Sara-Jane was the distant look on the woman's face, as if she were a mere spectator in this scene of her own life. Even though the child was clearly hers and the man was her husband, she herself seemed an outsider.

Sara-Jane transferred her attention to the man: a heavy, jovial man, wearing an impeccably tailored suit. He squatted down on his toes, forearms opened, ready to catch the child. But if you looked closely, there was in his pose a simple eagerness to embrace life.

The child was dressed in a white woollen jumpsuit with attached beanie. Even though the focus was the mother, who ironically looked as if she would rather fade into the paper, the viewer's eye was drawn to the infant, whose chubby little face, swaddled in the softness of wool, captured the full light. Sara-Jane read the address on the back of the envelope.

Sara La Rocca
Piazza Chiesa Madre 29
San Sisto (Messina)
Italia

La Rocca, it was Nonnu's surname, which meant that she was not married to that man, or perhaps that she had kept her maiden name. Quite without thinking Sara-Jane sat down to write a letter. It was a long time since she had used a pen other than to jot down notes, ideas, or agenda items for meetings. The only correspondence she wrote was business letters or email messages. This was something new for her, or rather, the beginning of a new her. She hesitated, bit into the top of pen with such force that she cracked it. Perhaps she oughtn't to. Was she ready or willing to enter the murky world of other people? She shivered, then spoke to herself. 'Take the initiative. Don't wimp out, Sara-Jane, it's just a letter'.

> *Dear Sara,*
> *I hardly remember you, of course, and you might not remember me …*

Nah, appellation too familiar and the opening sentence made too many assumptions, while the self-effacement suggested in the second sentence would convey altogether the wrong message.

Dear Ms La Rocca,

Hmm, too formal for a letter of a personal nature. Anyway, a lot of people these days took offence to *Ms*, for the same reason she discarded *Dear Madam*.

Dear Sara La Rocca,
(Hardly ideal, but it would have to do.)
> *My name is Sara-Jane, I'm the daughter of Sheryl Giffen. I believe you were best friends when you lived in Australia.*
> *Of course I can't remember much of you, but you might remember me, because I was named after you …*

Too many 'yous', best not be too familiar. Besides, should she go into this? Wasn't there some sort of rift between this woman and her mother? This was getting more complicated than she had anticipated. Then, an idea.

She should have thought of it earlier, because in fact the people she did remember, the ones she really wanted to catch up with, were Nonnu and Nonna. He, of course, did not speak English at all. Now her Italian was hardly up to scratch, but with the aid of a dictionary she could manage a few sentences. After all, she merely wanted to make contact and pay them a courtesy visit.

> *Cari Nonni,*
> *Sono Sara-Jane, vi ricordate di me? Spero così. In due settimane, cioé da 10 ottobre, visiterò Sicilia. Sarà un bel piacere per me visitare tua casa. Ecco il mio indirizzo in Sicilia:*
> *Albergo Ruggeri*
> *Viale Stazione 71*
> *Milazzo (Messina)*

There, that would do. A brief note that communicated what she wanted to say without giving too much away, or going into risky areas. Simply asking whether they remembered her, and her hotel and the dates she would be there.

As she ran her tongue along the glue line of the envelope, Sara-Jane wondered at the irony of how easy it was writing in a language not hers. This was not the language of Sara-Jane the adult, with all the risks and responsibilities, or the complications that adulthood entailed. Children are not held responsible and this was the language of her childhood, that part of her childhood when she felt secure and loved. This language gave her the most freedom, as if by reverting to it she was no longer an adult, with all the weighty responsibility it carried, but a little six year-old sitting at the laminex kitchen table in suburbia, smelling the comforting smells of Nonna's *ragù* simmering in a crock, of garlic browning in sizzling olive oil, as she waited for the pasta to be brought to the table. She still remembered feeling secure in the hands of two old people who had no other ambition in life but to grow their own vegetables. And when she fell they took her in their arms, kissed her *bubù* better, made a fuss of her.

Sara-Jane took those memories with her as she walked up to the post box in Mill Point Road, and hesitated as she held the letter balanced on the edge of the letter box, fearful of the consequences of such a simple act, until someone came from behind with letters to post. So she had no choice but to resolutely pop the letter in and press at the edge of the envelope with the palm of her hand. She shivered as she walked back to her apartment.

2

Sara La Rocca's hand shades her eyes from the October sun poised on the Verna peak, its rays clipping the top of the ancient olive tree. She enters the canopy of silver foliage and searches for green beads. Hardly any. Olive trees, she knows, are capricious bearers. Even so, she can't remember one year when this tree has not produced enough eating olives to last them out the year. What portent, such a barren season?

This is the tree of the eating olives. For some inexplicable reason, it's always the first to tender its fruit for picking. Perhaps it's the high position, facing the sun and shading the face of the old stone house, whose white-washed walls are discoloured to a patchwork of ancient maps; and the window frames – which have not had a new coat of green paint for a decade – are now ashen grey.

This tree would have seen it all: the Ottomans, the Normans, and the Bourbons. The wars, the Black Death and the Spanish fever. It would have stood by impassively to the passing of Garibaldi's one thousand heroes.

This trunk – desiccated by droughts, hollowed out by fire, bent by the wind and marked by time – was the effigy of her childhood. As a baby her mother would sit her here in the shade, while she put out the washing, fed the grunting pig in the concrete pen below ground, and milked the goats tethered by the blackberry *macchia*. In spring, when the blossom appeared imperceptibly among the leaves, the pollen was carried inside the house by the wind to announce the end of winter.

From a cross-branch, her father had hung a swing: two lengths of rope falling down to iron hooks inserted into half a car tyre. There she sat to dream and listen to the muffled calls of pigeons in the coop: kiwoo! kiwoo! kiwoo!

Now, since the death of her father, their nests are raided by rats and their calls are a sad echo of time gone.

This tree has belonged to her family, from the days when families were bound together by poverty and the will to survive, and households were alive with children's voices. Over the centuries it stood here, a muted witness to the courtships and the dramas played on the torso of these mountains.

Then, in the early seventies, a landslide damaged the house and there was no money to fix it. So they had to leave it, to save it. They went to Australia, just for two or three years, they said. Their exile lasted twelve. Twelve years of homesickness and longing, to save a house. And now she is going to lose it to progress, to a bobcat, to a new millennium marching in with the speed of unstoppable charge; to destiny, presenting itself in the unlikely face of Mimmo Urzì, the strong man from Barcellona.

*

Some people, like some plants, are not meant to be uprooted. They can only thrive in the very soil into which their seed is planted; in the same air, in the familiar landscape that feeds them through memory and stories, ghosts and myths. Not for them the illusory journey of self-discovery, the headlong leap into the sea-storm of change.

They – we, she ought to say – bow to the superior force of fate. They are the hardy, the stubborn, the clingy. Their roots dig down deep through generations, searching in depths of time.

People like her father who, torn away from this steep

mountain flank, pined away in the suburbia of another country for twelve years, only to come back to die in his plot of land. Like her mother who, though old and sick, resisted the move down to San Sisto. Like herself, who never wanted to leave in the first place, but then brought back a heavy legacy from the other side of the world: a seed, a language, a love, a consuming guilt. Like Sante, her son, who carries the imprints of both worlds, yet fits this landscape, like the olive tree and the fig.

Sante is coming up the steep ramp which is overgrown with spiky blackberries that threaten to overwhelm this ridge. In his step, light with youth and heavy with the burden of two worlds, you see the contradiction in the way that his sweet temper sometimes – rarely, thank God – flares up. And then the most surprised person is Sante himself. Not her, though. She knows the contradiction in his eyes, of a steel blue you do not see around these parts, which occasionally perturb you with their stillness.

Sante sprints up the track from the gate, waving something in his hand. 'Mamma, look what I found in the letter box.'

His voice rings through the air, his face radiates joy. How could she not love Sante? But her love straddles the hump of oblivion. To love him she made herself forget how he came to be. But now she can feel the heavy steps of the past approach with an insistent thud, like heartbeats through an ultrasound.

'Look, it's addressed to Nonnu.'

His excitement disturbs her.

He raises the letter aloft like some sort of trophy, 'It's from Australia …' His voice is pitched higher with each detail. 'Someone called Sara, like you. I'll open it.'

'No!' She snatches the letter from his hand. Her reaction shocks him, but he recovers quickly. 'I'll do it later.'

A letter addressed to a dead person does not augur well. She would have liked to destroy it unopened, consign the contents to fire, let the words waft away in smoke of oblivion.

But of course he would not let her do that. 'Who is Sara-Jane, Mamma?'

'The daughter of someone I knew in Australia, a school friend.'

'So, she called her baby after you. Mamma that's beautiful. Why did you not tell me before? You're so secretive. Open it.'

'Sante, this is not my letter. It's addressed to Nonnu.'

Pathetic really, seeing her father has been dead for two years.

He's too kind to remind her of that, instead he comes at her from the flank. It's all the more effective because she knows it's done without malice. 'Mamma, can I go to Australia soon?'

Sara feels the tension wind around her head in a tightening spiral. 'Don't be silly, Sante.'

'I want to, Mamma.'

Sante Marzano has dreamt about Australia every day. He imagines it big, of course, empty, flat, sun-drenched. He sees it in contrasts: young and very old, naked yet inscrutable, vibrant and sleepy, silent and rumbling; a lumbering giant in images of orange, gold and faded green under a canopy of powder blue.

This love of Australia must be encoded in his DNA, given he was merely conceived in that far-away land. She escaped before he could breathe its air, register its sounds, experience its moods, or take in the scents. Before he could know its inner reality: the insidious tragedy beneath a shell of laid-back jollity. It was a strange connective. Initiated from inside her womb, then stretched across the oceans, in an attempt to break it off. And yet, separated by space and time, draped away by her curtain of resentment, it turns out that he loves Australia, passionately, its mystery only feeding his obsession.

'Why this fixation with Australia?'

'I'd love to go. I love Australia.'

Love and destiny are a mystery, their workings are a mystery but the effect is too real. So there is no point in resisting them. It would be like resisting the thrust of these mountains which, in pre-history, rose into the sky and stood there as monuments to the power of the gods. Human affairs, in comparison, are trivial, a speck of lint hardly noticeable in the grand rug woven by Nature. The energy that weaves the pattern of destiny is love. Destiny and love. It's that simple and that mysterious.

For Sante, part of that mystery is his father, his natural father, that is. And to protect him from a destructive truth, she deceived him. One day, she lied, he had set forth for the interior on a safari. A *safari*, for god's sake! And never came back. He was swallowed up by all that orange, gold and blue, lost in the black of the night, vanished. Not a photo, nothing.

That he found strange, although he could understand his mother did not want to preserve painful memories, but where did that leave him? One day he will have to go. Not so much in the hope of finding his father. After all, if he were still alive, he would have found a way of getting in touch. If he is dead, better the certainty of a dead father than the possibility that he might be out there somewhere. So, it's a journey he needs to make, to give form and sharpness to that spectrum of colour swirling inside his head.

'This could be the best time to go, before I start University. I will try and find a job in Milazzo, save some money.'

With both hands she picks the olives that have fallen in the dry brush of grass, and remembers a song her grandmother used to sing:

Mamma mia mi dai cento lire
Che in America voglio andar
Cento lire io te le dono
Ma in America no, no, no

Such songs, about the pain of emigration and the fear of distance, folk sang while picking olives, or spreading tomato paste out in the sun, or embroidering pillow cases ... those songs spoke wisdom.

She turns to him. 'You know it's not the money, Sante.'

'What is it then?'

She knows it's unfair but she's only trying to protect him after all. 'You are our only child, does it seem right that you should go off to the other side of the world and leave us, does it?'

'It will only be for a few weeks.'

'Australia is not the safe country it looks from outside. How often do you hear about tourists going missing over there? Some disappear never to be heard of again. I do not want this to happen to my son.'

He has nothing to say to this. What can he say?

Time for a sweetener. 'One day you can go.'

One day, when he's settled, when he is ready.

But Alfio, her husband, sees it differently. 'The boy is nearly eighteen. You will need to tell him the truth about his father. You will need to let him go to Australia, soon.'

*

That night, back at San Sisto, with the olives soaking in water, Sara is left alone in the house with time to think. She knew that letter would come one day. Whatever the content, the past is about to march into her present. And so there is no way of avoiding its visit. She first catches its face in the mirror at the entrance, as she hangs her coat on the hook. She glimpses the shadow stalking her along the wall of the corridor, she hears its thud as she treads the terrazzo floor tiles, she feels its presence behind the turquoise drapes of the balcony door. Sara unlocks the lid of her wedding trousseau chest. She reaches down underneath the silken underwear she has never used, past the hand-embroidered bed linen, the place-mats, the lace doilies and tablecloths, the chenille bedspread and the Romeo and Juliet tapestry, whose tragic posturing is never likely to be gazed at by visitors, and takes out a box of carved walnut.

There she finds a letter she wrote so many years ago, but never had the heart to send, and reads it again, hoping to find in it inspiration out of her dilemma, or perhaps justification for her shameless deceiving of her only child.

> *Dear Sheryl,*
>
> *You've no idea how many times I've sat down to write you a letter and then gave it away. But now that things have settled, now that I have a father for my baby son, somehow it makes it easier to forgive myself, though I must tell you it doesn't make it any easier to open up to you.*
>
> *But maybe I am being too hard on myself, because one of the reasons I did not write sooner was to protect you from the knowledge I am about to reveal. And it doesn't matter that you probably suspect, that's not the same as having it confirmed. And for that reason I think*

you might hate me for writing it down as much as for leaving you the way I did ...

Abruptly Sara stops. She folds the letter back into its well-pressed pleats. There – better to keep these things well tucked away, in a trousseau of things that will never be used. Just this much of the letter is enough to add strength to her determination not to expose Sante to all that unhappy past. She lowers the lid and clips the padlock firmly down. She will take a Mogadon and go to bed.

3

On receiving the bad news from his doctor, Clem Franzetti's dimpled chin dropped in disbelief. There was no way he could have colon cancer, not he. He expected to die one day, of course, but not yet, the timing was all wrong, and certainly not this way. That's not the way it was played out in his mind. Since his wife and son had been taken away from him, so suddenly, death held no fear for him, just the natural outcome of living.

It's the dying that he feared, or rather, the kind of dying that ravages you slowly. Not for him though. That's for the bleeding hearts that make a life's vocation out of the dying. They play out their lives as melodrama, preparing for the arrival of that degenerative disease, a debilitating injury, a breakdown of the mind ... whatever. More often it's a chronic ailment, which stamps a permanent imprint on their personality and becomes an alibi for failure, before it morphs into a slow sickness of living. Such people spend their life watching death stalk on the periphery of their consciousness, squeezing out every drop of sympathy and self-pity, before taking the final bow to the slow clapping, and relief, of those left behind.

The world is full of bleeding hearts. He, on the other hand, was born to go out with a bang, a splash, a crash, a thud, a blow, the sound of gong, a hiss, a spin, or a silent heave. On those rare occasions – prevalently since the death of his wife and son – when he thought about his final encounter, he imagined death stealing upon him in the middle of some frantic activity, in the rush of a freak flood, taking him by stealth, catching him on the run, on the cusp of two major projects, on the way to somewhere else, as an aside, a detour, a distraction. Death, he always thought, would take him before he knew anything about it.

So this news was nonsense. He wasn't going now, not yet. His mission in life wasn't accomplished. Too many things left undone, needed his attention; too many people depended on him. The young doctor must have got it wrong when he gave him the news, going all unctuous with rehearsed sensitivity. Clem felt quite insulted. He wanted to shoot the messenger.

But even if – let's just admit for a moment the possibility that they had found something – he wasn't going to do anything silly or act on impulse. The last thing he wanted was to give it credence by behaving strangely. No, the best course was not to make a fuss, keep it quiet. A man in his position could not afford any suggestion of weakness. Too many vultures out there waited to take the spoils. Like his useless stepbrother, Danny O'Rourke, who was positioning himself to feed on his remains.

Then, in his moment of confusion, the Holy Ghost spoke to Clem Franzetti by means of two apparently banal incidents. First, his eyes fell on a tiny news item in the paper, one of those fillers easily missed when flicking through the pages.

Olive Leaf Cure for Cancer Claim
A Sicilian researcher, Doctor Emilio Troina, claims to have cured patients with advanced cancers on a diet of olive leaves juice from particular ancient trees found in the area...

Clem Franzetti was struck by the coincidence. There was no doubt in his mind that God had moved the hand of the hack in the editorial room to fill in a space with that innocuous news item, so that he, Clem Franzetti, would come to notice it. God moves in strange ways. True. Perhaps God had chosen a few insignificant lines in a newspaper to tell him to turn a corner, take the side road and redirect his journey.

Of course, there's no way of knowing whether this Doctor Troina was a doctor at all, or some quack posing as one. But that was a minor consideration. The significant thing was the manner in which events came together. While he was pondering over this article, that girl, Sara-Jane, walked into his office with her proposal. Her appearance was no coincidence, nor was it the free choice she imagined it was. No, she was part of the plan. Unbeknown to her, she had been enlisted by God to be part of the maze of His intentions.

*

Clem Franzetti would never admit it, of course, but he was a product of contradictory energies inherited from his parents. His father, Vittorio, was a well-educated Northern Italian from Treviso. He was quick-witted, urbane, agnostic and a snob. His conceit travelled uncomfortably close to racism. Apart from the Anglo-Saxons and the Jews, both of whom he admired for different reasons, he had little time for other nationalities. His greatest contempt was for Southern Italians, whom he considered lazy and untrustworthy.

Vittorio was no ordinary migrant. There were no economic reasons for him to go to Australia. What moved him was a sense of adventure and a feeling that Treviso was too provincial, too attached to its traditions to offer the kind of space a young man like him needed. News of a large gold nugget find in Western Australia was all the motivation he needed. So, in the spring of 1924, Vittorio, aged just twenty-one, set sail from the port of Genoa.

One might be tempted to read the hand of destiny in the fact that, within one week of his arrival in Kalgoorlie, the mining town, he set eyes on a young woman with sapphire eyes and tan-coloured hair. It must have been a proverbial *coup de foudre*, because even though the girl turned out to be a miner's daughter, poorly educated and a Sicilian, Vittorio asked her to marry him. It was a case of love triumphing over prejudice. The girl was Carmelina Ribaudo, or Carmel, as everyone called her.

Soon after the wedding, Vittorio left Kalgoorlie, partly to get away from Carmelina's family, to settle in Perth. Within a year Carmel gave birth to a son, Clemente, soon shortened to Clem. Meanwhile, Vittorio easily mutated into Vic, as he set out to scale the socio-economic ladder and reach the kind of position in which he knew he belonged. He bought into a jewellery shop in the city and before long, owned it. He introduced new designs, sponsored top craftsmen from Italy, and developed a keen sense for what rich people wanted. Within ten years he became the state's leading jeweller. Success in that field gave him access to some of the most influential men, and their wives. Vic Franzetti had arrived.

His wife had no choice but to get caught in the vertiginous climb up the spiral of power and social positioning. A shy woman, she became well adept at playing the role required of her: the quiet, demure, dutiful wife. She aired no opinion, for fear of being wrong. She dyed her hair a cool blonde and had it set at the hairdresser once a week. In public, she merely flashed her eyes, without ever resting them on anyone long enough for fear that they might see the desolation inside. Everyone knew her husband had affairs, as did Carmel. The trick was not to give the impression she knew. The important thing was that she be true to her own standards, set in the concrete of a millenarian tradition, to maintain her honour as a woman and her dignity as a mother.

*

Because Clem loved his mother he would have liked to respect her, admire her fortitude and constancy; be in awe of her. Instead he felt pity for her. He found his mother's submissiveness to her husband obscene. Such contradictions sapped his childhood energies.

Clem grew up in a whisper-quiet world, dominated by the solitary, timorous figure of his mother. He followed her as she moved about in tentative steps as if she weren't sure she should be occupying the space allotted to her. As far back as he could remember, he and his mother attended the little parish church in Baker Street. Every Sunday he and his mother sat in the same place, three rows back, listening to Father Murphy intone the Holy, Holy, Holy in his rich Irish lilt. Above them, the Virgin Mary smiled down from the alcove. Sometimes, if little Clem gazed up for long enough, the two faces: his mother's shadowy profile and the lighted visage of the Virgin Mary, merged into one.

His mother died suddenly at fifty-seven, slipping away unexpectedly, almost unnoticed. It was the kind of timorous death she would have wished. Less than a year later, his father married a woman the same age as his son Clem, with a twelve year-old son, Danny.

Clem Franzetti married eventually, at forty-three. His

father lasted another dozen years. In his will Old Vic left his widow the house and a life-long annuity. To Clem, begrudgingly, his business, which by then included a printing and publishing company.

4

The year before Sara La Rocca arrived at Thornton High School, Sheryl Giffen had started her first year there. She was a lonely scarecrow of a girl, with straw hair, a stick of a body and freckles that strayed even to her lips. Sheryl was then not quite thirteen, no parents to love or to blame, just the latest pair of foster parents to resent. Her natural father she had never known, while her mother had remarried and gone to New Zealand to have more children with a new man.

She spent the first year hiding around brick pillars. It took months to discover that if she gravitated to a group, kept her head down, and went with the flow of the throng, no one would notice she was friendless.

In year nine, she managed to fit a space on the periphery of a group of girls, whose sole purpose for being together was to sit out their lunch hour by the wall of the horticultural garden and watch Russell Toohey cavort with his mates. Russell was in the bottom class in year ten, one year up from hers. The kids in his class were referred to variously as the dummies, the morons, the spastics, but somehow these epithets were never applied to Russell.

And it wasn't out of fear that he would have thumped them, although it was certainly on the cards, it was more the fact that Russell was a leader. His total contempt for learning, for teachers, or for school rules was seen as liberating even by the studious nerds. To be accepted in Russell's group was the peak of cool. The requirements were simple: you needed to be male, tough and antisocial.

The birds, well, they had their uses, occasionally. As for the brains, they were just little pansies that couldn't crack a hard in a room full of Raquel Welches.

Throughout year nine, Sheryl's group watched the boys smoke, fart, swear, spit, brag, talk tough, wrestle each other to the ground, jostle for the ball, and slag off at the teachers. The boys hardly knew the girls were there. They occasionally flicked a cigarette butt in their direction, posted with a contemptuous leer that threatened unspeakable violence if they dared invade male space.

The girls put gloss on their lips and glitter on their eyelids, plaited each other's hair and watched. The only time the two groups acknowledged each other was if the ball landed in the vicinity of the girls. Then one of them would try and kick it back, getting a jeering for their pathetic effort.

All at once, midway through the second year, something happened to Sheryl. She started to fill out and get a shape, and suddenly she was being noticed from across the graffiti-ridden path that separated the boys from the girls. One day Russell procured a giant-sized bag of Samboy salt and vinegar potato chips, probably stolen or taken from one of his lieutenants.

He held it up. 'Hey you.'

All the girls turned, astonished.

'You, the skinny one.'

'Me?' Sheryl was incredulous.

'Yes, you. You wanna a chip?'

'Yeah?' Sheryl was not so sure.

'Well, whatchyou waitin' for. Come and get it.'

Feeling as if she had just been crowned queen in a beauty contest, Sheryl crossed the divide to take her reward. The other boys, who a moment before would have spat on her, now took notice. The girls too looked at her with envy and disbelief. Sheryl felt her skin pores dilate. She was faint with exhilaration. This was something new for her.

Around that time, an enthusiastic young teacher

arrived in Russell's English class. She started the first lesson by introducing herself, and went around the class asking the students to do likewise, and give a brief outline about themselves and their interests.

'Whatchyou mean, *intrests*?' asked Russell, licking his lips.

'Well, what you enjoy doing best,' she obliged, happy to get a response.

Russell looked around the class with a smirk on his face, making sure he got everyone's attention. 'Right, m' name's Russell Toohey, I gotta big dick and I like playin' with it.'

The story got around the school and Russell's reputation, already pretty formidable, got another boost. It wasn't long before Sheryl moved into the group, this time uninvited, and sat there, trying to blend, saying nothing, just sending shy glances towards Russell.

After that initial invitation, Russell hardly seemed to notice she was there, but he did not send her away either. If ever he acknowledged her it was to order her about, send her to the canteen to buy him a coke. Sheryl loved doing this for Russell, it made her feel needed, important – an importance she knew she did not deserve. And Russell hogged her admiration. Things moved on.

On Saturdays Sheryl worked at an old lady's house, Mrs Mullens, doing house duties. In the afternoon, Mrs Mullens took a long nap, which was when she sneaked Russell in, from the side gate into her garage. On one particular afternoon she was able to procure a bottle of sherry from the pantry.

'You beauty, Shirl!' Russell snatched the bottle off her.

They drank it in the garage, sitting on a blanket that had been used by the dog before it died, a loss that caused Mrs Mullens to fall into a state of depression, marked by lengthy sleeps.

Away from the gang, Russell was a different person. He displayed little of his tough posture, and was quieter, and more reticent. It was Sheryl who encouraged the necking, while he kept repeating, 'I gotta go. I don't want the old hag to find 's here.'

'She sleeps for hours, Russ.'

'She'll hear 's.'

'She won't – she's half deaf, I told ya.'

Despite all his bravado and being one year older, Russell had never gone 'all the way' before. As for Sheryl, she had been given some unwelcome instruction, by her previous foster-father, who had a panic attack at the last minute and lost his erection. Scared by the experience, Sheryl had nevertheless been made curious and thought she might like to reprise with Russell.

After a while, the sherry emboldened Russell. He started coming on to her. The sight of his tool snaking up her skinny leg made Sheryl panic.

'That's too big,' she said, 'I can't even get a tampon up there.'

Her resistance made his need greater, his desire more urgent, his advance more pressing. By then she realised that she'd allowed things to go too far, so Sheryl gave in to Russell and the sherry.

*

This first experience confirmed Russell's belief that sex was power, that his exceptional virility empowered him not just with girls, but with his friends as well. Once word got out that he and Sheryl had 'done it', he saw his power grow in the envious admiring eyes of the boys. It changed Sheryl too, but not in the same way.

During her young life Sheryl had been shunted from one set of foster parents to another and generally made to feel like a burden, or ignored, which was worse. Now she was no longer on the outer. Someone wanted her. And not just anyone. It was the spunkiest, toughest boy in the school. It was wild. She had an identity and status. She had a position other girls envied, she was Russell's girl. What else could a girl ask for?

Of course he could be tough on her, old Russ, the way he flirted with other girls, knowing full well she didn't like it. And if she complained to him, and started crying, he had a smart response. 'But I always come back te ya, don' I?'

Well, he had a point there, she had to admit. He always came back to her, which proved he must love her best of all. It made her feel immensely proud. Flirting was just part of his nature, for being the school stud. What right did she have to nag him?

So what if he made her do things she didn't want to? That was part of the deal. It was what pleased him, and she wanted to please him most of all. What she didn't like was when he went and bragged about it to his friends.

Once he did go too far, though. They were at a party at the house of a boy whose parents had gone away for the weekend. They were drinking and passing a joint around. Then he started looking at another girl. Well, he had done that before, and Sheryl had learnt to manage her anger. She pretended she didn't see a thing. She leant back on a pillow and pretended she was falling asleep. She didn't want to give him the satisfaction of her jealousy. But she saw the two of them get up and disappear upstairs.

And that's when she lost it. She went to the kitchen and got the biggest knife she could find from the cutlery drawer, one of those big pointy things you carve a Sunday roast with. She ran up the stairs and started banging on the door, screaming. Russell came out, holding up his unzipped jeans by the buckle with one hand. With the other, he reached for the knife she held in her trembling hand, shoved her down with a push of his powerful shoulder and kicked her.

'What do you think you're doing, you stupid bitch. What's wrong with ya?'

Sometimes she too wondered what was wrong with her. Why she lost control like that. Other people didn't lose it like she did.

The next day, when they had both sobered up, Russell was still furious with her. 'You do that again, you mad dog, and it's finished, you know that? Finished.'

'Oh please Russ, I won't do it again. I promise it'll never happen again.' She grabbed his arm and held it tight beside hers, even while he tried to shake her off, clinging to him because she knew she was nothing without Russell. Big, strong, confident Russell Toohey made her feel truly alive.

The prospect of him leaving her ... she would rather be dead, she really would. Sometimes she wondered, though, about living. It was hard. Sometimes she thought about doing herself in.

And then, a miracle, a rare incident whose importance she didn't recognise until much later.

5

Don Alfio Marzano, the Mayor of San Sisto, the village shut off from the big coastal town of Milazzo by the mountains and its own medieval traditions, was happy. The day ended very pleasantly, despite having had to deal with a couple of niggling matters.

He had started the day by paying a courtesy call to the shops and businesses along the Via Cesare Battisti, to ensure there would be no problems when Ciccino Cauta, Mimmo's bagman, came around to collect the monthly dues. Of course he perfectly understood the grievances of the shop owners. In these difficult times, nobody relished the added financial burden of paying the *pizzo*, masquerading as insurance. But one had to be a realist and avoid trouble. He did not want a repeat of the previous month's unpleasantness when, following a fee increase, some restive business owners had started to talk of a collective revolt. In the end, Mimmo sent a couple of heavies to make some inelegant visitations. Unfortunately, one of the shops, *Calzolerie Estetiche*, caught fire in the draft. After which all talk of revolt ceased.

Later in the morning, Ciccino did the rounds and everything went smoothly, much to Don Alfio's relief. Mimmo Urzì would be satisfied, and the likelihood of another fire on the Via Cesare Battisti had receded.

At one in the afternoon, he had gone down to Milazzo for lunch with some friends at Attilio's, one of his favourite eateries. Attilio, ever in good form, presented him with a dish of *polipetti* done with tomato, olive oil from Gioiosa, garlic, pine nuts, and capers from Pantelleria, washed down with a litre of Attilio's superb dry white, from his own small vineyard on the slopes of Castroreale.

For sweets, which he normally would pass up, he was tempted by fresh peaches in a mixture of Rosso Antico. How could any mortal resist such divine offering!

Unfortunately, later in the afternoon, he had to face the tedious business of Sara's land. Who would have thought that a strip of steep mountain land, with a few olive trees, such as you see hundreds of in this part of Sicily, should be of interest to the biggest olive-oil co-operative in the region?

And yet, this is exactly what's happened,' ruminated Don Alfio. What's more, they're willing to pay a handsome sum for it. Unfortunately this is one of those cases where luck comes to kiss you with barbed whiskers, because Sara won't hear of selling. He can understand her being so attached to a piece of land that has been part of her family for generations, although he himself has no such sentimental hang ups.

He had no hesitation selling his own family's much larger citrus orchard on the coast, when developers offered him what amounted to a minor fortune in those days. So if it were up to him he would sell.

The land is of not much use to them, he thought. Sante would hardly be interested in working such a small piece of land. As for the oil and the olives, they can be bought from one of the small local farms. More ominously, the co-operative has the protection of the powerful Urzì family, so rumour has it.

His visit to Avvocato Allia aimed to investigate precisely that rumour.

Somehow you knew Lawyer Allia would not approve of a man the age of Don Alfio wearing a pea green suit, over an off-white shirt with button-down collar, famously worn by the handsome Leader of the Opposition, Francesco Rutelli, at a pro-environment demonstration in Rome some months ago. The suit was matched by a light yellow tie, patterned with tiny blue and red diamond shapes.

He would think it too fashionable, too studied for an older man. Well, let him think whatever, thought Don Alfio, as he stepped off the footpath and into his *studio legale*, an office that befitted his position.

Lawyer Allia's suit was a safe smoky brown, with no pin stripes, thank God, and his shirt was predictably white with a wide, butterfly collar like the ones worn by Berlusconi, and his tie was a well-matching, if prosaic, silver with dark red diagonal stripes, as if he were a conservative American politician. Such prudent elegance wrapped the wily careful character of lawyer Allia.

The lawyer's responses were likewise considered and mostly non-committal. Yes, he'd heard the rumour that the Urzì family had an interest in the proposed venture, but could not confirm it definitely. What he could say was that there were moves in high places – as high as the regional government in Palermo – to encourage the buying up of small plots of mostly-abandoned land, which a couple of generations ago had provided a meagre living for thousands of *contadini*, and create bigger properties. The idea was to set up modern commercially-viable holdings, to counter competition from new emerging producers from places as far afield as Australia and Chile.

Lawyer Allia thought it possible that officials might have encouraged Mimmo's involvement, unofficially, of course. He was, as everyone knew, a man of influence instrumental in convincing smallholders to part with their plots. There was some concern that once these unschooled but cunning peasant owners of land realised the project had government backing, they would try and hold out for exorbitant sums of money.

'Understand, my dear Alfio,' concluded lawyer Allia, taking Don Alfio's arm and pacing in the direction of the door, in a not-too-subtle hint that the time he had set aside for the consultation had expired, 'all of this is still highly speculative, but I would hazard to say it has a degree of substantive plausibility.'

Uffa, what a bore that Lawyer Allia! Don Alfio had left the office in quite an ill mood, especially as the lawyer suggested by the all-too-smug voice and darting little eyes that he knew more than he was prepared to tell him, and most probably, he too was on Mimmo Urzì's payroll. In which case, he might as well tell Sara she had no choice but to sell.

Luckily for him, Don Alfio had the wonderful ability to temporarily tuck away grimness in a remote compartment of his brain, especially when faced with the prospect of pleasurable company. So, as the sun scaled down the walls of the far side of the thirteenth century Castello, which dominated the skyline over Milazzo, and the lungomare began to fill with strollers, Don Alfio's prospects could not have been more enjoyable.

*

He found Elia in a high state of excitability.

'*Carissimo*,' she gushed, in that champagne voice of hers, which for years had seduced audiences not only in Palermo and Catania, but as far afield as Naples. 'How sweet you are to come and visit me.'

She kissed him on both cheeks and hugged him affectionately. There was no other woman that gave off such powerful vibrations as Elia.

Proximity to her energised him. With her small slight figure held in a full-length loose floral number, she positively glowed. Her new play, Martoglio's *L'Aria del Continente*, was opening next week at the Teatro Stabile of Palermo. She stretched on the chaise longue where, many years ago, he had savoured the gifts of her body; before it all settled into a life-long friendship.

'Do fetch us some drinks, Quercia, Cinzano for me.'

Quercia, or oak tree, was the nickname she gave him, many years ago, on account of his large size and protective nature. 'Alfio is just like an oak tree, to shelter under,' she would say.

'On Saturday, come what may, I will be in Palermo for the opening.' He beamed.

'To tell you the truth, my dear Alfio, I am utterly terrified.'

'Why, Elietta?'

'Well, I play Milla Milord.'

'So?'

'How do you suppose the audience will respond to a woman aged … my age, playing the part of a thirty year-old?'

'What nonsense. You look no more than twenty-five.'

She took the Cinzano from his hand and brushed the sleeve of his jacket. 'Your flattery is so outrageous, it would annoy me if it came from anyone else.'

They touched glasses lightly, caressing each other with their eyes. She patted the fabric of the chaise by her side and Don Alfio's well-rounded rear filled the space near her feet.

'What brings you to Milazzo?'

'I've come to see you.'

'At five-thirty in the evening, and dressed like that? I don't think so, Alfio.'

'Well, I also had some business …' And because she was his best friend, he told her about Sara's land.

Elia listened, and from time to time she stroked him on

the arm, never taking her eyes off him. She was a good listener, unusual for an actress. 'That's terrible. Your wife is absolutely right in refusing to sell. That land is part of her ancestry.'

'Problem is, it runs through the middle of where they intend to site the *frantoio* ...'

'Well, that's their problem'

'If, as it appears, Mimmo Urzì has a major interest in the oil distillery project, it becomes our problem.'

'Oh no, not that grotesque *mafioso* from Barcellona!'

Don Alfio nodded, and added, 'Not quite. His ventures are strictly-speaking legal.'

'What about his protection racket?'

'Insurance, Elia.'

'That's despicable. Alfio, you can't let them bully you this way.' Elia sat up, looked across the room, to some imaginary figure sitting opposite and declaimed somewhat theatrically, 'Oh Sara, you poor darling.' She returned her gaze on Alfio, 'Quercia, we can't let him do that to her.'

'Well no.' Alfio tried to sound resolute and compensate for his lack of conviction, 'I'm trying to find a way out. What do you suggest?'

His flushed, well-fed face with the big doubting eyes looked sort of lost. It was a look that women loved, especially women with a mothering instinct and no children of their own on whom to lavish it. Elia would have taken him on her lap and held him tight against her bosom, had he not been such a large man. Besides, there was still a residue of past feelings, at least for her.

'Don't worry.' She soothed him. 'We will find a way.' And because she had the sort of personality that could not dwell on negatives for long, she turned on a brilliant smile. 'And how is Sante? He must be ... what ... eighteen?'

'Almost. Just completed the *Liceo Classico*.'

'Oh he is such a beautiful boy. Beautiful, bright and good-natured. You're very lucky to have such a son.'

'I know, God must have rewarded us for calling him Sante.'

'Is he religious?'

'Not really. Who is, these days? Except for Sara. He's … gentle. Something of a dreamer.'

'Like you.'

'Me!'

'Yes, yes Alfio. Not physically, of course. He is slight and dark, like his mother, but his nature is all you: gentle, averse to confrontation, *tranquillo* …'

Of course, knowing what he did, he could not stop a wry smile sneaking up around his mouth.

Elia misinterpreted his smile. 'Of course, you were quite cheeky in your younger days, as we know, but always *tranquillo*, even when you were deceitful, you did it with such style, that I could not be angry with you for long.' She was getting sentimental.

'Come,' he said, taking her hand, letting the action prevail over emotion, 'let's go down on the piazza.'

The idea brought her cheerfulness back. 'Beautiful idea, it's time for me to have one of Mauro's coffees.'

They spent the evening strolling on the Lungomare Garibaldi, *a bracetto*, talking and walking arm-in-arm, acknowledging the occasional acquaintance going by, smelling the gentle autumnal breeze blowing in from the dreamy Gulf of Milazzo, and luxuriating in the warmth of a friendship that had proved more rewarding, and certainly more resilient, than the passion they shared so many years ago.

By the time he took the winding mountain road back to San Sisto, it was after eleven. He felt at peace. Yes, the world was in a mess. In the Middle-East they continued to butcher each other, the air of the world was being poisoned, and so was the world of politics. Berlusconi had a stranglehold on Italy, and Bush *Fils* had snuck up on the hapless Americans. What a disaster! And yet, as long as you could have days like this, living could still be glorious, tucked away between the Peloritani Mountains and the Tyrrhenean Sea.

While the night mist descended on the mountain, Don Alfio counted his blessings. He was heading back to San Sisto, to Sara, to the woman he loved above all else. More than the food he enjoyed so much; quite as much as the good soul of his mother, whom he had revered like a saint.

*

Sara came into his life at a time when his mother's chronic illness had taken a turn for the worse. Twenty-one year-old Sara La Rocca was hired to look after her. Don Alfio, then a strapping thirty-six year-old with a fondness for flamboyant women, hardly noticed the dark, waif-looking girl with intense black eyes. Just days after her arrival, his mother, a devout woman, called Alfio into her room.

'I just want to tell you this young woman is pregnant. Now, I don't want you to send her away, I am growing fond of her. And another thing, you will not take advantage of her, unless, that is, you have honourable intentions in her regard.'

Alfio was crestfallen. His mother hardly ever spoke to him about such matters, since he had chosen to live what she called a dissolute life. She understood his weakness. Her long-departed husband had been a womaniser, so she could hardly expect anything else from her son.

Alfio accepted his life was flighty, but what could he

do? Had he been gifted with artistic talent, or even a head for business, then yes, it would have been a pity to waste it. But he knew his only talent was for appreciating life's many pleasures: food, conversation, good company and women. Ah, women he did love. Of course, he had to accept that, in his mother's strict religious code – her code, not his – he was a sinner. In his defence he could say, to the Supreme judge when he got to the other side, that he hadn't just taken pleasure, he had given pleasure also. So while he admitted his life was shallow, at least he could not be accused of entirely wasting it. That would be unforgivable.

His sick mother's words must have planted a seed, or rather given him her eyes with which to look at Sara. And he saw in her a strength he had not seen in all the women he frequented.

Alfio's courtship of Sara La Rocca was conducted over the fast-receding body of his mother, and Sara's expanding belly. It wasn't easy for Sara, whose only experience with one man had been traumatic, to accept this man's attentions. For Alfio, who had dealt with sophisticated and willing women, adept at the game of love, Sara was a new challenge. Amorous looks, suggestive phrases, subtle physical contact as he brushed past her in the corridor – all of these had no effect. And yet the more she ignored him, the more eager he became. Her coldness fed his passion.

He stopped going to Palermo to attend society functions and fashionable houses. Instead he took a personal interest in the family citrus orchard, which in those days was his sole source of income. At night, he came home and took his coffee at Ciro's, where he knew people were beginning to talk about the delicate situation, because by this time Sara's condition was beginning to show.

Devotees who went to early morning Mass on Sunday could not help but notice. People naturally assumed Don

Alfio was the father, but couldn't understand why the woman was still in the house. Otherwise, why had he not married her? It did not occur to them that Don Alfio might not be the father, or even less likely, that she may not wish to marry him, the most eligible bachelor in San Sisto.

Don Alfio's persistence was making little impression on Sara. If she thought about it, and that was rare – for she was too busy to think at all – she found Don Alfio frivolous and lacking in character. Although she could see how a lot of women might find him attractive, she didn't. Of course she couldn't say this to Alfio, there really was no point in unduly hurting his feelings. But some explanation was needed. One day, while Donna Rosamunda slept on a chair by the fireplace, Alfio came back from Agneddu with a pannier of early figs.

'Figs already!' cried Sara, who had a real weakness for them.

Alfio held out the basket to her and she took a fig, smiling. He was encouraged by her obvious relish. He watched Sara squeeze the top of the fig with her thumbs and forefingers, then split it down the middle and pop the two halves in her mouth. As she savoured the flavour, making appreciative noises, she licked her lower lip. On seeing the flesh smeared over with sweet fig juice, Alfio could not hold back and he made a clumsy attempt to kiss her.

Instinctively Sara recoiled and gave a muffled shriek. Luckily the old woman slept through it. 'Don Alfio…'

'Please, call me Alfio.'

'Don Alfio,' Sara insisted, 'I am hired to look after your mother. Please don't take advantage.'

Don Alfio went red with outrage; that his intentions should be grossly misjudged offended his dignity. 'I assure, Sara, I have the greatest respect for you.'

'You don't know anything about me.'

'Only that I am in love with you. I don't wish to know anything else.'

She grabbed him by the wrists – her skinny fingers hardly reached halfway around their thickness – and held him at arms' length. She looked straight into his eyes. 'Don Alfio, I'm going to have a baby.'

'I know.'

'You do?'

'Yes, I knew it from the first day,' he lied. 'I am sure there is a story. But frankly I'm not into stories. All I want is to be allowed to stay by you, in the same way as you have sat by the bed of my poor mother.'

'Well!' She gave such a burst of laughter it made her look her age, for the first time since her arrival. 'You are not an invalid, for a start.'

'I will make myself an invalid, to get me your notice.'

He was so earnest, like a child begging. Sara, who had held herself together for four months, suddenly felt something inside her rupture and the tears gushed. She began to tell him about that night of fear in far off Australia, the hurt and shame.

Before she had even got to mention names, Don Alfio placed a finger over her lips. 'Don't. I don't wish to know. If you will have me, I will marry you tomorrow and this child will take my name.'

How could she say no? Sara married Don Alfio, not out of love, but out of his need and her gratitude. Love would come later; this was God's direction. She could see that. Alfio was a good man, what she lacked in love, she made up with plenty of care and affection, and in time it became indistinguishable from love. They were married in Sant'Antonio Abbate, the tiny church on the rocky hill on the outskirts of San Sisto.

It was a very small gathering, but large enough for the news to get around town, that Don Alfio and 'the Australian' had a shotgun marriage. Everyone thought it was the best thing, although they found it difficult to believe that Sara, who looked so serious, so devout, could have been involved in that sort of thing out of wedlock. The unanimous agreement was that Don Alfio had seduced the girl, the old lecher, which did not surprise anyone, and then hired her to look after his mother, to get the full measure. But at least he had done the honourable thing and married her.

Not long after the wedding, Alfio's mother died. He was distraught, but as his mother's ornate hazelnut coffin went into the Marzano family crypt, he consoled himself that, partly thanks to his mother, he now had a devoted wife. It was more than he had hoped for. Soon he became father to a beautiful son. Which was just as well, because following some tests he had for a prostrate inflammation, the doctors discovered that his sperm count was so low as to make him virtually sterile. This suited him fine, for Don Alfio had one truly outstanding talent: the ability to enjoy life. The last thing he wanted was to be strapped with the responsibility of a large family.

As his Alfa Romeo reached the Piazza Chiesa Madre – which in the village was referred to simply as Chiazza, because it was not merely the only piazza, but the only flat surface in the area, for which reason it was always used by town kids as a sports pitch on which to kick a soccer ball – he looked up at the window of his home. No sign of lights. Good. He didn't want to feel his wife had been waiting up for him. And Sante was home too; his Fiat Punto was there, parked right under the balcony with the ornate wrought iron railings.

He parked the car outside the *portone*, and walked

across to the Bar Ciro for his tucking-in coffee. There were just a few customers at the Bar, Carmine and Paolo, the Borrello cousins who spent their evenings there since their wives had died in an accident at the Forcina. And Fausto, the bus driver, who had just done his last run from Milazzo. Ciro the owner was also sitting down at one of the tables, and looked as if he had not had a good night's sleep in months.

Alfio downed his corretto, and called out a collective farewell. '*Signori, buona notte.*'

'*Buon riposo, Don Alfio.*'

Once inside, he checked to see the light was off in Sante's bedroom. So as not to awake his wife, he undressed in the passage, down to his cotton vest and underpants, slipped quietly in the bedroom and laid his tired body next to Sara. Carefully, he tucked his arm inside her smooth thin one and took her hand to his chest, right in the centre where he knew his very soul resided. And he felt all warm and cleansed. Sara was the port to which he would always return, always. She was his touchstone, his redeemer.

Ah, how he loved his wife!

6

With Alfio quickly asleep and snoring next to her, Sara was able to relax, but no sleep came. Sleep was elusive for her. She spent most of her nights lying in bed: thinking, fretting, regretting.

She could say, with utter sincerity, that of all the feelings that bound her to her husband, gratitude was the strongest. There were many things she was grateful to him for, many. For being such a good father to her son, of course. For not prying into her past, and allowing her to bury large slabs of it. For not demanding from her what she could not give, and getting it from other women. For being patient and understanding. Most of all, for being so loving, while she … ah, well now… when it came to that phantasm of emotions she was mystified by its complexity and stumped by guilt. For her husband's uncomplicated love, the most she could manage in return was total commitment and a genuine regard for the person he was, which easily passed for love.

Actually, right now she was grateful for his snoring. It provided both a backdrop for her morbid ruminations, and a link to the present, to reality, to normalcy over a night heavy with remembering. Unwelcome ghosts from that ill-fated migration to Australia lit the dark of the bedroom and walked across the ceiling.

Enter Sheryl Jane Giffen, with trademark straw hair and freckles.

Sara put the palm of her hand between her and the snoring Don Alfio.

'Don't think for a minute you're getting into bed between me and my husband.'

Sheryl's mouth twisted in scorn.

'As if … I've come to tell the story my way. I don't trust you after what you did.'

*

Sara La Rocca came to Thornton High halfway through first term. Sheryl saw her for the first time one sunny lunchtime in winter, sitting alone on the library steps, like she herself had done some two years before. She was a dark slight figure, with a tiny face and black brows over big dark eyes. She sat crouched, legs drawn up under her chin, where her tiny face sat propped up by closed knees. With her free hands she was throwing what was left of her lunch to the crows.

Sheryl thought she should feel sorry for her, for being foreign in a school where she knew foreigners were given a hard time, and for not having any friends. But somehow the girl didn't seem to mind. There was such self-sufficiency in her expression, such calm confidence, that for this creature being alone was comfortable. It suggested certainty about who she was and what she was doing in the world. Her self-assurance belied her fragile appearance. Sheryl couldn't even look at her for fear she might look back and annihilate her. And yet, at the same time, Sheryl felt an urge to speak to her. If only she had the courage! Besides, she had Russell's lunch in her hand and he was waiting for it.

Russell was playing around with Moira Austin, the redhead who hung around like a painted crow waiting for crumbs. Russell had her right arm locked behind her back, and she pretended to be hurting.

'Don't. Let me go, Russ, you big bully.'

But you could tell by the tone of her voice that she was

enjoying it.

'Here's your lunch.' Sheryl slapped the paper bag down next to him.

'Where ya been? I been starvin'.'

He looked as if he should go on a starvation diet, thought Sheryl, suddenly feeling aggro. 'I can't help it if the teacher keeps us in, can I? Why can't you get your own lunch, anyhow?' The words were out before she could stop. It shocked her to be speaking to Russell like that, and in front of everyone, too.

Russell went psycho. 'Fuck off you dog, go on. You don't belong here.'

'Let her stay,' someone said.

But Russell was resolute. What was at stake was his power, his manhood and they were not to be compromised. 'No, she ain't stayin' and that's that.'

Sheryl spun around and strode off, shoulders stooping. Tears stole into her eyes, but this time they weren't tears of self-pity and rejection. They were tears of anger. She wasn't angry with Russell, he didn't know any better, he acted true to form, he had to assert his power. She was angry with herself for being who she was. She wanted to be someone else: with a different face, different hair colour. Somehow she knew the foreign girl she had just seen feeding the crows would never be in her humiliating situation.

Quite without thinking she headed back for the library. The girl was gone. At first she was relieved. Had she been there, Sheryl would have run scared and hidden somewhere. Then she became angry for being so stupid and began to sob. Groups of students chattering by ignored her. Sheryl Giffen's antics were well known around the school. A bit of an attention seeker she was.

After school, she would normally go with Russell to the back of his stepfather's garage, where there were a few wrecked cars, to have a smoke and whatever. But that afternoon, Russell was still mad at her and went off with his mates. Sheryl was left at the front of the school wondering what to do. She felt terrible. She sat down by the entrance wall and rested her head on her knees.

Someone wheeling a bike out of the fence enclosure stopped next to her without saying anything.

'Whatchyou lookin' at, hey?' Sheryl spat at the shadow, but looked up and saw it was that foreign girl. Embarrassed, she got up on her knees and straightened her back, grazing her spine along the wire fence as she did so.

'My name is Sara.' The girl spoke in a voice that was unexpectedly deep for such a slight girl. 'I'm new.' She spoke deliberately, as if she were reading words from a book inside her head.

'Sara? What kinda name's that?

'Italian. What class are you in?'

Sheryl told her. 'And you?'

'Not sure yet. They've put me in C12 for now.'

'That's Miss Kovic's class. She's a dragon.'

'I hope they'll change me then. Do you live around here?'

'Yes … no, not really. I usually catch the bus, but I've missed it today.'

They started walking in the same direction down Lawson Street.

'I'll give you a ride,' said Sara.

Sheryl looked at her as if she had suggested something subversive. 'What do you mean? How?'

'Here, you can sit on the rack.'

Sheryl eyed her suspiciously, but Sara had such cheeky *I dare you* kind of look. It was persuasive. 'OK then, but don't blame me if we fall.'

They had gone less than twenty metres when the bike

promptly toppled over and landed on the petunia bed in front of the school. Neither got hurt, and it probably wouldn't have mattered if they had. They didn't care. They were both in stitches over the incident and the giggles lasted until they arrived at Sara's house, by which time it seemed as if they had been friends forever. It was weird.

*

 Sara lived in one of those chunky 'Italian' houses, with high limestone foundations, a garage underneath, wide balcony with ornate railing, and cream-coloured bricks. It was an expression of cultural disorientation; an ugly allusion to the mountain 'cascina' in sterile suburbia.

They left the bicycle in the garage and Sheryl followed Sara up the external staircase to the back door and into a dark corridor that smelled stale. She opened one of the doors and quietly tiptoed in.

A soft, whining voice came from the bed. 'Sara, *trasi, ca nun dormu. Apri a finestra.*'

Sheryl didn't understand the words or see the person speaking, until Sara went and drew the curtains to reveal an old man lying in bed, wearing a woollen vest. He had sunken eyes and lots of white hair. Sara went up and kissed him on the forehead. The old man put one hand around the back of her head and held her to him for a few seconds.

'Dad, look how sweaty you are.' She spoke the sentence in English, for Sheryl's benefit, or perhaps to draw his attention to the 'Australian' guest, then continued in Sicilian.

She went to the linen cupboard on the opposite side of the room and got out a clean vest. She helped him sit up, pulled off the sweaty garment, and swabbed him down all over his face and neck with a damp face cloth, all the while chatting with him in their own language. Sheryl gathered she was telling him about her new school. Finally, she slipped the vest on him.

When he was done and looking a little revived Sara said in English,' Dad, this is my friend, Sheryl.'

The old man gave her his left hand and squeezed hers without saying anything. Meanwhile Sara changed the pillowcase. 'He's been sweating like a donkey.'

On the bedside table were some pills. Sara got one out and held the glass to her father who drank it slowly. Next to the glass was a twig of silver leaves in a vase.

'What's that?' Sheryl was curious.

'It's an olive branch. Dad thinks it'll bring him good luck. He's very superstitious.'

In the backyard, they sat at a white cement table over which twisted a canopy of branches.

'It's a grape vine.' Sara explained. 'In summer, you can stand and pick your own. I love grapes, don't you? Oh, look at the time, I've got to go and put the tea on.'

'Don't you have TV?'

'Of course. But we hardly ever watch it. My parents don't speak much English, and I don't have time.'

'What do you do?'

'Oh I got lots to do, 'specially now my father's sick, me and my Mum are looking after the garden. I feed the chooks, pick the veggies. And there's homework of course.' Sara had never taken homework seriously. She had followed Russell's maxim that homework's for teachers to show students who's boss.

'What's wrong with your Dad?'

'Had an accident at the factory where he works. Broke his pelvis. He's much better now. Before, he couldn't even sit up.'

'He looks pretty old ...'

Sara giggled. 'Don't tell him that. He's sixty-four, he got married late. Mum was pretty old too when she had me. Forty-two, I think.'

A voice came from inside. 'Sara, *vidi ca to mamma arriva.*'

'*Vegnu.* Better go in, my Mum's coming. Dad can hear the car coming a kilometre away. I don't know how he does it.'

A woman came, carrying a bagful of shopping. She was quite short and dark, with a mousy face like her daughter's and hair tied back in a pointy bun. A mole stood out on the side of her neck, but otherwise her skin was smooth.

What Sheryl found disconcerting were her eyes: they were dark and set in deep sockets, and looked at you out of some unseen depth.

'This is my friend from school.' The girl spoke to her in English.

The woman sized her up and down. 'A frien'? Good. Very good.'

Sheryl thought the woman was judging her suitability to be her daughter's friend, and felt sure she didn't like her.

Yet, after letting go of her hand, she turned to her daughter. 'You frien' she look too pale. Make a Marsala drink for her.'

Sheryl followed Sara to the kitchen and watched her crack an egg into a glass, whisk it vigorously with a fork until frothy, then add milk, a dash of Marsala and a sprinkling of cinnamon.

'Is that wine?' Sheryl pointed at the Marsala bottle.

'Yeah, sort of, like a sweet wine.'

'You mean you're allowed to have it?'

'Why not? Try it, it won't kill you.'

Sheryl stepped back, as if she were offered poison. 'Do I have to have it?'

'No, you should try it though, it's good for you.'

Sheryl took a sip. It was just an egg flip with a bit of taste. She drank most of it.

Sara finished the rest. 'It'll please Mum if she thinks you finished it.'

*

Sheryl and Sara became best friends: best friends at first sight. They joked about it. And when Sara was put in the same class as her, the two girls became inseparable. They sat together, worked together, laughed, teased, and gossiped. It was fun.

'Sheryl, do you think the Ram and the Koala are having an affair?' Sara was referring to Miss Ramsay, the English teacher, and Mr Kawala, the art teacher, who were often seen together.

'You're a gossip, Sara.'

'I know, pass me the protractor, will you?'

'I think Mr Kawala's too old for her. I think he might be married.'

'Oh I know he's married, that's why I said 'an affair'.'

'Honestly Sara, you're such a busybody ...'

And they giggled until Miss Ramsay would call out to them, 'Come on you two, get on with your work.'

Having a best friend was wild.

Russell didn't like Sara from the start. He first saw them together outside of science walking side by side in between periods. 'Who's that foreign chick you was with today?'

'Who do you mean?'

'The dark runt with the fuzzy hair.'

'That's Sara. She's new.'

'Toldya. She's a dago, ain't she?'

'Don't be awful, Russ. She's very nice.'

'Oh yeah, and what was you doing with her?'

'Just talking, what do you think?'

'Don't snap at me, or I'll sock you one.'

God how she hated Russell when he put on his bully manner!

*

Pickering Brook was a community of stone fruit orchardists, nestled on the city's escarpment, where the sand of the coastal plain gave way to the gravelly soil of the hills.

Here post-war migrants from Southern Europe attempted to transplant what they had left behind, with replicas of Valtellina, Sicily, Dalmatia. They planted orchards of apricots, peaches, apples and pears, built churches and community halls. They replicated festivals.

For the feast of St Anthony, some 600 people came together in the paved space in front of the church of the same name, in the soft autumn sun. A statue of the saint with his chalk face, monk's tunic and sandals was hoisted up on a frame with four wooden handles. On a blue silken sash adorning the saint's breast, people pinned five-, ten-, or twenty-dollar donations. As the procession started, the brass band headed off first, playing *O Santa Vergine Maria*.

The statue of St Anthony, with its rouged cheeks and a silver ring over its small, bald head, was carried over the shoulders of four brawny men. Others flanked them, waiting for their turn to take on the honour. They were followed by children dressed as little angels, with wings of sky-blue feathers. The dignitaries came next, headed by the bishop, the priests, and the president of the St Anthony Devotees. Finally, came the rest of the congregation.

Sara and Sheryl walked together, alone, because Mr La Rocca, although much better, was still not strong enough to last out the length of the procession, so Mrs La Rocca stayed with him back at the church. The people paced behind the statue, talking. Some older women prayed, children skipped along.

Sheryl felt protected and happy. 'It's nice here.'

'I wasn't sure if you'd like it. I mean, this is very traditional stuff.'

'I do.'

Without warning Sara tucked her forearm under hers and drew her to her side. The unexpected closeness made Sheryl shiver.

'You cold?'

'Not really… a bit.'

Sara pulled her closer. They walked arm in arm, past rows of apple trees with gold and brown leaves. Women had intense whispering conversations with each other, children held their parents' hands. Men in suits, ties and hats chatted with friends in familiar subdued tones below the shrill sound of the brass band. The elderly prayed with rosary beads in hand.

'This reminds me of my village in Sicily,' said Sara.

'Do you still remember it then?'

'Of course, I've only been in Australia five years.'

'Do you think … you'll wanna go back there?'

'Probably. I don't know. I'd like to go and visit anyway. We can go together. Would you like to?'

'Yeah, I'd love that.'

And they held each other so close they nearly tripped as they walked. Sheryl sniffled as she wiped a tear with the back of her hand.

'What's wrong?' Sara wanted to know.

'Nothing, I'm just happy, that's all.'

7

Disaster arrived on the back of an exotic fruit. Prickly pears made an unhappy journey to Australia. In Queensland, their adaptability proved to be their downfall. As they threatened to overrun newly-cleared land they were quickly declared invasive. In Western Australia they came to be tolerated, begrudgingly, in the confines of a home garden, so that nostalgic Mediterranean people could add a prickly pear to their olive tree, fig tree, lemon tree and grape vines in family orchards. Sara's father had planted theirs at the back of the sandy block, tucked away beyond the corrugated iron roof of the shed, between the chicken pen and the asbestos back fence.

When Sara took them to school in her lunch box, Sheryl eyed the two egg-shaped fruit – one golden, the other the colour of pomegranate – with the same mix of fascination and caution with which she had regarded all the other strange foods she had sampled, since the friendship had started.

'They're a cactus,' explained Sara, 'the skin's covered in prickles. My father peels them. Take your pick, they're really nice.'

Best friends had to share everything. Sheryl took the golden one. Sara ate the other one, savouring the sweet, seedy succulence.

'What do you think?'

'Mm, they're different.' She was unconvinced.

'I love them,' said Sara. 'One time, when I was little, I ate so many that I blocked up. '

'You mean … you couldn't go?' Sheryl giggled into her hand.

'Mm, mm … my mother had a hell of a job getting me

started. It was painful.'

As Sheryl laughed, juice ran down the side of her mouth, to her chin. 'Messy too, I bet.'

Sara gave such a hilarious account of the ordeal it had Sheryl in stitches. They laughed in each other's lap, not caring who was watching. There they go again, those two weirdoes, thought the other students.

An hour later, Sheryl was sitting in the infirmary, having left the fruit in the toilet bowl. The nurse asked a few questions, gave her something to settle her stomach, and suggested she should take some tests. When she came out to Sara, who was waiting for her in the foyer, Sheryl's cheeks were on fire.

'What's wrong, Sheryl?'

'I got somethin' to tell ya.' Her voice was strangely elated. 'Not here though.' Her body seemed to be straining to contain some pressure cooker of a secret from exploding out of her. It was scary.

When they were finally alone in the darkness of the house, Sheryl took her hand and led her down the narrow corridor, through the fly-wire door, and out on the back porch. Down the steps they went, over the patch of buffalo lawn and beyond the vegetable garden into the orchard. In the cosy privacy afforded by wall of the shed and the canopy of the juvenile olive tree, Sheryl took both her hands and pulled her close. She was all animated, eyes beady, as if she were about to propose marriage.

'I been dying to tell you … we're going to have a baby.'

So great was the shock that Sara did not think her use of the pronoun strange. 'Don't be stupid, Sheryl.'

'I saw it. The nurse showed me the red dot on the tester.'

When the truth finally sank in Sara felt shaken by a great surge of anger. She pulled her hand free from Sheryl's grip. 'You're so stupid...!' She screamed, pacing up and down. 'Stupid! Stupid! Stupid!' Her face was all twisted up. You told me you'd stopped doing that stuff.'

'I'm sorry. It's just that I get lonely when you're not around.'

'What are you going to do?'

'I don't know.' Her eyes filled with tears. She had expected Sara to be delighted with the news, make a fuss of her. This was big news, this was awesome! This was their baby, a living icon of their love for each other. Instead, Sara had only made her feel guilty, scared. So, prompt came the tears, and then a frightening thought. 'Russell's gonna kill me.'

Sheryl was wrong. When Russell was told, in the presence of the school counsellor, his reaction was unexpected. He seemed pleased, already basking in the glory of his mates' acclaim of his prowess. He did not consider the implications; his imagination did not stretch that far. All he could think was that this pregnancy was a further, irrefutable proof of his superior manhood. He imagined himself walking around the school grounds, in the shopping centre, at the bike track – with Sheryl at his side, her protruding belly a trophy to his unassailable virility. And to show manly stiff-dick Russell could also be tender, he went straight to the canteen and spent his last fifty cents buying a diet Coke to present to Sheryl.

*

If Sheryl was undecided what to do about the pregnancy, her foster parents had no doubt. If she wanted to have the baby, she would have to move out. Their house was a foster home to two other children, and they had to think of their welfare too.

'They want me to … lose the baby.' Sheryl burst into tears and fell into Sara's arms. She clung to her constantly in that period; she wanted to be held, comforted, have her tears wiped, her hair done.

'And what did you say?'

'Sara, I can't. I don't wanna. It's … our baby.'

'What about Russell? What does he say?'

'I don't care about him. I don't want him around ever again. I hate him.' The pregnancy brought out the fighting spirit in Sheryl. She was a bit like the old hen back in Sicily, the speckled one, pecked and put-upon by every other bird in the yard. Then each spring, she punctually went clucky and sat on the eggs for weeks. When she came off the roost with her brood of chicks, she had more fight in her than a cock. She puffed out her feathers as a warning, and if any hen came near her chicks she would chase it ferociously.

Every afternoon, after school, Sheryl came to her house and stayed there in Sara's bedroom, lingering as long as possible. She was scared of Mrs La Rocca, who saw that this girl was in deep trouble, and wasting her daughter's time.

One day, after she had a good cry and Sara was comforting her, Sheryl looked her friend in the eye. 'Maybe I can stay here, till the baby is born.'

The thought had occurred to Sara, but the niggling worry she was getting herself deeper and deeper into a muddy situation restrained her. Now, she suddenly found the idea captivating. Despite herself, Sara admired the new Sheryl. There was a maturity and softness about her. Sara loved those long embraces, stolen in the privacy of the bedroom. Looking back on it now, with a quarter of a century of hindsight, it was clear that it was the devil, tempting her through Sheryl Giffen, and she had caved in.

Sara took her friend's case to her shocked parents. 'She doesn't have anyone, Mum. She's pretty desperate.'

'We'll speak to Father Cassani. They may be able to help at the parish.'

It turned out Father Cassani was away in Melbourne for a month, and his place had been taken by a priest from the Philippines. He was a young man, full of missionary zeal, which over-spilled into a plenitude of social conscience. 'This child seems to have lost her way. What she needs most of all at the moment is a good, stable, Christian home.' He looked at Mrs La Rocca. 'Yours has the added advantage that she would have her best friend for support...'

*

For the last four months of her pregnancy, Sheryl did not attend school, but spent her day waiting for Sara. She made lunch for Mr La Rocca, whom she called Pop. The La Rocca household was a busy one. No all-day TV watching: there was too much to do. Mrs La Rocca went to work while Pop, still convalescing from his accident, spent his day pottering around in the garden.

When autumn came, Sara and Sheryl picked the green fruit off the olive tree. Sara went up the ladder and picked the upper branches, Sheryl did the lower ones. They crushed them on a wooden cutting board, banging on each individual olive with the bottom of a milk bottle, splitting the olives so they could be stoned. They left them in a bucket, changing the water several times a day, until the lime colour changed to dark green. Then her mother seasoned them with garlic, chili, fennel seeds, bay leaves, slices of lemon, and salt. Sheryl became addicted to these olives.

'You maybe need da salt,' said Mrs La Rocca.

'It's not me, it's the baby.' Sheryl smiled. Everybody

thought it was hilarious. Even Pop, who was a sad, distant man, laughed.

But there were tears too. For no particular reason, and at the most inopportune times, tears would steal into Sheryl's eyes. Then she had to hold them back, fearing that if Mrs La Rocca noticed, she might send her away.

But at night, in the bedroom, it was different. The girls shared a room with two single beds, separated by a small chest of drawers on which stood a lamp. When Sheryl cried, Sara would slip into bed with her. She comforted her friend, running fingers through her blonde hair, whispering soothing words. When Sara made as if to return to her bed, Sheryl held her tight and pleaded, 'Don't Sara, don't go yet.'

Some nights they fell asleep in each other's arms and in the morning they'd wake up in the same bed.

Sheryl never mentioned Russell. Russell was the past, a world she wanted to close the door upon. He was probably with someone else now, making some poor girl's life miserable. It amused her to think how jealous she had been just a few months ago. Now she couldn't care less if she never saw Russell again.

'Know what, Sara?' Sheryl whispered one night, as they were about to fall asleep holding each other's hand. 'There's one part of me that wants this to last forever.'

As her belly grew, Sheryl would lie on her bed naked and they watched a leg or arm push up under the skin and arch across the belly and both would stare and wonder at the miracle. Sheryl's breasts also began to enlarge, to swell and got sumptuous.

Sara could not stop looking at them. Around the dilated pink nipples, a circle of follicles had appeared. Sometimes the ends of her blonde hair – grown long and unkempt, now other parts of her body occupied her mind – curled around her breasts and the nipples peered through blonde strands like big buttons of satin.

Even now, a quarter of a century on, lying next to a man she'd been married to for over seventeen years, the vision comes through so fresh she can smell the skin. The devil is surely in her; it visits her at her most vulnerable times. And yet, never during those recurrent visits did her lips and Sheryl's breasts make contact. It was her just punishment.

*

One night, Sheryl went to bed earlier than usual, complaining of feeling tired. She fell asleep almost at once. Sara, working at her desk, could hear her breathing. A light film of sweat had appeared on her brow, she looked fragile but at peace. A girl just turned sixteen, younger than herself, hurled into the role of womanhood, long before she was ready. Suddenly she stirred, wriggling, and started to kick the cover off the bed.

'What's wrong?' Sara was concerned.

'I'm hot.'

With the palm of her hand she felt the sheet. When her finger came into contact with a warm, melmous patch she gave out a scream. Maternity classes had not prepared her for this moment. It was Mrs La Rocca, woken by the screaming, who sprang into action.

The birth was quick. Sheryl barely made it to the delivery room before a bald pink head forced its way through the cervix and the slippery body of a baby girl slid into the world.

'What name are you going to give her?' The nurse had not been informed that the baby was marked for adoption.

'Sara.' Sheryl spoke promptly. 'Sara Giffen.'

Sara was moved to tears. She leant over the bed and

hugged her. 'That's so sweet, Sheryl.'

Later in the morning, when the nurse brought the baby into the room, she had something else to say. 'Of course, the name will probably be changed.'

'Why?'

'Well, her adoptive parents might want to give her their own name.'

Sheryl, the child-mother who could never make a decision on even the most mundane matters, this time was resolute. 'Sara, this is our baby. We are the parents. I'll never give her up for adoption.'

Jane, Sheryl's middle name, was added later to the birth certificate. So the child came to be known as Sara-Jane, to distinguish her from the older Sara.

8

A wet October Saturday morning and, once again, his lie-in is spoilt by a headache and screaming kids from next door. A couple of Panadols might fix the first, but there's no remedy for the kids.

He does of course have a grown-up daughter of his own, the one with the hoity-toity name and attitude to match. Hasn't heard from her in ages. She's going places and keeping her distance. Suits him. He's got enough on his plate. Still, he has to admit, it's good to see her doing well for herself, considering all the shit her mother put her through. Good old Sheryl, there's a stuffed-up mind if ever there was one. To be honest, she managed to stuff him up too. Looking back, all the women he's had since – and there've been a few– they've just … flitted through his life. Forgettable mock-ups, they've been. The one he'll never forget is that ticked-in-the-head sixteen year-old with the whiney voice, who used to follow him around like a mange dog.

He can never figure out what it was about Sheryl. Maybe it's because she was the first and the craziest. It's like her face was tattooed inside the walls of his brain. And it's not as if she was a great looker; he's had plenty better-looking women since. As for brains, old Sheryl was a bit on the thick side, let's face it. Personality? Nothing to write home about either. Boring.

Nah, it was something else. Something about her that hit you unexpectedly when you were daydreaming or watching the box. You saw it in a flash sometimes, when you caught her profile. She looked kind of waiflike. She reminded Russell of this picture he once saw of a single garment hanging from a wire on one of them clothes hoists, being tossed about by the wind. It made you want to trap her, contain her in a space, keep her steady, because Sheryl was out of control. Something anarchic about her. With Sheryl you felt you had to keep a tight lid on things because, if he let that loose cannon have it over him, she could do some real damage.

So, when she whimpered or looked at you with her stupid dog eyes, you were caught between competing urges to either screw her or belt some sense into her. Of course he didn't know at the time the risks he was taking, he didn't think. Just kids getting into grown-up games, tossed about in a world of anger and desire.

It's weird to think a chit of a girl like that, without brains or personality, could have left such a mark on him. Maybe it came down to this: he loved Sheryl, and after a quarter of a century he is convinced that love it was, although at the time it was just a game. He loved her for her weakness, because her weakness made him feel strong.

Then out of the blue, she turned against him. It happened so quickly, like someone catching you from the rear, grabbing you by the nuts, wrestling you down. It was all the fault of that foreign girl, the one with the olive skin, the crow-black frizzy hair and the lizard eyes that unsettled you. From the first time he set eyes on her, he knew she would be trouble, that one. After the foreign girl arrived at the school, Sheryl wasn't the same any more, she took over her mind, changed her personality. Overnight, his girl, who had clung to him like a leech, became moody and wilful: a rebel he could no longer control, a resentful bitch that bit back. That dago girl had poisoned her.

Well, you can fight off a male rival but a female … it takes a different approach, a different method. He knew he would get his chance sooner or later.

When he was given the news, Russell was

disappointed. A baby girl wasn't part of the picture he had in his head. Still, he was a father, and just seventeen. It was certainly good cause for celebration.

That afternoon he called a couple of his mates, Ronnie and Darryl. The latter had a car and, more importantly, at eighteen, was allowed to buy alcohol. They drove to the nearest liquor store and bought a dozen VB stubbies, headed for South Beach, and got stuck into the celebrations, as any man who had just become a father would.

'It's not every day you become a father, hey.' Darryl expressed the very thought in Russell's mind.

General agreement accompanied gulps of beer and appropriate manly burps. Having given due regard to the great feat accomplished by Russell, the conversation soon moved to cars, and whether a MK II was faster than a Mustang. Russell, who had always said he would be buying a sporty red Mk II when he had his own business and made heaps of money, said that undoubtedly a MK II was the fastest.

'Ok then, how ya gonna carry your baby in a MK II? Tell me that.'

Russell was stumped for a moment. 'What d'ya mean?'

'Well, it's got no back seat for starters. Where you gonna fix the baby seat then?'

Of course, the baby was going to be adopted anyhow, so the question was academic, but it didn't stop the trio arguing the point for a long time, as long as the grog lasted, anyway. Then, for good measure, they had a tussle in the sand. When the twelve empty stubbies lay scattered around a sandy mound, it was time for him to face up to the responsibilities of fatherhood.

*

When he got to King Edward Memorial Hospital, with his mates flanking him, the matron, a no-nonsense woman, nearly as broad as she was tall, seeing the state they were in, got stuck into them. 'Just where do you think you're going?' She spoke to the three of them, eyeing them at once. 'This is a maternity hospital, not your local boozer.'

But Russell was not going to be intimidated by the woman, not in front of his mates, most definitely not on the day he had become a father.

'I'm the father.' He stood tall.

'It looks to me as if you could do with a father yourself. Whose father are you?'

'Of the baby.'

'Which baby? We've got twenty-three in this ward alone.'

Russell realized, to his dismay, that he didn't know his daughter's name.

'Sheryl …'

'Sheryl? There's no baby Sheryl here.'

'Sheryl's the mother. Sheryl Giffen.'

The matron knew the girl. They didn't get too many sixteen year-old mothers. 'She's in 2.36 down the corridor … Ah! Ah! Just you. Your mates can wait outside.'

Bitch! Russell said the word under his breath.

Approaching the bed, he had not counted on meeting Sheryl's mate there. They were sitting together, their heads touching, studying some baby magazine with such absorption that they seemed insulated from the world. It made him angry to see that. The alcohol was beginning to wear off and that always made him morose.

Sara saw him first, and nudged Sheryl who, on looking up and seeing him there, gasped as if the devil had walked in on her.

Russell had not seen Sheryl for some five months and she had changed. She was not Sheryl, but a grown-up woman who didn't need him anymore. An impenetrable aura wrapped the two girls. Russell understood that whatever they were sharing – the space into which they were huddled for companionship and comfort – that space, would always be denied to him. Being ostracized by those two females at such a moment hurt so badly that to stop himself from crying, he grabbed a clump of hair from the back of his head and tore at it.

Looking back, he now understands what he felt is what millions of men feel: the desolation of being male. It's only now, at age forty-one and counting, he has come to realize that – for all the posturing, the physical strength and the power-play of men – real power resides with the woman. The physical weakness in a woman is a ploy. It's the appearance of weakness, a trap. What passes for weakness in women is a surfeit of that ability to focus all their energies to love, and to submit, not to the man – that's just an illusion, part of their genius – but to the strength of their own feelings. This gives them a quality men can't comprehend and so deny, at their peril. Women have the power to make a man or to destroy him. Women are witches, anarchic; the weaker they appear, the more dangerous they are.

Sheryl stonewalled him with an icy stare. 'What are you doing here?'

'I come to see ya.' He felt intimidated and hated it.

'You could have called …'

He was the father, why did he have to call? He wanted to give Sheryl a piece of his mind, the sharp piece, but with what's-her-name there, looking on, it was a case of grin and bear.

'I'd better be going.' Sara started to rise from her perch on the end of the bed.

Sheryl grabbed her hand. 'You can't go yet, Sara. They'll be bringing the baby soon. Don't you want to see her before you leave?' She said 'the baby' like it was 'our baby', a shared thing between the two of them.

'I thought you was going to adopt.' Russell looked confused.

'I've changed my mind.'

He was stunned as much by her tone as by the news. It was like, this is what I've decided to do and you'd better not argue with me. No by-your-leave. Such sure-fire decisiveness was not a trait of the Sheryl he knew.

'You mean, you gonna look after her yourself?'

Sheryl looked at Sara. 'Yeah.' Her voice was firm. 'We're going to.' She looked him straight in the eyes, confronting him like a featherweight squaring up to a heavyweight in the ring.

Sara stood. 'I'm going down to the canteen.' Before Sheryl had a chance grab her hand again she whispered, 'I'll call in before I go home.'

With Sara gone, he was able to really take a good look at her and was astonished. When he last saw her, five months ago, she was still the same gawky Sheryl he had always known. Now, her teenage body had filled out and she was a strange, self-assured, intimidating woman.

Russell sat on the bed, the way Sara had done. With the weight of his hefty body the mattress dipped and sagged. Sheryl's lighter body slid forward and her leg came to rest against his knee. Quickly, Sheryl hoisted herself on her elbow and went to rest back against the headboard. Her breasts swelled up under the embroidery of her nightdress.

A flush of desire filled Russell's loins, heightened by a weird kind of tenderness. He was almost in tears, and found himself saying embarrassing things. 'Sheryl, I want us to get back together ... I'll get a job ... I'll look after you ... and the baby.' His pleading voice disarmed her for a minute.

Then her face hardened. 'Would you mind not sitting on the bed? The nurses don't like it.'

'What about your mate then?'

'She's not as heavy as you are.'

What really hurt him was the contempt in her voice, and the hatred in her eyes. Of course, he realized it wasn't her. Sheryl wouldn't be so hard, Sheryl he could handle. It was the foreign tart who had turned her, and poisoned her against him.

Russell moved his weight off the bed, but didn't sit on the chair. He stood, so his laddish bulk towered above the bed. 'Where you gonna live?'

'I've applied for a State Housing Commission flat, which I'm entitled to, as a single mother ...'

She had it all worked out. Or rather, the other one had it all worked out for her. Sheryl didn't have the brains for it. He knew one thing; Sheryl would not be his again, not the way it used to be, until the dago girl was put back in her place. Russell knew what needed to be done, and he was just the right person to do it. It was a case of waiting and getting her all by herself.

9

Don Alfio went to the bathroom to lighten his body. Normally, he would have stumbled back to bed, this being a Sunday, but he sensed Sara had had one of her nights. The cold of the mattress next to him attested to the fact she had been up a long time. So he rinsed his mouth, and gave a quick brush to what was left of the hair around the crown of his head. His smile, emerging from the collar of his burgundy shaving coat, brought light and ease into the living room, heavy with Sara's thoughts.

One look at her, and he understood this was no physical ailment: no migraine or stomach upset. No, Sara was having a very athletic tussle with her demons, and she had a plenitude of them. Sara was at the mercy of her thoughts, her memories, her scruples, her guilt, her religion. Enough baggage to fill a train compartment.

Still, Don Alfio did not judge or feel pity for her. He understood all that baggage was as essential to her existence as pleasure was to his. So their union seemed to him fortuitous and, in its own way, perfect. Human perfection, which of course was as illusory as a magician's trick, was all about balance, about extremes weighing out each other. By the rules of his rudimentary philosophy – he couldn't cope with anything more complicated – her heaviness was the perfect antidote to his frothy approach to life. Likewise, her piety counterbalanced his earthiness; his straightforward nature was a fitting counterweight to her convoluted psychology.

Like a good prosecco, in which acidity and sweetness were perfectly balanced, so were Don Alfio and Sara.

Sara had been smoking, unusual for her at this time of the morning. Usually she did not start until after lunch. As he walked in, he caught her with a cigarette in her fingers, over a coffee. Ash and two stunted butts on the bottom of the tray betrayed her turmoil. He wondered at the reason. Probably that business with the olive grove.

'Have you had your breakfast, Sara?' He kissed her on the cheek, avoiding smoke billowing past her shoulder.

'Alfio, I don't have breakfast on Sunday, you know that.'

Of course, Holy Communion. One must receive the body of Christ on an empty stomach. Hopefully Christ does not object to the smell of tobacco, he mused. Don Alfio did not mind the contradiction. He saw it as the rich, mysterious vein that ran through all women and made them such fascinating creatures.

Don Alfio loved women. He liked men too, but women … women were a miracle. He mused and pondered as he sat down to his breakfast. They were the reason for his existence, his oxygen, his saviours. Their beauty complemented a man's plainness, their wonder his banality. Women, whether they love or hate, did so intensely, totally. And sometimes, at their most miraculous, did so contemporaneously. Women gave of themselves fully, and were equally exigent of their man, hence the eternal conflict.

Men did not have the courage, the daring, or the power to give totally of themselves. In short, men were trapped by their egos. For that reason, thought Don Alfio – happy to be able to conclude his train of thought with an appropriate aphorism – a man's philandering is an escape from his inadequacy; his stronger frame a cover-up for his moral frailty.

He wanted to share all this with the woman he was devoted to, but how could he? Would she understand? Certainly not at a time like this. This was the time to assuage her fears. 'What's wrong, *cara*?'

Sara stretched out her arm and from inside the sleeve of her dressing gown retrieved a single sheet of paper folded several times – and probably scrunched into a ball at one point, judging by its condition – and placed it in front of him.

Don Alfio understood. His wife had told him about the other woman in Australia and her daughter. That whole business stressed him, but only because he knew his wife viewed it with such intensity. To tell the truth, he'd rather not have known about it, but he had to take on board his wife's burden sometimes. So he sighed. 'I see.'

And because he didn't know what to say, he drank down his coffee, tilting his head back and keeping it there for longer than was necessary.

'I am not going to contact her,' she said. Then, because he still did not say anything, she added, 'I suppose you think I should.'

Of course she knew what he thought. They had discussed the matter before. Left up to his wife, she would have had Sante still believe Don Alfio was his natural father. It was recently, barely two years ago, that the boy was told the truth, or rather, a portion of the truth, seasoned with some syrupy invention to make it more palatable.

'Sara, if I am not mistaken, this girl is Sante's natural sister ...'

'Half-sister.' She corrected him, blowing smoke away from him.

'Well, he'll want to meet her. He's entitled to know.'

'That would mean having to tell him the truth about ... his father.'

'He will find out eventually, and it is better that he hears it from you.'

'I can't Alfio.' She stubbed out her cigarette and almost shouted, 'I can't!' Then more sedately, 'Not yet.' She pleaded with him, as if he were some kind of condemning judge.

Love and pity did a little pirouette in Don Alfio's heart and stopped him from pressing the point. Besides, he could see that in time she would come round to his way of thinking, all by herself.

10

At last, with Clem Franzetti dozing behind her, stretched out in his first class sleeper, she had time to relax and enjoy the moment. Franzetti had fidgeted ever since he arrived at the airport. He was morose and ill-tempered; his nostrils flared as if attempting to keep out a bad smell, his double-breasted jacket was undone over a retreating stomach, his complexion doughy.

He hardly looked at her. On the plane he had complained about the seat being too close to the window, the temperature being too hot, the air too dry. When he finally settled down, he asked for a glass of water, took something, and promptly fell asleep.

Sara suspected he was aviophobic. Flying first class was a waste on Clem Franzetti.

From the airport, the taxi lumbered along a dirt road, through low-lying bamboo clumps, toward Villa San Giovanni, to catch the ferry to Messina.

Behind the wheel was a stocky man in his late fifties, with a crown of hair that once might have been red, then mutated to dark brown but was now definitely – what was left of it – a few strands away from white. His small chestnut-coloured eyes were quick and lively. He blinked a lot.

Perhaps a nervous tic, thought Sara. The comparative thinness of his upper lip was compensated by a fleshy pink bottom lip that protruded like a beak, which he moistened frequently as he spoke.

At the ferry queue, they dovetailed on a ramp and a strange ritual began. Each car revved its engine with intimidating thrusts, pushing and lurching forward to gain that extra centimetre over the cars on either side. All this went on while the driver conducted an animated conversation with Sara-Jane, in his basic English.

'Ah, you Australian! Beautiful! Beautiful! I 'ava … *parente*, in Australia … many, many long time in Australia he stay.' The bulk of his chatter was pretty well incomprehensible, though it did not deter the man.

Franzetti sat in the back seat, his head slumped back, eyes closed, suffering the driver's chatter, finding his familiarity overbearing. Sensing her boss's irritability, Sara did not encourage the conversation, even though she wanted to try out her Italian on the man.

'Ask him how long it'll take to get to the other side.' Franzetti spoke without moving.

As the driver seemed unsure of what she said, she repeated the question in Italian. This delighted him and made him even more loquacious. He told her his name was Rocco Masiti, and though his folks originated from Reggio, he was born in Messina itself. 'Messina is a city.' He was inordinately proud. 'Reggio is only a town. *Un paese.*' He added the word with a dismissive wave. He glanced at Franzetti in the rear-vision mirror. '*Suo padre non sta bene?*'

Sara smiled and replied her companion was exhausted by the journey. She was going to add that, no, he wasn't her father, but couldn't find the Italian word for 'boss', so let it pass. She sensed mutual antipathy between the two men. Rocco Masiti probably found Franzetti's manner unfriendly and his dress shabby.

'*Signorina*, your mother, she must be Italian, true?'

'No.'

The fact she had no trace of Italian ancestry and yet spoke the language impressed the man even more. While the queue was getting sorted out, Rocco kept firing questions in Italian. He had never heard of Perth, but he knew Fremantle because of the America's Cup.

With the car finally in place, the driver invited them up on deck for a coffee, but Franzetti stayed in the car. Rocco insisted on getting the coffee from the on-board canteen, while Sara sat looking at the sea as the *Centauro* detached itself from the Villa San Giovanni pier.

Across three kilometres of sea, Sara-Jane watched the city of Messina splayed around the sea edge, its back resting against sharply rising hills in a tuft of haze. She felt like an ancient explorer approaching the island for the first time.

The land seemed as if it had gathered folds and stretched skyward, over the sea. Sara-Jane looked for a connection between those mountains and the old people she knew as a child. She thought instead of the other woman, their daughter, whose face she could only capture as a shadow, an outline. What else had trickled through that distillation of time? A voice punctuated by long pauses, a smell left on the bed linen, which wasn't her mother's …

Somewhere beyond those inscrutable peaks, people whose breast she had curled up to for comfort and warmth were sitting down to an evening meal. It was over seventeen years since she last saw them. The old couple must have been in their sixties, which now put them in their eighties. Perhaps they were dead.

Rocco came back with a coffee, disappointingly in a plastic cup. As he handed her the coffee, she noticed he wore a wedding ring and two other rings, with matching sapphire stones, one on each little finger.

He caught Sara looking at his hand and smiled. 'I will show you.' His words were enigmatic.

From the inside pocket of his jacket he pulled out a brown wallet, worn out and frayed at the edges, incongruous in such a neat little man. He sifted through various cards until he found what he wanted. He held a photo in between index and forefinger and placed it on the table in front of her.

'My family.' He spoke with as much pride as if he were introducing royalty. It was a miniature studio photo of himself, wife, and son, with a green curtain for a background and a bunch of fake irises on a small round table. It must have been taken some years before, because Rocco's hair was thicker and rich brown. His wife was a little taller, even though she was wearing flat shoes, no doubt in deference to his masculine ego.

'This is my son, Gianpaolo.' He ran a ringed little finger under the image of a boy of about fifteen, with shoulder length frizzy hair and a freckly face.

He told her he was now twenty-nine years old, and living in Milan. 'He is a very beautiful young man, very tall, taller than yourself, *Signorina*. He designs jewellery. He's a genius, *Signorina*. I don't say so myself. His *principale*, his boss, offer him a partnership in the boutique jewellery shop, a small share, but he will build on it.' He placed his hands palm-down on the table for Sara-Jane to admire the two rings. They were his son's creations, were they not stupendous? He wore them always, always even at night. Gianpaolo wasn't married, and he was not in a serious relationship. He was not the kind to indulge frivolous dalliance.

'Yes, yes, when he finally chooses it will be for life.' Rocco spoke dramatically. He emphasised with quick flashes of his lively eyes and a pouting of his fleshy bottom lip, which somehow attested to the seriousness of character in his son. Gianpaolo was a very serious, serious boy, committed to his work. He would surely make a wonderful, wonderful husband for a lucky girl some day soon. All this information was delivered at breakneck speed.

It was time to go back. Not a pleasant prospect, given that Franzetti would still be in that foul mood. She would rather spend more time on deck, entertained by the congenial taxi driver.

Rocco was not ready to go down either. How long was she staying in Italy? Only ten days, what a pity! Gianpaolo was due to visit next month, it would give him great pleasure, great pleasure if he could introduce such a beautiful girl to his son.

Here the penny dropped. She realised, with amused astonishment, that in the twenty minutes or so it took for the ferry to cross the three kilometres of sea that stretched from the mainland to Sicily, she had received what amounted to a proxy proposal, on behalf of Rocco's beloved son. Must have been something about the air of the place.

*

The *Casa di Cura* Madonna dell'Ulivo stood on an old olive estate of six hectares, some seven kilometres up the slope from the coastal town of Falcone. From the back of the property you caught a glimpse of the sea over the hills, but not from the clinic itself, a nineteenth century villa that was once the property of the Barons of Mammolici, before the Baron sold out and moved his family to Palermo.

The property was chosen by Dr Troina, not merely for its imposing three storey villa, but because the trees on the estate were said to be the oldest in the region. Tests showed that some were over 500 years old.

The estate was enclosed by a dry-stone wall, along which grew pink and white oleanders for greater privacy. Inside the wrought iron gate a drive led to a granite escalade on top of which rose a nineteenth-century villa, with stuccoed walls freshly painted in ochre, and dark green shutters. From the way the building and the grounds were maintained, it was clear things were going very well for Dr Troina, at a time when deep cuts were being made to the Italian health system. It was because the *Casa di Cura* was entirely funded by private patients. Here the patient was also the paying customer, and nobody was more aware of this than its director Dr Emilio Troina. The success of the clinic was entirely due to the director's skill, both as a doctor and PR man.

For years the clinic had struggled financially, until a Tunisian financier was successfully treated there. In gratitude, he left a bequest large enough to bring to the clinic the standard of comfort of a luxury hotel. And even though its success rate was the same as it had always been, the quality of the patients it attracted ensured its profits multiplied.

Doctor Troina had left instructions to be alerted immediately the Australian arrived. As a consequence, while the party was going through the procedure of signing in at the desk, the doctor came down to the foyer to greet the new arrivals. He appeared at the top of the marble stairs, with a brilliant smile on his handsome face, and even at a distance you could tell he fitted his well-appointed establishment like a tortoise its shell. He was quite tall, slender and distinguished. His teeth were white and perfectly straight, but by the time he reached the bottom step, in a poised stride, and he smiled ingratiatingly, you wondered whether his teeth were in fact his own.

'Welcome, sir, I am very much pleased to meet you.' He bowed to Franzetti as he shook his hand.

Dr Troina was in his early forties, tanned and prematurely balding. This was no disgrace. If anything it served to complement the air of mature elegance that was his trademark. His shoes were English and had a matt finish; his suit, although of the best Frescolana quality, was not of the latest cut. He did not wish to give the impression he was a slavish follower of fashion. Sobriety, not frivolity, was the proper image for a man in his position. A measured attention to appearance was his preference. His hands were fine and long-fingered, and the flesh was pink under the well-clipped nails.

As Franzetti failed to introduce her, Sara-Jane offered her hand. 'Hi, I'm Sara-Jane.'

'*Enchanté.*' He bowed as if he were going to kiss her hand, but desisted at the last moment, perhaps put off by Franzetti's abrupt manner.

'Ask him if he knows any English.'

She wanted to say, *You've just heard him speak English,* but realised this would upset her boss, so she did as directed.

'Not very well. ' Dr Troina replied self-effacingly. In fact his English was very good, which he demonstrated as he took his guests around the establishment. The clinic was indeed impressive, more like a well-appointed hotel. The rooms were all equipped with private facilities. There were no patients in the beds, since it was lunch time and they were all having their meal in the dining room, which through the smoked glass had the appearance of a pricy restaurant.

The only thing that reminded them of the nature of the clinic was the radiography room, where the patients' progress was regularly tested.

'Our testing equipment is the best in Sicily.' Dr Troina felt entitled to boast.

It was difficult to argue with him. The good doctor tried to leave no doubt in the mind of his potential client as to the state-of-the-art quality of his equipment, the comfort of the rooms, the thoroughness of the testing, and the efficiency of his staff.

Unfortunately, it was not enough to impress Clem Franzetti. At the end of the tour, Sara-Jane went with him to his room. He looked quite as miserable as the moment he had boarded that plane back in Perth. Sara-Jane wished he'd clip those eyebrows of his, because they made him look imperious, unkempt, and even older than he was.

'What do you think?' He looked straight at Sara-Jane.

'Very impressive…'

'I don't reckon. The bloke's a fraud. He talks too much for a start, and I bet he charges like a wounded bull.'

For a moment she thought he was going to order the luggage back in the car and leave. When they got down to the bottom of the stairs, he noticed a statue of the Virgin Mary tucked away in the alcove. It was small and fine-lined, with alabaster eyes, straight nose, perfect lips, and dimple on the chin. Her long garment was powder blue with a gold line along the collar. In her right hand, raised higher than her left, she held an olive branch. Franzetti found it arresting and stood there gazing at the statue. The taxi driver came into the foyer.

'What would you like me to tell him?' asked Sara-Jane.

'Oh well, I suppose having come all this way, I should give it a go.' Franzetti spoke without taking his eyes off the statue.

11

As always, Sara La Rocca was first to rise in the Marzano household. She lay in bed waiting for the fluorescent hands of the alarm clock on the bedside table to reach 5.30 before she got up. Any earlier would have made the day unbearably long, filled with too many cigarettes and too much coffee.

At exactly five-thirty she stepped down on the rug, leaving her husband cocooned in the duvet. Out of habit, she didn't turn on the light, because the bedroom window looked out onto the Piazza Chiesa Madre, and anyone out there at that time would notice the light in the bedroom. To her mind there was something weird, even shameful, in her insomniac behaviour. In the dark, she ran her fingers along the ribbed surface of the wicker chair, feeling for her dressing gown, the one Alfio gave her only the year before. She slipped it on, and groped her way out of the room. In the corridor she turned on the light and made her way past Sante's room and into the kitchen to make coffee. She placed three heaped scoops into the *caffettiera* filter, filled the container with water from the flagon marked *Acqua Sorgiva di Fichera*, screwed the top on, and lit the gas burner. Then she went on the balcony to water the pot plants: geraniums and stocks, coming to the end of their flowering, and the large rectangular cement pot with the herbs: mint, parsley, basil – all gone to seed now – and rosemary, which threatened to take over the pot.

Beyond the railing, the piazza was yet to emerge: a mystery in a double wrapper of dark and mist. Sometimes when it was like this, an absurd notion came to her, that when the dark lifted she would find, not the familiar piazza whose every nook she knew so well, but a foreign world in which she found herself a stranger, unhappy, and unwelcome.

The hiss from the *caffettiera* brought her back inside. She poured her first cup, but resisted the temptation to light a cigarette and fill her head with smoke so early in the morning. But caught as she was between the rock of Sicily and the hard place of Australia, a little confusion, obfuscation, partial loss of memory might be the way to go. She feared the past was about to crash into the present once again, and there was nothing she could do to stop it. Two worlds: Sicily and Australia, worlds she thought she had successfully separated by thousands of kilometres of sea and air, not to speak of the stretch of time ... the worlds were about to touch, scrape each other's edges. Who knows what tremors might ensue?

Why was it all coming to a head like this? The grove at Rovaro would be taken from her. This girl, her namesake and almost-daughter, was coming to stir the quiet waters of her existence. Secrets, painful and jagged, would rip through the surface. The landscape would be dislocated, rearranged. Of course, if she were young or – crazy notion! – of a different mould, she might welcome this, be energised by the prospect, wonder at the possibilities. At the very least, the bond that attached her to this girl's mother, to the girl herself, should prevail upon her fears.

But, what was she afraid of anyway? Of the truth being known in this town, with its medieval houses banked upon one another, walled in against the march of time? Did she really fear that, once the mist lifted from her secret, she would be crushed by a moral code that changed little in centuries? Whatever the weight of the town's judgement, it could not be as heavy as that of her own conscience. Perhaps her fear was that Sante should discover the dark side of his conception. That secret, as Alfio wisely advised, would have to be revealed, now that Sante had grown. No, it wasn't that either. The truth she did not want to face required uncompromising candidness; and what better time to get down to the rawness of it than now, under the protection of darkness? The truth that lay beneath a carefully choreographed exterior of alibis and deception was … that once upon a time, in a far-off country there was Sheryl; that is, Sheryl and Sara. Two girls, a love, a … bed. Ah there, she admitted it.

*

Following the baby's birth, Sheryl was given a low-rent duplex and Sara spent more and more time there, often sleeping over, particularly at weekends. Her mother, who had never really warmed to Sheryl, was now giving Sara worrying looks.

'Why do you spend so much time there?'

'She needs me, Mum. She's got no family or friends.'

If only she had been a better sleeper, things might not have gone the way they had. As it was, even at seventeen, Sara was bedevilled by insomnia and had to suffer the consequences.

No such problems for Sheryl. Once she finished breastfeeding the baby, she put her down and fell asleep, sometimes leaving her breast exposed over the loose neckline of her nightie. Sleep was elusive for Sara, blocked by the vision of Sheryl's breast cascading over her upper arm.

At eight months, the nurse suggested the baby could be weaned. They got a secondhand cot from St Vincent de Paul's and placed it on Sara's side of the bed, as it was she who inevitably got up at night if little Sara-Jane cried. The toddler adjusted to the weaning quickly enough. The one who felt it more was Sheryl. She had enjoyed the whole breastfeeding thing. It gave direction and purpose to her daily routine, and she got plenty of attention from everyone, not least Sara.

Now she was fretting. 'I really miss feeding the baby.' She complained often. 'I miss the closeness.'

Now that the baby was in her cot and the nights grew colder, Sheryl drifted closer to Sara who turned her back to her, hands crossed over her chest, fists clenched. One night in her sleep, Sheryl's face came to rest on Sara's back. Her heavy breathing blew hot air on the side of her neck where it met the shoulder.

A tingling lassitude spread all over her body. Sara wanted to move, but couldn't. Against her better judgement, she allowed her body to distend in the soothing draught. She turned and a threshold was crossed. Sara buried her face in the cleavage of Sheryl's breasts.

Sheryl's voice echoed drowsily through the dark. 'What are you doing, Sara?'

Silence. Sara held her breath and shivered.

'What's wrong, Sara, are you cold?'

'Yes, yes, Sheryl, I'm cold.'

So they snuggled up to each other, clinging tightly so they heard each other's hearts. Thump-thump, thump-thump, thump-thump. And then, in the dark, witnessed by God and the ghosts of her ancestors, Sara La Rocca finally gave in to the devil in her.

In the morning, with the sun making a splash into the room through the vertical blinds, darkness did not lift from Sara's soul. She got up and made some coffee – ah, how life repeated itself through daily rituals! She wanted to go back home, but her mother would be up by now and the last thing she wanted was to meet her judging eyes. She went into the tiny living room, which also served as her study, and pretended to do her work. In reality she was filling in time, and couldn't work in that house any more. She wanted to go back to Sicily. She wanted to be as far away as she could from what happened during the night.

Sheryl shuffled in, the child in her arms, and went to boil water, saying nothing. She was too intimidated by Sara's silence to talk. She went and sat on the sofa, and gave the bottle to the child. Every now and then she looked across at Sara who paid no attention to her. Finally she spoke. 'What time are we going shopping this morning?'

'I've got work to do. I'm not getting any study done.'

'This afternoon then.'

'No, I'm going home this morning.'

'What do you mean? Why?'

'I told you, I got study to do.'

'But … but … we always spend the weekend together. You can study here.'

'No I can't, it's too distracting with the baby. I've got exams in less than two months.'

Sheryl could hardly argue with that. 'OK, OK, I'll see you tonight then?'

'I'm not coming. I'm studying, I told you.'

Sheryl's forehead knotted up.

'But, Sara, you always sleep over on weekends.'

'Not any more.'

Sheryl put the whimpering child down on the floor and went to Sara, and although she wanted to touch her, she did not dare. 'Why? Why, Sara?' Panic gave Sheryl's voice a whinging tone. 'We always do things together.' Her pleading eyes looked for Sara's, but her friend refused to meet them, and looked down instead. Sheryl took two steps, touched Sara's shoulder.

Sara shook her off.

'What's wrong Sara? Is it because of ... what happened in the night? Is it?'

Sara looked away.

'Sara, I loved what we did. I loved it. I love you, Sara.'

That's how she was. Saying the unsayable. No restraint at all. Things that nearly a quarter of a century later had the capacity to make her squirm, Sheryl just came out with them.

If only she could be like that. Sara was torn by guilt. What she had done wasn't right according to her religion, her culture, her mother ... but the one who cried was Sheryl. Down came the tears, easy and copious as the milk in her breasts. Of course they were not tears of guilt. Sheryl was utterly devoid of conscience. They were blackmail tears. Tears designed to melt down resistance and entrap you.

The baby, who was crawling around in the kitchen, getting pots out of the cupboards, now started to cry. Sheryl was too caught up in her own misery to take notice, so Sara went to pick her up, but the child's vest was caught around the table leg.

Sheryl spread her arms to form a protective circle around Sara and the child. 'And I thought you loved us too, Sara.'

'I do. Of course I do, but ...' She looked away.

Sheryl grabbed her upper arms and shouted into Sara's face. 'Sara, look at me, what we did was beautiful.' Sheryl's face was right up above little Sara's bottom. Her nostrils flared suddenly and an unexpected grin distended over her face. 'Oh, oh! Can you smell something, Sara?' She put her nose down over the baby's bottom and laughed. 'Shit, Sara, look what little missy has done. She smells like Pepe Le Pooh. Quick, let's get a nappy.'

Sheryl ran to get a clean napkin and they changed the

baby, or rather, Sara did, because Sheryl was still squeamish about it and carried on about the smell. After that, no more was said about 'that business'.

*

Four years passed. Four years of happiness. Well, mostly happiness, punctured by drama. During that time, Sara all but moved in with Sheryl, and her parents accepted the situation. Her mother made peace with her because she had no choice. As for her father, his emotions never strayed beyond love. Love for the little child he adored, love too for Sheryl. So his conflicts easily evaporated through the endless space of his love.

When she turned eighteen, Sheryl got a job at the local tavern as a barmaid, and worked most nights, while Sara studied to be a schoolteacher and kept herself busy day and night. The young mother often stayed out late, after the tavern closed, and when she came home, often after midnight, Sara was beside herself. She worried about Sheryl, worried about what was going on. Each time she thought about her at the tavern, being ogled by drunken men as she poured them a beer and she, no doubt, looked back coyly. Whenever her friend returned late they would row. That was when Sheryl started going out at night, even when she wasn't working.

'What's the point of me stayin' home when all you ever do is study? There's nothing for me to do around here.'

'You've got your daughter to look after.'

'She's fine with your parents, she loves it over there.'

That, at least, was true. Once she started to walk, little Sara-Jane spent more and more time in the other household.

They became Nonnu and Nonna and Sara-Jane became Sarina, to distinguish her from the older Sara. The old people had plenty of time, and although they dreamed of going back home to retire on their land, there was no more talk about it while they had Sarina to care for and to love.

*

Russell did not bother contacting Sheryl after the encounter in the hospital. 'Pissed off' as he was with the mother, he showed no interest in seeing his child. Nearly four years later, when he finished his police cadetship and started earning a wage, the family court caught up with him and demanded he pay maintenance to Sheryl for the upkeep of the child.

As a compensatory measure, he was given access to his daughter one day a fortnight, to begin with. He was to pick her up at 9am and bring her back by six in the evening, every second Saturday.

The first time, he arrived at Sheryl's doorstep punctually at nine, and took the unwilling child, who didn't know him at all, for the day. Little Sara was so unhappy, however, that he brought her back by noon. After that, he took her for a couple of hours, usually for a feed of fish and chips at Cicerello's by the seaside, and then brought her back. Sometimes he had to work, so his visits became even less frequent.

On this particular Saturday, Russell hadn't turned up: nothing unusual about that. Under normal circumstances, the child would be taken to Nonna's, because Sheryl was due to do her shift at the tavern and Sara wanted to get on with her studies. This time, Mrs La Rocca rang to say that the husband of a friend had just died, and they wanted to go and spend some time with her.

In the afternoon, when Sheryl had gone to work and little Sara-Jane lay down for her afternoon sleep, Sara had just sat at her desk when there was a knock on the door. It was Russell, eyes glazed and looking none too good.

'Sheryl's not in.' Sara kept the door ajar, with her foot behind it, ready to push it shut again.

'I didn't come to see Sheryl, I've come to get me daughter.'

'You were supposed to be here at nine o'clock.' First mistake – she should not have engaged him in an argument.

'I was working, see.' He pointed to his uniform with his thumb.

She resisted the temptation of asking him how come he smelt of beer, when he was supposed to be on duty.

'I can have her all day. I got a court order. She's my daughter.' He was very insistent.

'She's asleep.' Second mistake. She should have said she was at the grandparents'.

'She can sleep at my place.'

'She's only just gone down. I'm not going to wake her up.'

Russell's reaction took her by surprise. 'Ok then.' He gave the door a shove with his elbow, nearly bowled her over, and pushed past her. 'I'll wait.' Once inside, he seemed to relax a bit. He crashed down on the sofa and smiled. 'Well, do I get a coffee? I been told you make a great cup.'

What else could she do? There was no arguing with him in this state. When she came back, he seemed to be dozing off with his head slumped back on the sofa. She put down the coffee on the cane table, and turned her back to him.

Fatal third mistake. As she went to straighten up, she felt a grip on her calf. She struggled to turn and her hand caught the coffee mug. The contents spilled all over the table and ran down his leg, between the trouser cuff and the upper edge of the sock.

'Fuck! You've just scalded me!'

Sara saw her chance to escape, but his reflexes were sharpened by anger and primal urges. As she went to turn, he grabbed her wrist. His eyes, bloodshot and dangerous, mesmerised her. She started to scream, but he stifled the sound with his hand.

'Ah, ah. None of that.' His voice had an eerie calm.

Sara became a silent participant in an unspeakable act. She remembered his nightmare voice whisper.

'This is whatchyou been wantin', you little dyke. Isn' it? Isn' it?'

She heard herself groan, and realised he had taken his hand off her mouth. What stopped her from screaming was the sight of the child standing there in the doorway, rubbing her eyes with tiny fists and whimpering.

*

The sun heaved over the hump of the eastern peak, lit up the spire of the Chiesa Madre, and a new day was born in San Sisto. The first long rays slanted over the roofs, and soon shadows from the buildings patterned the granite ground of the piazza. The great bronze door of the church, framed by a sandstone portico with double columns, would be opened by the wobbly figure of Tazio Monteleone, who lost a leg back in the seventies, in a Mafia shootout. After that, he 'gave himself up to God' and was appointed sacristan of San Sisto's main church.

The roller door went up at Ciro's, and the smell of newly baked pastry inundated the piazza. Sara loved this moment, when she knew her memories would be engulfed by the rush of the day's activities. She welcomed the first signs of life, the sounds; cars crossing the piazza on the way down to the coast, driven by those who worked at Milazzo or Barcellona.

Cosimo's boys were leaving to get fresh fish and other *rifornimenti* for his shop. Worshippers would come to church, fewer and older, for the daily morning service. Ciro meanwhile got his bar ready for the tradesmen, shopkeepers, municipal workers and teachers calling in for coffee and a cornetto on the way to work.

Sara drank her coffee and took a decision.

*

'Hello, I am looking for Sara-Jane.'

It was a deep voice, a little husky, but clearly a woman's. It echoed as if the person were speaking inside an empty room with bare walls and a hard floor. The young woman was stumped. 'Sara' was pronounced with the strong Italian R, while the A in Jane was definitely Australian.

'Speaking.'

Silence, a breathless pause. Was she going to hang up? Instead, after a little stir, a rejoinder came, slow and deliberate. 'My name is Sara La Rocca, we have received a letter from you …'

'Oh I see, you're …' Now, how was she going to phrase it? Mother's friend? My namesake? No, better to avoid the possessive at this stage.

100

'The other Sara,' said the voice, followed by a short, mock-conspiratorial laugh, which managed to distend the tension across the line. Perfect.

The younger woman took up the cue. 'The original one,' said she brightly, congratulating herself on finding a good riposte, and even throw a compliment into the bargain. A connection was in the making, or was it?

'I'm sorry I had to open your letter,' said the woman, her words flowing freely now, 'unfortunately my parents are deceased.'

'I'm sorry, I wasn't aware.'

Two sorries: would they suffice to establish a line across a wall almost twenty years wide? Perhaps not, because now a silence, made heavy by the two dead people that connected the two women, weighted over the distance. Then, the words fell knife-sharp across the line and sliced through it.

'I hope you have a nice stay in Sicily, good bye.'

12

News travels fast in the province. When Mayor Marzano left his office at the municipal chambers, he had news for his wife. It wasn't pleasant news, and he wished he hadn't been told, or at the least, that he had been told later in the afternoon, so that it wouldn't spoil his lunch, to which he had been looking forward all morning.

Apart from a couple of truly great restaurants, of which Ristorante al Castello in Milazzo was one, he knew of no better fare than what his wife served. In order not to think about the unpleasantness of having to tell her the news, Alfio tried to imagine what it was that Sara was preparing for him. This being Friday, it would be fish of some sort. *Spezzatino di Baccalà* with potato puree and a few green olives and chillies, followed by stomach-refreshing *verdura*, seasoned with olive oil and lemon. But maybe not, the weather was still warm for *baccalà*. Perhaps a nice steak of swordfish, done in garlic sauce and grated over with lemon rind.

When he arrived at the piazza, he saw Sante standing in front of Ciro's with a couple of his friends. Seeing Sante put him in a good mood. He decided to go across and share an aperitif with him. But just as he set off, the group headed for Sante's car that was parked just outside, with the left back wheel on the curb. Don Alfio called him.

Sante turned, strode over in that unhurried, leggy gait of his. 'Ciao Papà.'

Don Alfio gave Sante a pat on the arm and shook hands with his friends.

'Coming up for pranzo?'

Sante looked at his watch. 'Is that really the time? I'll be up soon. I've just got a get a CD from Leoncarlo.'

'Don't be long. You know Mamma, she will not start without you and I'm hungry.'

Don Alfio went into Ciro's and ordered a prosecco.

*

The trout was superb, and he did like being surprised, they hadn't had trout in a long time. But now, with Sante gone to Tindari, where he held a casual job as a guide for English-speaking tourists, he had the opportunity to talk to Sara.

He went to the kitchen and helped her put the dishes in the washer. 'A superior meal, as always, my love.' He gave her a hug from behind. 'Where do you get all the ideas for such dishes?'

'I enjoy it, Alfio, it gives me pleasure to see my family well satisfied. How was the day? Any news from Mimmo Urzì?'

'No, it is better this way. Mimmo is one person I don't mind not hearing from. Ever. Actually I have some other news, *cara* …'

Sara closed the dishwasher door, but did not turn it on. She scrutinised him with her dark eyes. There was a nervous tone to his 'cara' which alerted her senses.

'Marsiti, you know Rocco Marsiti, who drives the taxi, he tells me that he picked up an Australian girl from Reggio airport yesterday, a splendid looking girl, by his description. Anyway, it appears her father is travelling with her.'

'What?'

His wife jumped as if she had been jabbed on the arm.

'Apparently. I find it hard to believe myself.'

'That can't be true. As far as I know they have never got on.'

'Things change, Sara, maybe after the death of the mother there was a reconciliation. According to Marsiti, he has booked into the *Casa di Cura* near Falcone. What are you going to do, Sara?'

'Nothing.'

'Sara … ' Don Alfio put his hand on the dishwasher door.

'I don't want my son to know his father is a rapist.' Directness was one of Sara's most effective tools.

'I know, Sara. But isn't it better that he hears it from you?'

'I can't Alfio. Not now, not yet, and certainly not while that … man is here. They must not meet.' Sara went out and watered the pot plants for the third time that day.

Don Alfio proceeded to take his afternoon siesta. This whole affair was stressing him out, it was a good thing he was such a good sleeper; one hour's sleep would recharge him and restore his good humour. He went to the bedroom, closed the shutters, undressed down to his underwear and lay on the bed, trying to think of something pleasant.

Of course, Elia's opening was that night, he nearly forgot. She would not forgive him if he did not go. He would have to leave early. It took a good hour to drive to Palermo. Better get a good rest. It would be great to see all his friends at the Teatro Stabile, not to speak of the pleasure of seeing sweet Elia on stage again. And on this very happy image, he fell soundly asleep.

Upon waking, Don Alfio realized that *quell'affare Australiano* had been stewing in his brain during his sleep. Damn it! He was caught between loyalty to his wife and certain conviction that Sante would want to know the truth. At the very least he was entitled to know he had a sister.

Of course he understood Sara's unwillingness to have to recall that sorry business. He doubted any man could fully realise what was felt by a woman who had been subjected to such an ordeal. When he thought about it – rarely, thank God – his civilised mind became polluted by primeval visions of revenge, like personally castrating the man who had done that to his wife. But when the anger subsided, and he was able to consider his emotions rationally, all that was left was pity. Pity for the victims, of course, but also pity for the perpetrator.

To think there were people out there who were so unhappy, so profoundly dysfunctional, that they had to do that to a woman … it left one numb with incomprehension. Don Alfio just didn't want to think about it.

Now, circumstances were forcing him not merely to think, but to act, something which did not come easily to Don Alfio. Thoughts must have been ruminating inside his head during the siesta because now, as he sauntered back to the municipal offices for the afternoon meetings, he found himself formulating a plan. There was no point in trying to persuade Sara to change her mind. His only option was to contact this Australian girl and speak to her.

Good thing she spoke Italian – Marsiti could not stop talking about how beautifully she spoke Italian – so at least there was that much in favour of his strategy. Once he had established exactly how much she knew about the situation, he would decide whether to arrange a 'chance' meeting between the two siblings.

He hated the surreptitiousness of this plan, but he excused himself in the knowledge that his intentions were good. Besides, the child in Don Alfio – still very much part of his personality despite his age – enjoyed a little intrigue, and if truth be told, he found the prospect of meeting this Australian beauty a most enjoyable one.

First thing, though – he had to contact the girl. He remembered reading the name of the hotel in the letter Sara had shown him, but he had forgotten. Besides, there was no mention of her father in the letter, so her plans might have changed. If she were staying at the *Casa di Cura*, which he doubted, he would have to contact Troina, something he would rather not do. Dr Troina was one of those ambitious men he tended to avoid.

Don Alfio did not mind ambition; it was just that he found most ambitious people so single-minded they had no other conversation outside their area of operation. In the last few years, the success of the *Casa di Cura* – regular reports appeared in La Gazzetta del Sud and other publications – had rendered Troina more pompous, more arrogant than ever. Anyway, it was the girl he wanted to speak to.

A better option was to contact Marsiti the taxi driver: he would certainly know where the girl was staying.

'Marsiti?'

'Ah, Mayor Marzano, what an honour ...'

'*Ciao, senti* ... I need to get in touch with those Australians you were telling me about yesterday – as you know, my wife lived in Australia for many years – so she is eager to make contact. Would you know um ... where the girl is staying?'

'Yes, the Hotel Ruggeri. As it happens, I am about to collect her from there, to take her to Tindari.'

'What? Tindari? Is her father with her?'

'No, she's on her own. She has hired the taxi for the whole afternoon, on a charge account I suspect.'

Don Alfio could not believe his luck. This was one opportunity which simply demanded to be seized.

Not usually a decisive man, he had no hesitation in making another call. What a genius, the man who invented the mobile phone!

This time, a call to his son. However, his phone was shut down, which meant he must be taking a group around.

'Send him a text message,' suggested Miss Racina, the municipal secretary.

Now, this skill was beyond Don Alfio's limited range, so he enlisted the assistance of Miss Racina who, despite her age – older than him and showing it – had a surprising talent for absorbing new technologies as fast as those ITC people were able to inflict them on the population.

> *'Ciao caro. I believe a certain Signorina Sara, from Australia, is visiting Tindari this afternoon. You might wish to seek her out.*
> *A presto,*
> *Papà.'*

There, Don Alfio was satisfied with his little ruse. After all, the gods were pointing in the same direction, and had created the perfect situation for the young people to meet. In fact, even if he had done nothing, the chances they would meet were very good. Tindari was tiny, and tourists tended to congregate around the same sites: the church, the Roman ruins, the theatre. In the circumstances, a little human manipulation would not go amiss.

13

She had, of course, considered the possibility that her Italian grandparents could be dead, but that was not the same as knowing it. Now it seemed as though that part of her childhood, the only aspect worth remembering, never happened. It felt like someone had just vandalised the canvas of her life and blotted out a whole section from it. She felt damaged.

Hey, what about this woman, Sara La Rocca, icy or what? Just about frosted up the phone line. Sara-Jane searched her earliest memories for traces of her. All she could recall was a smoky outline, a puff of frizzy hair without a face, a pair of dry lips, a close smell.

Perhaps it was just as well they were not meeting. If they had, Sara-Jane would have to be very wary. This woman must have known things about her, secrets. She might harbour complex, subterranean emotions and nurse wounds that had not healed. She could tell – by the echo of her deep voice, by the gaps in her sentences – that there was a lot of shit still simmering in the pot of her memory.

Did she really want to sift through it? Was she being morbid after all? It was comforting to know that, within a few days, she would return to the present, to her uncomplicated life in Western Australia. Meanwhile, she got ready for her day ahead: a trip to Tindari for photos, and an interview she had managed to line up with an official at the Santuario. She got together her camera, tape-recorder, mobile, and waited for Rocco's taxi to arrive.

*

The cliff on which the shrine of the Madonna of Tindari stands grows out of the sea and rises into the sky for some 300 metres. As you leave the autostrada at Falcone, the road coils up the incline, giving the traveller ever more vertiginous glimpses of the landscape below: the sharp ridges, the fields and the groves. A dreamy sea in a wrapper of silver sheath invites the eye to the Aeolian Islands, faintly stamped on the horizon: mysterious monsters looming through the haze of time.

The taxi left her at the car park, from which Sara-Jane proceeded on foot, navigating through the stalls, which were crammed with assorted paraphernalia. Most common, of course, were miniature images of the Black Madonna and child, in a range of materials: resin, plastic, wood, ceramic, metal and stone. If you fancied it, you could have the relic sealed inside a water bowl with imitation snow-flakes. The local produce too was adapted to the religious theme, like rosary beads made from locally-grown hazel nuts. In other stalls, the religious and profane mingled in such items as T-shirts, aprons, hats and sunglasses; chocolates and biscuits; CDs of pop and religious music. Sara-Jane was not surprised: it all reinforced her natural cynicism towards organised religions.

The church was packed with pilgrims from all over Italy and beyond, milling around in obsequious confusion. The object of their worship was the black figure of the Madonna and Child enthroned above the altar, or rather, their crowned heads emerging out of a gold-embroidered, stiff mantle. From the distance they appeared remote, surreal, imprisoned within the metal-like texture of their extravagant garb.

Sara-Jane felt pity for those people, trapped in myth and religion. Give me the scepticism of Australia, any day, she thought.

An English-speaking voice over the whispered hubbub, caught her attention. 'According to tradition, in the seventh century AD, this effigy of the Madonna came over the sea on a ship, from somewhere in the East. When it reached this coast it was caught in a storm, and the ship was grounded at Marinello, which you would reach if you decided to take a jump down the cliff.'

The audience laughed.

'The local monks believed it was a miraculous event, so they build a shrine on top of this hill …'

Sara-Jane hardly listened to the words. She knew the young man, although she had no idea where from. She knew the timbre of that voice. Weird. He did not look much older than school age, even though he must have been old enough to hold a job. There was a stillness and poise about him, quite remarkable for a person so young. Was it arrogance or self-confidence? Probably the former because, as he spoke, he hardly seemed to look at his audience.

They, on the other hand, were focused on him, although not necessarily on what he was saying. The reason for this was all too obvious: he was – she had to admit – irritatingly good-looking, with raven-black hair, opal eyes, and fleshy pink lips. Probably gay, she thought uncharitably, and vain, no doubt. Then, as if he had been aware of her attention all along, the young man turned directly to her. Over the heads of his listeners, he asked, 'Do you have a question about this?'

The group fell silent as the young man kept looking at her, waiting for a response. It was quite disconcerting at first, but her discomfiture caused her to react, she wasn't about to let this precious little creature intimidate her in front of an audience.

Sara-Jane straightened her back, gaining both height and self-confidence in the process, and obliged. 'Are there any recorded instances of miracles that have occurred here?'

There was a pause, as if the young man had been somehow stunned by the question. 'Several people claim to have been granted a cure by the Madonna of Tindari. I cannot say, however, if it is really so.'

The group parted to make way as he moved a few paces in her direction. In a lower tone he added, 'Some people say that a miracle is only a manifestation of faith.'

'In Australia we call it positive thinking.'

'Ah, so you are *the Australian*. I knew it.'

Sara-Jane was left wondering. Was it some kind of standard opening gambit he used on foreign women? The very idea he might be trying to chat her up, despite their obvious age difference, made her smile.

He was about to engage her again, but someone else intervened to ask a question, leaving Sara-Jane free to exit the church and visit the profane side of Tindari: its Greco-Roman amphitheatre and the Roman excavations. Strictly speaking, not part of her brief. But she knew you cannot really understand the sacred without the profane. Not that Franzetti, or the readers of *Escapes,* would be interested in such conceits.

As she covered the short distance that separated the church from the excavations, the image of the young guide strode alongside her. She decided he wasn't gay after all. From the sensuality of his lips to the light in his eyes, his features suggested a male in fine balance between spirit and body. Strangely though, she still couldn't decide whether she liked or resented him.

She stood in the centre of the amphitheatre and smelled the stones that someone had carefully manoeuvred into place some two millennia before. In fact, there were relatively few stones left. Apart from the archway and the remains of the columns in the arena, the seats were lost to history and its pilferers.

Only two wings remained; the rest had steel trusses upon which wooden seats were bolted during summer performances. But it did not dispel the sense of timelessness, all the more eerie for the fact that, with a group having just left, she found herself alone in the theatre for a moment. She listened for ancient voices in the wind declaiming words of good and evil.

The silence was soon broken by a shrill voice coming from the top tier of the theatre, where a girl was having an animated discussion on her mobile. Her male companion, tired of waiting around, ran down to the arena and called out in Italian. '*Mi senti?*'

The girl did not respond.

'*Dai, Ennia, parlo con te, mi senti?*'

This time Ennia covered the mobile with her hand and shouted back. 'Of course I can hear you, you're shouting. Speak normally.'

The man whispered. 'I want to make love to you.'

The girl giggled. 'Don't be an arsehole Mauro, everybody can hear you.'

'I want them to.'

The girl ran down giggling to join her companion, leaping over stones, irreverent of the antiquity she was trampling under her feet.

Sara-Jane climbed the steps to the top and took some photos; then stood by the cypress tree and breathlessly took in the view that had brought audiences to this cliff for centuries. Beyond the arches of the arena, a patch of land precariously held together by cane stubble, prickly pears and ferns, sheered away to the sea. What a spectacular backdrop for the great dramas of the gods!

An eagle appeared, riding the airwaves over a curling sandbar, which was said to represent the figure of the

Madonna and Child. Well, if you say so, thought Sara-Jane. She thought of another legend that recalled a child falling down to the sea from that height, saved in the nick of time by the Madonna.

She took several photos of the sandbar and shot a few more inside the theatre. The sacred and the profane, side by side. Though of course, the theatre was no less sacred. As she moved the lens around, the figure of the group guide came into focus, looking right into the eye of the camera.

'I'm sorry to startle you.' He was suddenly up close.

Sara-Jane wondered briefly if she were being stalked.

'I wanted to ask you before, but there were too many people around, are you from Western Australia?'

'Ye ... ah.'

He leapt up the steps to where she stood, stopping just one step below hers. A film of perspiration had appeared on his upper lip. 'Ah, you must be Sara, yes?'

'Sara-Jane ...' She corrected him automatically, wondering how on earth he knew her name.

'Yes, yes, you are she.' He opened his arms as if to hug her.

Sara-Jane stepped aside to avoid him.

'Oh, sorry, sorry, my name is Sante Marzano. You have written a letter to us from Australia.'

'Oh I see. You must be related to ... the other Sara.'

'Yes, she's my mother.'

Sara-Jane offered her hand.

He took it inside both of his.

'Well,' she said. 'What a coincidence!' She tried to keep it formal. She didn't cope well with effusion.

'In Sicily we call it fate.'

'Let's not get into that again.'

He didn't seem to mind her abruptness, or perhaps he hadn't noticed. Perhaps, she mused, nuances of tone are lost in cultural interchanges.

'Maybe in Australia you don't believe in fate, yes?'

Sara-Jane felt the stones beneath her low-heeled sandals, and cringed at this kind of talk. This kid is such a poser, she thought. She looked into his face for traces of condescension. His eyebrows, perfect like the rest of his features, did not arch. His face, still waiting for the whiskers of manhood, looked open and earnest. He was simply too perfect, too carefully-groomed to be interesting. Life's lines of experience and struggle had not made their mark. The shadows of disillusionment and self-deception had yet to gather around his eyes. Here was a young man molly-coddled through life in the soft wool of love and protection. Did she resent him, like she had resented those private school girls many years ago? No, definitely not, she felt sorry for him for being so naïve, so vulnerable. She felt much older than him and, much to her shock, vaguely protective.

She was moved to speak. 'You speak very good English, did your mother teach you?'

'A little. Also, during summer vacation I studied in London, in a language school, in Oxford Street.'

Just as she thought: a protected, privileged background. 'I must get going. I have an interview to do.'

'Yes, my mother told me, you are a journalist. That's one profession I have considered.'

'And...?'

'Maybe yes, maybe not ... I don't know. Very difficult for me to decide. Also because prospects in journalism are rare in the provinces.'

They headed back to the main strip, when her eye caught a long inscription on a white marble plaque covering the wall of a building. Sara-Jane stopped, curious to know why those words should be given so much prominence.

He said, 'Do you know Quasimodo?'

'Not the character in Les Miserables, I take it.'

'No, this poem is by Salvatore Quasimodo, Sicilian Nobel Laureate. Shall I read it for you?'

She could hardly say no.

Sante read in a voice still impassioned with a schoolboy's declamatory pitch.

Vento a Tindari

Tindari, mite ti so
fra larghi colli pensile sull'acque
dell'isole dolci del dio,
oggi m'assali
e ti chini in cuore…

The young man stopped, his eyes floated back to the present.

'It sounds gorgeous,' she conceded. 'I'm not sure I understand though. My Italian isn't that good.'

'It's about loss and longing. It speaks to me about Australia.'

'Oh, really?'

'Many people in Europe dream about Australia: all that space, beautiful beaches, clean air…'

Sara didn't correct him about the latter. As a travel writer, she was paid to enhance people's dreams, not to dent them.

Then he proceeded to tell her he was the love child of a liaison his mother had when she lived in Australia. The father, who was some sort of adventurer, had subsequently disappeared during a journey into the desert. 'Soon I will travel to Australia. I want to experience my father's country. Perhaps I can find him. I dream so many times about him, that he is alive. I see him in some vast pastoral property on the edge of the desert, with orange soil and open blue sky.'

No doubt about it, he is going to be disappointed, thought Sara-Jane. Dreams always disappoint.

*

In Sicily things don't work out quite the way you plan them, thought Sara-Jane. No sooner had she finished her interview with Vincenzo, the resident artisan, than, outside the workshop, she was met by Sante again. He had finished taking through his last group and was ready to leave. Would she like *un passaggio* back to Milazzo?

His reappearance unsettled her a little, not because she didn't want to see him, but precisely for the opposite reason: she realized she had wished all along he would turn up again. And she didn't want him to know that. She felt vulnerable. She mistrusted enthusiasms and quick emotions. Her tendency was to ask what exactly was behind them. Inevitably there always were strings attached.

'Actually, you know Sante, my expenses are covered, I have a taxi waiting…' But even as she spoke, she knew she would accept his invitation. She had a few questions to ask and besides, he might be useful to her: he might provide her with some quotes for her feature. 'Bugger it!' she said aloud, 'why not?'

He drove a Fiat Punto, near new. Not bad for an eighteen year-old. No doubt a gift from doting parents.

Sante became animated when he talked, and talk he did. Sometimes he got so caught up in the conversation, trying to explain himself in English, that he went perilously close to the edge of the steep road that dropped to a breathtaking valley, in which a dry river bed wound its way to the coast around the base of steeply rising hills.

Sara-Jane, who did not cope well with heights, was too scared to look. Each time they reached yet another sharp turn, she closed her eyes and held her breath. She caught up with her breathing – and regained her thoughts – once they reached the coast. As they turned into the Via Nazionale, carved out of granite rock rising from an amethyst sea, Sara wondered how she would be able to steer the conversation to a subject she was eager to discuss, when Sante, with typical directness gave vent to his thoughts.

'Our mothers were best friends. That makes us best friends too, true?'

'I suppose.' Sara-Jane adjusted the length of her safety belt. 'Although …'

'What? It is not possible to be best friends instantly, right?'

'No, no that. I think something must have happened to the friendship.'

'What do you mean?'

'Sara left Australia suddenly, I know that much. Following her departure my mother went away too, and I was left in the care of Nonnu and Nonna La Rocca, for some years. So it's a bit of mystery…'

'You mean, my grandparents?'

'Well …yes, I suppose.'

'Why, Sara, we are like brother and sister then.' Sante leaned across the seat and planted a kiss on her cheek. In so doing he had taken his eye off the road and strayed just over the centre strip. A small truck traveling in the opposite direction tooted and the driver's fist flailed at him. Sante took no notice. His face glowed at the discovery. Had he not been driving she was sure he would throw himself at her.

Now it was his turn to ask. 'What about my father? Has your mother mentioned him?'

'No, nothing. I don't even think she knew him, or

about you. I'm not sure.'

'Well, she's the only person who can answer some of these questions.'

Sara-Jane didn't want to think about La Rocca, too much murkiness there. As a diversion, she turned to look at the sea below. Such a stunning place this is, she thought. Quite surreal.

There was no way that she would have connected this with her Sicilian grandparents, not this postcard of a coastline, anyway. And yet in these rocks, perforated by the sea, wind and rain, she recognized something of theirs, a timelessness … something. More strangely still, and for the first time since she had arrived on the island, she felt at ease. She felt as if this were a return, not a first time visit.

'You have been there before?' Sante pointed.

'What?'

'The island, look.' His arm stretched in front of her, a finger pointing to the distance across the sea, where the contour of an island could just be seen in the afternoon haze. 'That's Lipari. You know Lipari?'

'Yes, Sante, I can see, but don't take your hands off the steering wheel.' She pulled a face. 'You nearly had us collide earlier.' But this time, she was surprised by a familiarity in her tone, like she was fondly scolding a younger sibling.

He must have detected it too, because he looked at her and chuckled. 'We will visit there, if you want. We go to Lipari together.'

14

You really had to wonder about Sante. Was he the ingénue he appeared to be? Or was he *furbo*, underneath? Did he have more than a pinch of Sicilian foxy guile beneath that exterior of child-like innocence?

Don Alfio was beginning to suspect the latter, which pleased him no end, because goodness knows, if he stayed the way his mother wanted him to, he would be all too easy prey in the jungle of the world.

Later in the morning, Don Alfio met him in the corridor, coming out of the bathroom, already showered and about to return to his room to get dressed.

'Ciao caro, to what do we owe such an early rise?'

Sante's face, still damp, glowed. He grabbed his father's arm and pulled him close as if to whisper something.

Don Alfio smiled. 'It's OK, Mamma is out. Did you get to meet her?'

'Yes, yes Papà. I am so excited … I haven't slept all night. Thank you for the message.'

Sante's exuberance ignited him too. 'Fantastico! And what is she like? No, no, no … don't tell me, let me guess,' Don Alfio parted his hands in front of his eyes, framing the picture of his imagination. 'Let me see, she's. … tall…'

'Yes.'

'Umm … Blonde.'

'Yes.'

'Like … that famous actress, what's her name, la Kidman.'

'Papà, she's beautiful.'

'There, I knew it. Australian women are all beautiful and the men too. They are the best athletes in the world. It's a new country, what do you expect? They breed super humans down there. '

Like a couple of fanatics, their arms entwined in a rugby hold, they danced around the room, singing in English. 'We are the champions!'

In the process, Sante's bath towel, which he had wrapped around his waist, fell to the floor.

Don Alfio picked it up for him. 'Better go and get dressed.'

At this point Sara walked in. 'What's all this *baccano*? You two are waking the neighbourhood.'

'Ciao Mamma.' The young man tucked the towel around his waist and gave his mother a morning kiss. 'Mamma, you will never believe what happened to me yesterday…'

Don Alfio held his breath. The boy was going full frontal, with no preliminaries, no tentative toe-testing. He was going to deposit the hot potato right on her lap, with that naïve face and a disarming smile, as if he were presenting a bouquet. 'I saw Sara, no, not Sara, her name is Sara-Jane.'

His mother's brows pressed together above the eyes.

'You know, the Australian girl,' he persisted. 'Your friend's daughter.'

Sara's bottom lip quivered. She tugged at the tassel of her shopping bag, from which surfaced the head of a brioche. Bits of lace came off and fell to the floor. It made Don Alfio nervous to look at her, but Sante did not seem to notice.

'Why didn't you tell me this last night?' Her tone was accusatory.

'You were in bed.'

'You could have called me. You know I never go to sleep until you come home.'

A shadow flitted across Sante's forehead, then distended as he smiled broadly. 'Mamma, I knew straight away when I saw her that it was she. Isn't that strange! I'm going to collect her this morning from her hotel. You will meet her.'

'What? ' She looked as if she were about to have a fit, but again Sante did not seem to notice. 'Did you meet her father too?'

'What father, there is no father.'

'No?'

'Oh, I see, the man she travels with? He is her employer.'

'Are you sure?'

'Of course, Mamma, Sara-Jane told me. Why do you doubt it?'

Sara relaxed her grip on the bag. She put it down on the kitchen table and looked as if much more than the weight of the bag had been relieved off her.

'Better I go dress.' Sante was still smiling. 'I am to collect her at nine.'

'What about Mass, Sante?'

'I can go this evening. Maybe Sara-Jane will come too. Mamma, you will love her, she's beautiful.'

'There you are, Sara.' Don Alfio seemed relieved, 'You have nothing to worry about. Do you know what Faraone was telling me the other day? In Australia there are around twenty million people in an area the size of the whole of Europe. Imagine all that space for such a few people. No wonder they all look so perfect in those TV shows. It's all that clean air and natural food they eat.'

Sara La Rocca knew when she was beaten. This girl, stealing upon her from that unseen, sneaky side of the sphere, from a land that had caused her so much pain – and had bequeathed her a child she had never asked for – now demanded a seat at the table of her life. There was little point in resisting. What she feared – and experience had taught her that fears were almost always a prediction – was that she had come to deconstruct her life and reconstitute it on her own terms.

And now, as she got dressed for church, she knew there was no way out, she would have to tell her son some unhappy truths; fill out the omissions she had so carefully guarded to protect him.

She did not want to think about this girl. She feared her coming threatened to stir her world. That fear prevailed over all other feelings, including a discernible sense of attachment to a child who, so many years ago, had been almost a daughter to her. She could not help but notice a certain curiosity bobbing up in the troubled sea of her consciousness. What was this young woman like? How far did she resemble her mother? How much did she remember? Would she remember that fateful day when she stood in the doorway, clutching a rag doll in one hand as the other fisted over her eye, as she witnessed Russell Toohey commit a despicable act?

*

Don Alfio didn't always attend the church service with his wife. Firstly, because she was an assiduous churchgoer, often to three or four services a week, which made it impractical for him to join her. And secondly, because he was an avowed agnostic. Being agnostic of course didn't mean he refuted the possibility of a Higher Being. He liked to keep his options open.

So he went to church intermittently, as a partial insurance, just in case. Besides, he liked standing in church next to Sara, since he found her utter absorption sublimating. And because he lacked both devotion and the concentration for sustained prayer, he liked to think his wife's effort in that department sufficed for both of them.

Don Alfio Marzano was proud of his agnosticism, it was a sign of a free-thinking man. It might be a surprise that the first citizen of this conservative mountain town in Sicily should wear his agnostic colours so publicly, and with such aplomb, when politicians the world over make a display of their religious belief, real or faked. In the close community of San Sisto, however, Don Alfio's lack of religious conviction was regarded with the same degree of tolerance as his dalliance.

It was just part of his 'artistic' personality, although no one in town could actually point to any artistic achievements that could be attributed to the mayor. Others saw it as a sign of enlightenment and modernity. And anyway, even when he didn't attend Mass, he always made it a point of accompanying his wife to the church door, therefore demonstrating his allegiance to traditional values.

So there was no surprise at the Bar Ciro when Don Alfio appeared in the piazza, next to his wife, in full suit and tie, walking his Signora the hundred paces or so from their house to the *portone* of the Chiesa Madre. As they strolled past the Bar Ciro, Mayor Marzano called out a collective *buon giorno Signori*, and his Signora conceded a smile and a brief nod to the men sitting in the autumn sunshine, taking their coffee, while their wives prayed to God inside the church.

Though no one actually said so, it was accepted in the

town that it was a woman's role to intercede with God for her own sins and for the sins of her man. As for Don Alfio himself, his view was that if God existed, and He was male, He would certainly give women a more sympathetic ear.

As a result, Sunday Mass was attended by a preponderance of women worshippers. Men had more pressing things to do, like sorting out the political mess of Italy, and the world, to the aroma of roasted coffee in the Bar Ciro. And that's where Don Alfio headed for, during that Sunday's church service, to sit at his favourite table, with his friends: Pino Siracusa the retired school principal, Giancola Vinci the municipal secretary, and Carmelo Radice the surveyor.

This morning, they had plenty to discuss. What with the troubles in the Middle East going from bad to worse, Berlusconi defending another charge of corruption, and the EU constitution being debated in Parliament, there was no shortage of issues.

The four friends had one common interest: international politics. It was their way of fleeing the claustrophobic world of San Sisto. This was one of the best times of the week for Don Alfio. He enjoyed a good debate, pitting his wits against the sharpest brains in town, particularly those of Pino Siracusa, whose opinions he really valued, despite his being a Communist through and through. This when everybody else had abandoned the Party, after the fall of the Berlin wall: but then, Don Alfio admired dogged perseverance in the midst of adversity, probably because it was one of the qualities he himself did not have, and preferred not to take on, because martyrdom was just not for him.

He, the mayor, who always bought a copy of the Gazzetta del Sud, never read the articles in their entirety. Most of the time he would not get much past the headline, before someone's comment provoked a reaction that sparked off a debate. Sometimes they would refer to parts of the article to back up this or that point of view, but in most cases, the paper was merely a pretext to soap-box their political views. This morning, the discussion promised to be more lively than usual, as controversy over Berlusconi's gaffe in the European Parliament, in which he offended a German MEP, was still raging.

'What an embarrassment that man is for Italy. *Che figuraccia!*' lamented Radice, 'He brings shame on the entire country.'

'*Eh sì,*' agreed Don Alfio with a sigh, ironing out the creases in the newspaper with the palm of his hand.

But Giancola Vinci, who owed his job to the good offices of the pro-Berlusconi UDC party, could not let it pass. 'What shame? What embarrassment? *Signori*, let us consider the situation with clarity. The German offended our elected Prime Minister, true or not true?'

'What do you mean? How?'

'How? It is obvious, no? By suggesting that the *Presidente del Consiglio* is a crook...'

'So? He only stated what we all know to be true ...' Carmelo, who was getting very little municipal work since Vinci had been promoted Secretary, had to interrupt.

Giancola merely gave him a side glance and did not deign to address him personally. 'The fact is,' he continued, 'he had to defend himself, not just from a personal attack, no, no *Signori miei.*' Here Giancola's clenched hand rose dramatically. His index finger, slightly curved, lanced through the air, upon reaching the level of his cheek paused, then dipped down and tapped on the relevant article in the newspaper on the table. He declaimed, 'He was defending the honour of Italy.'

'UuuH!' Carmelo raised his hands to his forehead, and

turned his head to one side dismissively. 'What drivel!'

The comment would have surely led to a serious spat between the two men, had not Pino Siracusa intervened. His low, steady voice always had the effect of calming animosities. 'What Berlusconi has done ... he has put on display before the world the Italian character, more particularly the insecurities of a nation. What is our preoccupation with elegance but another symptom of those insecurities? We are a people with opinions, too many opinions. We react, we dream, create and fantasise, but we cannot organise ourselves as a nation, only in metaphor. Real life does not interest us, or perhaps we don't think it important enough to give it our attention ...'

'Now listen, Siracusa, what you say has some merit, I don't deny it, but here the matter in question is nothing to do with the Italian character ...'

'Do you not agree that this man's behaviour has made Italy a laughing stock in Europe?'

'Absolutely not ... No...'

The furore was suddenly arrested by the appearance in the piazza of a Lancia, with its unmistakable wide reinforced grill and bulletproof glass windows.

General silence fell as Mimmo Urzi's car slid silent and heavy onto the piazza, out of nowhere. It skirted the church, circled around the monument to the fallen soldier, whose face resembled a young Mussolini, and came to a stop in front of the Marzano house.

The driver, a heavy man, whose weight seemed to be suspended above the waist, got out of the car and went to ring the bell on the *portone* of the house, with its black satin badge in remembrance of Sara La Rocca's late father.

Don Alfio Marzano winced, but was too conscious of his position to show the fear inside him. He stood up. '*Signori*, I'm sorry, I have a visitor this morning. Please go on without me.' He left the Gazzetta del Sud on the table.

Everyone noticed he had forgotten to drink his coffee. Something he never omitted to do.

15

Since the death of his father, when he and his bodyguards were blown up inside their car as they left the Catania airport, Mimmo Urzì had found himself at the head of the family's 'business' empire. The many people whose livelihood depended on the goodwill and protection of old Leone Urzì, were shocked.

Prior to this disaster the Old Man had seemed invincible. He was ruthless, shrewd, highly respected and widely connected to people who could make things happen: politicians, businessmen and the enforcers, both inside and outside the law. Unfortunately, as everyone in that highly precarious business knows, you're only as good as your luck. When that runs out, all the other power props are of little use and tend to collapse with it. After the shock, people were considering how to best cut their losses and change allegiance to the new guard from Cefalù.

Initially, nobody gave the new boy on the block much of a chance. He was young and considered somewhat of a *scapestrato* by all who knew him. There was talk of him being a junkie, a gambler, a womaniser … you name it. Worse still, everyone agreed the boy was none too bright. His own father, who had all but disowned him, was quoted as saying his son's brain matter had all drained down to his penis, presumably in reference to the size of that part of his anatomy.

Be that as it may, once his father was out of the way, Mimmo astounded everyone by the swiftness with which he took over the reins, pounced on his enemies, and established order. Now, at thirty-one, and after a string of successful operations that left a few corpses riddled with bullets, incinerated in cars, and in one case, drowned in a vat of olive oil, he had rightly gained respect. It seemed that what Mimmo lacked in brain cells he was endowed with in cunning, swiftness of action, and good old survival instinct.

When Don Alfio arrived, the driver had given up on the doorbell and was heading back. Don Alfio stood outside the car, on the passenger side, where he knew Mimmo to be sitting, although all he could see was his own reflection in the bulletproof glass. Already tense, that face in the tinted glass made him feel faint.

'Signor Mimmo.' He called feebly into the glass.

An interminable pause of silence ensued. Finally, the glass lowered to reveal the chubby inscrutable face of Mimmo Urzì.

'Don Alfio, *i miei ossequi.*' Despite the obsequious words, Mimmo's face had a smirk and his voice a tone of contempt.

Don Alfio swallowed hard and touched his hat. 'To what do I owe this pleasure?'

'Nothing.' Mimmo's slow drawl made him seem even more dense than his repute. 'I was going for a *passeggiata* to the mountains, to get some fresh air. I've heard your wine this year is exceptional.'

'Oh, signor Mimmo. It would be a great pleasure, but … my family are all out this morning.' He accompanied the words with a quick glance at his watch. 'Would you honour me … over at Ciro's …' He looked towards the bar, like a man desperate to be rescued.

Mimmo dismissed it with a wave of his bejewelled hand. 'You know me, I'm a private man, Don Alfio …' He looked up to the balcony.

Don Alfio had no choice but to invite him up. He was glad there was the coffee to be made; it gave him an activity through which to channel his tension. He poured a cup for each of them, lacing his with a generous drop of grappa.

Normally he wouldn't, not on a Sunday morning. It seemed sacrilegious. But he needed something to steady his nerves. He knew that Mimmo would not be venturing out all this way unless there was something heavy on his mind.

Mimmo put three generous teaspoons of sugar in his coffee then proceeded to stir. As he did his bracelets clanged on his wrist. The sound further destabilised Don Alfio's unsteady nerves. Mimmo loved jewellery. The gold Cartier watch on his left wrist was augmented by a matching bracelet of thick spun gold. His right wrist sported yet another bracelet which strung together little silver bells, whose clappers had shapes of hearts and horns: love and luck, the two essentials in his life. When the *mafioso* raised his arm and shook his wrist, something he did regularly to emphasise a point or simply to fill in a silence, all those shiny trinkets glittered and jingled like decorations on a Christmas tree.

The luck theme was pursued beyond his wrist to other pieces of visible jewellery. From his left ear hung another golden horn, a further bastion in his barricade against ill fortune. The man felt, with some justification it must be said, that in his profession he needed to have plenty of luck on his side. And so far it seemed his lucky trinkets had served him well, given he had already escaped a couple of serious assassination attempts, by rivals keen to get their hands on his fast growing empire. But the pièce de résistance of his collection of jewellery was without doubt his chain. Chunky and solid, its reputation preceded its impressive appearance. Legend had it that it was instrumental, at least once, in the elimination of a rival, by strangulation. So many uses for jewellery.

Having downed his coffee, the guest got down to business, 'Have you considered the offer on that piece of land, Don Alfio?'

His host cleared his throat, knowing it was the reason he had come and yet, true to his old habits, instead of preparing for this visit, he had chosen instead to avoid thinking about it. Now he was lost for a reply.

'Yes, of course, it's a very generous offer ... Personally, I would sell right now... I could certainly do with the money...'

'You are ready to sell then?'

'Well, no. I mean not yet. You see, the grove has sentimental value for us; it's been in my wife's family for ... well ... forever. So, it's not really in my hands. I mean, if it were up to me, I would sell. Times change, and one must adapt. We must be realistic, but ...'

Mimmo didn't like talk, he liked words he couldn't understand even less. He felt threatened by them. He was sure they had been invented by clever dicks to confound people like him and to let themselves off the hook. So he shook his wrist in a show of impatience. At the sound of all those bells Don Alfio stopped talking, but the ensuing silence felt even more terrible.

'Maybe we can wait until my mother-in-law passes away,' he ventured, in a plaintive voice, hoping to appeal to Mimmo's sense of family. Too late, he realized, much to his dismay, that he might be giving Mimmo ideas. 'She loves it there. She would die if she were forced to move.' Don Alfio realised the futility of his plea.

Clearly death did not have the same import for Mimmo as it did for ordinary mortals. 'Don Alfio, this is an important project, one that will bring work and prosp ... *money* into our region. With all respect to you and your family, my clients are not prepared to wait for the good soul of your mother-in-law to leave us. Long may she live.' And here Mimmo dutifully crossed himself, causing an orchestration of jangling that just about traumatised his host. 'The property is required now, or my clients might take their business to Cefalù.'

Cefalù was under the control of his rivals and that did not suit Mimmo at all.

Silence.

'Don Alfio, *al buon intenditore, poche parole.*' Mimmo looked away on uttering the ambiguous adage. He never looked you in the eye, not out of shyness, but rather, so as not to deign you with the privilege of his whole attention. The effect was most disconcerting, because when the light fell obliquely on Mimmo's eyes it highlighted the yellow specks in his pupils, giving him a menacing appearance.

Don Alfio sighed. 'I'll speak to my wife. I'll need time to try to persuade her.'

'How long do you need?'

Don Alfio did not want to be held down to a date. 'Well, if I know her, she'll take some persuading.'

Mimmo's hand went to his ear, he winced and pulled at the golden horn with some force.

Staring in horror, Don Alfio saw the ear rip open and the ring come clear of the bleeding ear. Fortunately, it was his imagination playing a cruel trick, but the message was all too real. There was nothing to do but for Don Alfio to cave in, which he would have done, had he not feared his wife's reaction almost as much as Mimmo's threat.

The poor mayor, modern man that he was, did not believe in supernatural intervention, but what happened next was so timely that, in the days following the incident, it induced him to think that he might reconsider his philosophical position on this issue.

Just as he was about to sweat out another shirt, and Mimmo's patience was reaching a point of consequence, he was rescued by excited voices coming from the corridor, just outside the study where this private interview was taking place. Like a prisoner in a dark tunnel, who had just seen a spiral of light, Don Alfio excused himself and went out to investigate. His son's arrival was always a pleasure for Don Alfio, but never before accompanied with so much relief and gratitude.

'Papà, is Mamma with you?' Sante was out of breath.

As Don Alfio replied, his eyes fell on the girl next to Sante.

Seeing a beautiful woman would have gladdened Don Alfio's heart at any time, but at this moment of intolerable distress, her appearance attained the power of a miracle. In his eyes she became a veritable Angel of Rescue. She was, he guessed, the Australian girl, as Sante was about to confirm.

'Papà, *ecco* Sara-Jane.'

Gladness and admiration gelled in Don Alfio, producing an impetuous outpouring of affection. 'Ah *carissima Signorina*, we've been expecting you.'

It quite overwhelmed Sara-Jane, but there was no time to hold back, because Don Alfio had already tucked his arm under hers and led her into the study, where Mimmo sat, miffed at the interruption.

'*Vieni, vieni. Ti presento il dottor* Mimmo Urzì.'

'Oh, hello.' She chose to speak in English, even though she didn't have the foggiest whether the two men understood her. In the midst of what she perceived to be a tense situation, she thought she would retain the advantage that speaking her own language gave her.

Upon setting his eyes on the girl, a strange transformation took place in Mimmo Urzì. His face twisted and reset itself in a painful grimace, as if he were being tortured. His brow broke into a sweat and for a moment he froze in his chair, unable to return the girl's greeting.

To fill the silence, Don Alfio said, 'Mamma has gone to

see Nonna.'

'Ah, *perfetto*. Come Sara-Jane, we shall go and visit Nonna.' Sante moved to the door.

Sara-Jane thought she misheard.

'Nonna? You mean my Nonna?'

'Yes, of course, our Nonna, but I cannot say she will know you.'

Sara-Jane was dumbfounded. Just yesterday she had been told that both grandparents were dead.

Sante took her hand and started to retreat towards the door. The prospect of the girl's departure shook Mimmo out of his paralysis. He now sprang to his feet as if a spider had stung his backside, bowed very low and proffered his chubby hand.

Sara-Jane took it in passing, her mind still grappling with a contradiction perfectly mimicked in the fact that her hands were being held by two men pulling in opposite directions. Perhaps to compensate for her curtness, given the funny man's gallantry, she allowed him a wan smile. Never in her wildest dreams could she imagine the impact this perfunctory little gesture would have on Mimmo's heart and on subsequent events.

*

Such things only happen in books, thought Mimmo. Or rather, he imagined they did, for Mimmo had never read a book in his life. His eyes remained fixed on the door, beyond which that luminous creature had vanished just as quickly as she had appeared, after wreaking havoc in his heart. He wondered whether the apparition was real or whether it was one of those airbrushed things you see on magazine covers. He stared at the door, waiting for it to open again and confirm the reality of the vision.

Don Alfio noticed the change in his guest, how could he not? The man had been transformed by a passing spirit, though not quite spirited away, as Don Alfio would have wished. Mimmo seemed immobilised in a space of his own. This was a new situation for him, outside the realm of his experience. He turned his attention to his jewellery, hoping to find inspiration out of his state of bewilderment. But none came. None of the rings or bracelets; earring or chains provided him with a clue. So he sat there looking at the door and as his eyes scanned the room aimlessly, they came to rest on Don Alfio. They were little eyes, hazel, the specks of yellow lost in the ample space of his cheeks and the immensity of what he felt. They looked at the mayor pleadingly, as if to ask, *what is happening to me Don Alfio?*

Of course, Don Alfio, who had loved women above all else in his life, understood perfectly well. He sympathised and commiserated with him, especially as his experience in these matters indicated to him that Don Mimmo was in for a long haul of suffering, as the object of his nascent passion was unlikely to requite his feelings.

Nevertheless, Alfio was also a survivor and it was this very instinct which prevailed upon him. It occurred to him that this new state in which Mimmo had fallen relieved him of the pressure of having to make a decision now. It was a god-sent turn of events to be exploited to his advantage. For a start, he saw a chance to get rid of his uninvited guest and to obtain some respite.

Mimmo himself gave him the opener. 'Is that Sante's girl?'

'Oh no, Sante is merely a boy. She's a relation of my wife's, from Australia. The girl's mother and my wife were very close. She carries the same name as her. Unfortunately, she's an orphan, the poor girl, and looks to my wife as her mother.'

'She's a *Signorina* then?' One could feel his heart suspended on the filament of Don Alfio's reply.

His host paused, intoxicated by the feeling of power over such a tyrant. 'Certainly, my niece…' Imperceptibly, he upgraded the level of his relationship to the girl. 'My niece will not give up her independence for just any man. When the time comes, she will choose a strong man of character. I feel that a Sicilian man would be just the person for her.'

The mayor tried to discern the effect of his words on Mimmo without looking directly at him. Having satisfied himself that he had sown the seeds of hope in Mimmo's heart, he got up. 'Signor Mimmo, I would ask you to stay for lunch, but …'

The large guest sprang to his feet with such force his bulk teetered and the jewellery jingled, but this time it played sweet music to Don Alfio's ears, for it announced Mimmo's departure.

'No, Don Alfio, I … I am expected somewhere else. Thank you for receiving me.' The terrifying bully was suddenly bowing respectfully.

Don Alfio thanked unpredictable old Cupid – and Sara-Jane – that Mimmo, who had marched into his living room with the arrogance of a *mafioso*, was now limping back to the door, wounded by the arrow of love.

16

On arriving at the track that led to the stone house on the rise, Sara-Jane was in shock, for this was the house of a recurrent dream as a child: the blackened stone walls, the long narrow windows with grey unpainted frames and cracked putty, faded roof tiles overgrown with moss, the olive tree, whose upper branches cascaded into the gully on the roof.

This was not the tree of her childhood in Australia, growing in the sandy soil of a suburban backyard, which was young and smooth of trunk. The trunk of this tree was knotted and hollow; marked by centuries of elemental struggles: fire, wind and droughts ... With its gash opened to the sun, it inclined precariously in a gravity-defying pose. This was nature at its most resilient.

Back home, the landscape was flat and undemanding, the sky was wide open, her life busy. Her concerns were the minutiae of her day: planning meetings and activities; meeting deadlines, setting goals, looking forward. Here, among these stony ridges and dips, which intimated at cataclysms, things seemed mysterious, unpredictable. In this landscape of ancient villages – which looked like perennial rookeries – past and present moved in unison.

As the car trundled closer over the rough track, Sara-Jane turned to Sante. 'This is really strange.'

'What?'

'I've seen this house before.'

'You mean like ... *deja vu*?'

'Yes ...' Sara-Jane struggled to explain, 'No ... it's more like ... I don't know, it's crazy.'

There was an echo here, a correspondence with her childhood, a recognition. How could that be? Sara-Jane had to concede there were things in life, in her, which defied logic.

Sante slammed the brake and the car lurched, the back wheels dropped into a dip on the track and stopped.

Sara-Jane's face had the absent intensity of a sleep-walker.

Sante took his hand to her face, gently stroked the back of his index finger down the contour of her upper arm. 'Sara, Sara-Jane.' He whispered and his voice was strange.

Sara-Jane gave a start and he quickly retrieved his hand. She realised she was afraid of deep imperceptible forces working inside her, which had brought her here. The possibility she was not in control, but somehow an instrument of complex energies beyond her comprehension, was intolerable to her.

Such superstition was for simple villagers, because they needed them. Not for her though: she was a modern woman, a woman of the world, an educated, ambitious woman. Through the car window she watched skeins of mist where the land dipped. Did she dare go beyond the mist?

She would have told Sante to turn back, except she didn't want to appear irrational. Besides, two figures had now appeared in the courtyard, both women. One tiny, wearing a brown scarf over sun-bleached white hair, standing by the doorstep as if unsure whether to come forward or bolt back inside. The other, in a dark blue frock, and matching coat and hat, looked incongruous in that mountain setting. Neither woman moved.

Sante approached the house tentatively, as if he weren't sure he was doing the right thing, turning more than once to ensure Sara-Jane was following. On reaching the women, he embraced the older one, who then ran into the house, before Sara-Jane was introduced.

'Mamma.' Sante said the words for all to hear. 'I have brought you a guest.'

The woman stood there, unmoving, erect like a bastion defending her territory, waiting for Sara-Jane to come to her. A heavy cold wind whispered through the thistles.

As the young Australian crossed the space between them, she had the sensation of cutting through the ice of time. When she offered her hand, the other woman hesitated before accepting it. It was coarse, and her grip, when it finally came, was masculine and firm.

'You must be Sara-Jane.' She spoke in English, surprising the younger woman by conjuring up a smile out of her inscrutable face, and then, even more surprisingly, she gave her the briefest of hugs. Was it of love or betrayal?

Sara-Jane dismissed the first, she looked for evidence of the latter, and noticed the woman spoke with an Australian accent, unlike her son. This relaxed her a little.

The woman spoke again. 'You have certainly grown up.'

'Well, I hope so.'

'You were this big when I last saw you.' Sara La Rocca set the palm of her hand at knee level.

Ah, but that doesn't give you licence to patronise me, thought Sara-Jane. More to the point, it doesn't give you the right to lie to me.

There was nothing in the older woman's expression to suggest embarrassment. Nor did Sara-Jane expect that any mention would be made of that telephone conversation. That piece of deception was now superseded by events. What Sara-Jane wanted to know was the reason for the dishonesty. And while she considered her move, the woman spoke again.

'Your mother … she's … passed away.'

Sara-Jane nodded.

'I'm sorry. She was very young. An accident, I believe?'

She would not be surprised if this woman was well acquainted with 'the accident'. She suspected Sara La Rocca knew a lot more than she knew herself. The woman had a way of looking at you as if she were not seeing you, but someone else. Most discomforting. This was a woman who spoke her language, and had known her as a child, knew secrets about her. Sara-Jane felt violated. Just how much did she know? What was the relationship between Sara La Rocca and her mother? A week ago, in Australia, it didn't matter. Here, now, in this country, meeting her for the first time - although of course it wasn't the first time at all – it unsettled Sara-Jane. Bad sign. She picked invisible specks off her dress.

'How long are you going to stay in Italy?'

'I leave on Thursday…'

Despite her impassive expression, Sara-Jane just knew the Italian woman was relieved.

'So short!' Sante looked truly disappointed.

Sara-Jane mused silently. So this was the woman whose name she carried, and had played second mother to her, who had changed her nappies and put her to sleep. She felt spied upon, on the other side of a one-way mirror.

And then Sara-Jane became her mother, Sheryl. As the wind rose up the valley and crickets played their exhausted calls through the dry stalks of autumn, Sara-Jane was ushered into the old farmhouse, whose door was so low she had to bend down for fear of hitting her head on the cross frame.

Coming in from the midday sunlight into a small rectangular room, Sara-Jane smelt onion cooking on the stove; but it was merely a surface sensation hiding the feeling that here, time was stagnant, measured by the occasional drip of a tap upon metal. When her eyes adjusted, she could see the room, with lime-washed walls and exposed wooden beams, coffee-coloured by smoke. She stood next to a credenza, whose mirror top was cluttered with religious figures and an amazing array of *bombonieri*: angels and bridal figurines, silver spoons and crystal hearts, glasses, candles and jewellery cases, miniature violins and pianos.

There were framed photos too, among which Sara-Jane spotted one of two old people and a young girl, perhaps five years old. Strangely none of them was looking into the camera. Not the child, who clung with both hands to the arm of the old man, and held a questioning stare in his direction, not the old man who had a look of utter helplessness, and not the woman, who stood next to the man, some distance away, as if she were observing them. Sara-Jane studied the photograph, and it was only when she noticed the red ribbon that bound the child's fair hair on top of the head that she understood.

A voice reached her through the expanse of time and brought her face to face with the woman in the picture.

'Nonna,' Sante was saying, '*a conusci a chista?*'

The old woman was tiny. Sara-Jane towered over her. Eighteen years ago, it would have been the other way. She looked for traces of recognition in the frail figure.

Nonna looked at her severely. '*Ma si, certu, chista e' Sherula.*'

'Sherula?' Sante turned to his mother. '*Ma cosa intende dire la Nonna?*'

Sara La Rocca turned to Sara-Jane. 'She has mistaken you for your mother.'

Sara-Jane understood. The old woman could not reconcile the little child she had nursed, dressed and put to sleep a generation ago with this blonde giant. What she saw instead, standing once again inside her house, was the woman who had brought so much upheaval upon her family.

So, beyond the mist of time and space, Sara-Jane discovered an uncomfortable truth: that despite all appearances, she was after all more her mother's daughter than she wanted to be. It was a truth she could cope with, because she was able control the Sheryl in her. She had to, or she would decline into self-contempt.

More unsettling was another truth, the confirmation that the world she remembered, the world of Nonnu and Nonna no longer existed, and much of it was probably constructed out of her need to escape the pain of her later years.

This journey to Sicily, to this house, was valuable after all, for it demolished a dream castle, each cloud puff lifted, one by one, to uncover the rawness. It was better this way. Now she could be free of the past, free from memories she no longer needed.

But the other did not relent. This dark, inscrutable woman – with a shadowy face that suggested nooks full of skeletons – was setting the agenda. She stood there, looking intent, filling the space with her thought, holding power over Sara-Jane with her silence.

She turned to her son . 'Go and pick some prickly pears for Nonna. We'll take some home. You know how fond your father is of them.'

*

Now it was her turn to stand outside the house that smelled of damp wood, in the luminous October light, taking in how, in the distance, a breathtaking landscape of hills precipitated down to a dry riverbed. And how did it come about that two of them, the two Saras, found themselves here, in the very same spot on earth?

Sara-Jane felt sure, to her annoyance, that Sante's mother had planned it. Sara La Rocca was about to eject, volcano like, a rare outflow from long-dormant memories. You could almost hear the thoughts rumble inside her.

Sara held a long cane stick to the olive frond and beat it furiously. She picked up a fallen branch, and felt the beads with her fingers. 'These olives are not done yet, it will be another month before we can pick them.'

What a life! They're slaughtering each other all over the world, the Amazon forest is receding as fast as you can say the word, people are despairing everywhere ... and here the life question is when to pick the olives. Nothing idyllic about this, thought Sara-Jane, rather out of touch. Depressing, actually.

Sara-Jane wanted to say something to derail the woman's plan, something like, *Excuse me, but why exactly have you got me out here?* She wanted to confront her, stop her in her tracks. Instead, a lassitude overcame her.

Again, Sara La Rocca seized the initiative by turning the dark side of her face to her. 'What do you think of Sante?'

Sara-Jane was stunned, not so much by the question but by the look on the woman's face. It was challenging, accusatory.

'I've barely met him ... I mean – he's just a boy.'

'That's true. And he is younger than his age. He knows nothing of the world. I don't want him to be hurt.'

Don't want him to grow up, more like it, thought Sara-Jane, but desisted. 'I have no interest in him, if that's what you mean.'

'That's a relief. The problem is he seems to be very

fond of you.'

'Not in that way, I'm sure.'

'No. Tell me, did your mother ever talk to you about me?'

'Only that you were best friends and I was named after you.'

'Did she ever mention that we lived together?'

Sara-Jane felt irritated. She was the journalist after all: she posed the questions. 'Why are you asking me all this?'

'I'm sorry. The thing is …' To her surprise, the woman was nervous, she was about to make a revelation. Sara-Jane hated revelations, they usually carried the kind of payload she didn't want to be burdened with.

'You'd better sit down, Sara-Jane.' It was the first time she had used her name. 'I have a story to tell you. It's the kind of story you might prefer not to hear, I'm sure. But now that you have come to Sicily…' She looked at the younger woman accusingly as if, by daring to come to Sicily, she had committed a punishable crime.

It was the kind of story that should have been told in the evening, as the sun descended the far back of mountain, not like this, now, in the midday sun, with the glare bouncing off the leaves of the olive tree. But if the time of day was all wrong, the tone was adequately set by the tired monotone of one lonely cicada, stranded from the passing of summer, playing a terminal tune in the canopy.

The older woman's story left the Australian girl incredulous. 'That means … Russell Toohey is Sante's father.'

'Yes.'

'I really find it hard to believe. We're talking chalk and cheese.'

'Well, luckily there's not much chalk in Sante. But I suggest you take a good look at his eyes.'

This was the sort of melodrama Sara-Jane abhorred, the entangled past she didn't want to know. Now it snuck upon her like a betrayal. At this moment, she felt she could hate Sara La Rocca for the rest of her life. She regretted ever coming to Sicily. 'Does Sante know?'

'No, of course not.'

Again, that anger rose inside her. 'Why not?' She knew why not. Sante was too young, too gentle, too precious, to be burdened with such a past.

The older woman confirmed it. 'I wanted to spare him the details of his conception.'

'You mean … you were *raped*?'

The savagery of that word shocked Sara La Rocca, but then, she had to admit, there was something liberating about telling a blunt truth. There and then, she looked like she felt the intoxicating power of it, and was grateful to this young woman.

Did she really believe all that stuff? Was she just playing it to comfort herself? Was she just using it as a diversion? If so, a diversion from what? The more she stayed among these people, the less she understood them: their world of guilt and religion, of tradition, customs and social checks and balances, of appearance and pretence. It all confounded Sara-Jane. She countered it with a simple appeal. 'He needs to be told.'

'Maybe, maybe not. In these mountains we can live out a lifetime without needing to know certain things.'

Sara-Jane had to admit, on the face of it, that there could be no argument with a mother's desire to protect her son from the sordid details of his conception. She had constructed her life as a buttress against a reality too harsh to know. But then, this touchy-feely world, this world of mountain villages, of piazzas, of sun-massaged groves, of myth and conventions – all in pursuit of preserving ghosts –

this was not Sara-Jane's world. And glad of it she was, too.

Sara La Rocca stared up the track to where Sante and Nonna had disappeared, past the squat building that was now used as a rabbit enclosure, whose stones were blackened by a recent fire. She took a deep breath. 'They're taking a long time.'

Sara-Jane, eager to escape, seized the opportunity. 'I'll go and see.'

*

A stand of prickly pears grew at the lower end of the property. Its roots helped bind the terrain which fell away in a sheer cliff wall some hundred metres below. Sante, his shirt sleeve rolled up, was holding a long stick at the end of which was nailed an aluminium can. Nonna stood by, directing him to which fruit he should pick. Her mind might be gone, but her visceral connection with the land she had known all her life had not been damaged by decline into old age. He manoeuvred the contraption over the fruit, gave it a twist to break the stem, then dropped it into the bucket.

Sara-Jane stood and looked at Sante, but wasn't listening to his words. Rather, she had caught sight of his eyes in profile and made a shocking connection: Sara was right, this was Russell Toohey's son. She feared that once this sank in, it would change perceptions forever. Already she detected sensations of belonging and responsibility, about Sante, about this landscape.

Across the deep cut, on the opposite side of the ravine a mountain stood, like a bald giant. That's where Sara-Jane wanted to be right now. Or better still, back in Australia.

Nonna's wheezy voice reined her in. '*Fa presto, me*

figghiu, aiu a ghiri a cucinari pi to Nonnu.'

Sante explained. 'She say she has to go and prepare lunch for Nonnu.' For Nonna La Rocca, her husband would live on until her death.

While Nonna returned to her ghosts, Sante and Sara-Jane took the bucket of prickly pears back to the outdoor table. Sara La Rocca came out of the house, with a bowl in one hand and clutching two paring knives and forks in the other. She too was in a hurry.

Mother and son proceeded to skin the fruit. Sara-Jane watched Sante stab each one with the prongs of the fork and hold it down, while he sliced off both ends. He then slit the skin along the belly of the fruit from end to end. With the point of the knife he curled the skin away from the flesh, inserted the tip of thumb and finger into the open slit, pressed, and the skin came away. Behold, out of the thorny jacket came the sweet flesh of the fruit.

Sara-Jane thought this is a metaphor for something, but what? She watched fascinated as Nonnu's image materialized from the dark to perform the same delicate operation. The eye of her imagination moved swiftly from Nonnu's gentle face to that of Sante, who smiled as if he were holding up a trophy.

He came to her with a golden fruit pronged upon a fork. *'Provalo.'*

Sara-Jane wondered if this was a test.

'This is one of the authentic tastes of Sicily.' He sounded like the script on a tourist brochure.

Sara-Jane hesitated. What kind of fruit of temptation was this? What intimate ritual was Sante luring her into? Would she be burdened with this island's passions, its secrets, its guilt?

'Try it.' He insisted. 'You cannot come to Sicily and not savour its fruit.'

Impetuously, Sara-Jane pulled the fruit free from the fork and sank her teeth in. The recollection did not register until its sweet fleshy pulp passed through her gullet. Then the memories flashed. She knew a point had been crossed, a bridge to her childhood had been rebuilt. Sara-Jane looked at the older Sara, then at the young man. 'Sante, your mother has something to tell you.' Her tone suggested a resolution had been reached,

Sara La Rocca smarted under the blow, but managed to stand her ground. This foreign girl was taking control of her world, a world she had painstakingly constructed over nearly twenty years and protected with a wall of stone-upon-stone of secrecy. She set her eyes upon the younger woman. 'No, I have nothing to say. We are going now.'

For a moment Sara-Jane felt faint under the intensity of that stare. She understood the woman's game. Drawing on millennia of superstition, she set the *malocchio* upon her, the evil eye, to bend her will. But her only weapon was fear and fear was the weapon of the desperate.

This realization gave the young woman heart. She talked to herself, just as she had done in the dark years of her childhood: you are a rational woman, Sara-Jane, and this will only harm you if you let it.

The real pity was that this woman – who had been gifted incredibly beautiful dark eyes, the eyes of a civilization, eyes that should be conduits of light, form and knowledge – had chosen fear and superstition instead.

So, there they stood facing each other, the older and the younger, the dark powers of fear and the powers of hope.

The impasse was broken by that most intrusive of modern inventions: Sara-Jane's mobile phone. The interruption annoyed her. This was one confrontation she wanted resolved right there and then.

She ignored the persistent, jingling of ABBA's *Money*

Money Money. 'Why don't you tell him?'

Sara La Rocca was mute.

Sara-Jane taunted her. 'Why don't you tell him who his real father is, Sara?'

Sante's voice cut in, urgent and plaintive. '*Mamma, che sta per dire?*'

There was nothing but silence, but when the older Sara found her tongue, it came sharp as a knife, slicing through years of pretence. 'You tell him then. Go on. Tell him. You're his sister.'

The words shook Sara-Jane. Amazingly, she had not made the connection inside her head. Perhaps there was a part of her that had never accepted Russell Toohey as her father. Now the impact of this simple truth hit her. The three of them stood there speechless.

Sara-Jane, desperate for a diversion, instinctively snatched at her mobile that was still demanding attention. 'Yes!' She shouted the word into the phone.

Dr Troina, sounding positively lugubrious, was summoning her to the *Casa di Cura* because Franzetti had taken a bad turn.

*

His mother always said 'we're in the hands of destiny'. Are we mere puppets playing out a script set in stone? Are we locked inside some eternal stillness? Yesterday, Sante thought he was the natural son of a romantic adventurer, today he was the son of a rapist. And yet he felt the same, had the same face, the same hands, the same heart. The same heart? Perhaps that was about to change.

Now this girl says, *forget destiny, it's down to you.* But then, she came from a land where there were no ravines and landslides; no rumbling earthquakes or spewing volcanoes to remind you there were other powers at work; no history to pave the course of your present.

Destiny is you. If she was right, what a huge responsibility to carry! Was he up to it? And what if, after all the doing and posturing, the struggles and the achievements, the dramas and the revelations, the winning and the losing … what if she was wrong?

Nonna came ambling out of the house, wiping her hands on her apron. She noticed her daughter's distress, and drew her own conclusions. She pursed her lips, and shook a threatening hand in the direction of the gate. *'Meno male ca si nne iu.'*

'Who do you mean, Nonna?' Sante wanted to know.

'Sherula. '

'Nonna, that's Sara-Jane.' Sante spoke in Sicilian.

But his grandmother proceeded in her language, addressing her daughter. 'I have spoken to your father. She must not be allowed inside our house any more. She's trouble that one. She will bring us bad luck.'

Having delivered her sententious words, Nonna left. Mother and son watched her retreat to her cryptic memories, to her ghosts.

17

Sara-Jane could tell there was an air of despondency at the *Casa di Cura*. She felt the heaviness of incipient tragedy as she trod the marble steps. She saw it on the face of staff who strained to smile as they greeted her. Most of all, it was visible in the dipping eyebrows of Dr Emilio Troina, which seemed to have gone fuzzier and greyer in the six days since Sara-Jane last saw him.

His efforts to appear calm were undermined by an involuntary twitching of his upper lip. 'I'm afraid the news are not very good about your father.' For the doctor to make a grammatical error like that ... well, it went to show just how in how parlous a psychological state he was.

Sara-Jane resisted the temptation to correct him. Clearly the moment was too solemn and any appeal to accuracy just seemed frivolous.

He proceeded to give the news in a mixture of English and the occasional Italian phrase, when the narrative became too convoluted. Franzetti, he said, appeared to have suffered a severe allergic reaction to the treatment.

'It has happened before, on some rare occasion. We know some people do not tolerate our juice.'

That did not surprise Sara-Jane. The polished-leather texture of olive leaves hardly augured well for the palate, let alone the insides of the human body.

'*Che peccato*! Mr Franzetti was responding so very well in the beginning. For three days ... no problem. Then Sunday last ...' Dr Troina's cheeks fell closer to his moustache as he recalled the moment. 'Mr Franzetti, he have a collapse, all of a suddenly... for three days he has been like in a coma. I frankly cannot understand, his pulse is a little high, nothing to be alarming for a man of his age, and yet he has such high fever, and perspire, perspire, perspire all the time …'

'Can I see him?'

Dr Troina tilted his head over his left shoulder, in resigned assent, as if to say, 'If you must'. Clearly Franzetti had let him down badly. The old man's threat to die on him was in poor form, and Dr Troina was understandably miffed.

He led the way to the upper floor and the end of the corridor, to Franzetti's room, the remotest in the building. No doubt the good doctor did not wish to divulge this impasse to all and sundry.

Clem Franzetti looked peacefully asleep, face up, in a pose of supplication to the heavens. At first Sara-Jane feared the worst, so still and pale he looked, until she saw the catheter attached to his arm and the tube coiling up to a drip bottle. His forehead, the crown of which was still bedecked with a fine crop of hair for a man in his seventies, was clustered with pearls of perspiration.

'We have to put him in a drip for fear he might dehydrate.' Dr Troina was full of explanations.

Sara-Jane could not believe this enfeebled and prostrated body belonged to the man of bluster and fury that was Franzetti.

'What do you think?' Dr Troina's face pleaded for rescue.

A mischievous thought crossed Sara-Jane's mind that Dr Troina's radical method might be a cure by death. But this was no time for cynicism, less still for humour. She felt sorry for the poor doctor, who looked quite pathetic; his little grey eyes reeled as if he was about to faint. He unleashed some desperate words on the nurse standing by, which caused her to flee, and took out a white handkerchief that had been tortured into a scrunched ball during the course of the day. First he blew his nose, then wiped his eyes. A little filament of membrane attached itself to his left eyelash.

Oh dear, he should have followed the reverse order, something he would have surely done had he been in a better state of mind. He was such a clean, well-groomed man that at the sight of the unsightly worm, he squirmed and nearly fainted, before he quickly flicked it off his eyelash.

What made the situation unbearable was the fact this patient had aroused a lot of interest, both in the local media and further a field in continental Italy. Not only did his patient hail from the opposite end of the globe – which attested to the growing reputation of Dr Troina's wonder cure – but he was also a rich and recognised public figure back in Australia.

The *Gazzetta del Sud* had called him *un intellettuale*, a term that flew in the face of jealous spoilers who criticised this *Casa di Cura* for attracting only the gullible, the uneducated, impressionable new-agers, and other discredited riffraff.

And now this. Dr Troina did not wish to think about the effect this would have on his business and his reputation. He cringed at the thought of the headlines that would appear in the *Giornale di Sicilia* and the *Gazzetta del Sud*, not to speak of the *Telegiornale*. Uhh, *Madonna mia!*

Dr Troina's world was growing gloomier by the minute, and Sara-Jane wondered whether he would be able to stop the tears that pressed in a rear-guard assault on his red-sore eyes. Fortunately, a diversion was provided by the return of the nurse, carrying a photo album, its cover tastefully decorated with the clinic's logo, an olive branch woven in lime-green silk. Dr Troina snatched it from her.

His eyes were like fiery flints as if, somehow, he held her responsible for the *disgrazia* that had befallen his clinic.

He threw open the album with a wide flourish and placed it right under Sara-Jane's chin. 'Look, *Signorina*, how many testimonials we have, from patients with terminal illnesses, which we have cured. Read what they say about us. Come, come please read. It's through the generosity of these patients that our *Casa di Cura* survive.'

Eager to ease his sorrow, Sara-Jane ran her eyes over the page filled with expressions of praise and gratitude – some of them in English – for Dr Troina and his staff. They were, she was sure, genuine cases, and no doubt the doctor's unassailable belief in his formula was the contagion that worked the cure. Trust old Franzetti, she thought, to go and wreck a life's work by perversely failing to respond to the treatment.

*

When Sante entered the room, Sara-Jane stood with her back to the door. He dreaded that first look. Would she reject him? Would she be angry with him? Was he changed in her eyes? On the other side stood a man, who Sante assumed to be Dr Troina, flanked by a woman, whose face was even more tragic than his.

When Sara-Jane turned, she presented him with the best gift: a private smile he had not seen on her before, one which allowed him inside her personal space.

'Thanks for coming,' she said.

In gratitude, Sante placed his hand on her shoulder and stroked it.

Dr Troina found their show of affection in poor taste, given the situation. The thought crossed his mind they might be lovers, which made it even worse as far as he was concerned. He left the room in disgust, with his assistant treading in his every step.

Sara-Jane and Sante stood by the bed and forgot about the ailing Franzetti. A strange quiet descended in the room, but something was stirring outside. A whisper rose through the canopy of the grove and came murmuring through the window. They did not look at each other, there was no need to. It was the instant they were overcome by the momentous realization that they were brother and sister.

*

Drip, drip, drip: a thick liquid entered the vessel of his body, smelling of absinthe, filling him with joy. It had been building up for days, or maybe years, or even centuries in the misty past of his ancestry; reaching the brim of plenitude, flushing a complete transfusion of life through him. Franzetti wished he could stay forever as he was, just this side of consciousness, forever buoyed in this timeless stream.

A tingling behind his ear demanded his attention, but Franzetti resisted the urge to scratch, for fear of breaking the idyll. From somewhere rose whispers. He realised, with profound disappointment, that they had been there all the time, only muffled by the sound of his urges. The itchiness became more insistent by degree and finally he could not bear it any longer. He gave out a great sigh; his hand levitated to the ear and started to scratch madly. A fiery beam of light invaded his pupils and he began to writhe on the bed as he continued to scratch. Glass fell and shattered.

A foreign voice rallied. '*Fermatelo, per carità. Se no si fa male!'*

Arms swooped on him and held him down.

'What's going on? What the hell!'

He stopped. Now he luxuriated in the comfort of that hold. There was about the figure that appeared a golden glow, a sweet smell of jasmine, the arms were powdery butterfly wings. The man, a young man he thought by the strength in his arms, moved out of his range of focus, for Franzetti was short-sighted. All he could see was the outline of a head of very black hair.

He sat up and asked for his glasses to be brought to him. He put them on, and his eyes scanned the people around the bed. First the nurse came into focus, then Sara-Jane flanked by a young man, the one who had held him down.

'Who are you?' His voice was reproachful.

'Mr Franzetti.' Sara-Jane approached. 'He was just trying to...'

The old man pointed a finger without looking at her. This peremptory gesture stopped her mid-sentence.

'I am Sante...'

'You're a *saint*?' Terror and wonder, pulling in opposite directions, twisted Franzetti's face.

Sante laughed.

Franzetti looked at his chest, at his arm, followed the tube up to where the flask of liquid hung from the drip column. His gaze moved around the walls and paused on a framed copy of the Madonna of the Olives, the statue he had seen in the foyer. He stared at the picture as if he saw it for the first time.

After what seemed like an interminable pause, weighed down by the silence, Sara-Jane had to speak. 'Are you OK? '

Was he OK? Franzetti's hand went to his head, to help

him decide. 'Take this damn contraption off me.' He started waving his free arm, while with his left hand he tore away at the bandage that held the tube to his wrist. Before anybody could react he had freed himself of all attachments. Blood trickled down his wrist, of that took no notice, busy as he was kicking off the sheets and getting out of bed.

Sante and Sara-Jane looked to the nurse for direction.

'*Che facciamo*?' Sante wanted to know what to do.

The nurse had hardly recovered from the shock, now she ran around the bed ineffectually, yelling. '*Madonna mia, fermatelo…fermatelo*!' She tried to cover the old man with the bed linen, while he was getting on his feet.

At this point Dr Troina rushed in and could not believe his patient, who he had left in a coma fifteen minutes before, was now standing by the bed, stark naked, face flushed and, like a man imprisoned for a very long time, at last escaping to freedom.

'You, sir, get out of my way.' Franzetti warned the doctor, who could not move for shock.

'But *Signore* … Mr Franzetti, you very sick man.'

Franzetti took two resolute steps towards the doctor, grabbed him by the shoulder with his right hand and shoved him to the floor. 'Nothing wrong with me, let me go.'

Before anyone could stop him he bolted, hurtling down the stairs, heading for the exit. At the final step, as his foot hit the cold terrazzo of the ground floor, the clamp at the end of the tube caught in the gap of the railing that enclosed the statue of the Madonna of the Olives, and he was stopped in his tracks.

This enforced pause allowed the pursuers, who chased him down the staircase with a great clatter, to catch up to him. None of them, however, dared make contact with him, for fear of finding themselves flung to the floor. They stood some distance away, watching as he sat on the lower step and slowly proceeded to free his body of the remaining attachments.

When he stood up again his face had altered. Gone was the fury, leaving in its wake a look of intense contemplation. His face glowed, his tall frame teetered, as if he were trying to balance on his toes. The next moment he went down on his knees before the statue and began to cry.

The sight of a grown man sobbing arrested the four pursuers. To Sara-Jane it was positively shocking, for she knew Franzetti's reputation as a tough, even callous man.

Fortunately Franzetti's trauma was as brief as it had been abrupt. Soon he was again in charge of himself. Getting up, he turned to Dr Troina and asked him to follow him back upstairs, indicating he wanted to be alone with him.

Sante turned to Sara-Jane, his expression amused and conspiratorial. He whispered to her in Italian. '*Mamma mia, che tipo strano è questo. Ma che gli è preso?*'

Sara-Jane had one simple thought. This is Sicily.

No more than ten minutes later, Dr Troina came running down the staircase, muttering to himself. This time it was he who seemed possessed by the spirits. 'That man, he is mad.' He tapped his temple with the tip of a hooked finger. 'He say he has been cured by a miracle!'

'What?'

Sara-Jane and Sante looked at each other not sure what to make of this.

'By the Madonna.' Dr Troina pointed contemptuously in the direction of the statue.

'But, how does he know he has been cured?'

Dr Troina raised the palm of his hands skyward as if to say, heaven only knows. 'He want to ruin my reputation. This is a medical clinic, not a cabal.'

When Franzetti returned, his arm was bandaged where the catheter had nicked his skin, but otherwise he looked healthy and vigorous. Even his pasty skin had gone pink. But the real transformation was in his eyes. They positively glowed; so much so that Sara-Jane thought he might be running a temperature.

'Are you alright?' she asked.

'Yeah, never better.'

Dr Troina by contrast looked positively ill, as if the cancer had suddenly transferred from Clem Franzetti's body to his.

Proud as he was of the empirical basis of his medical training, Dr Troina was apt to dismiss Franzetti's claim of a miraculous cure as the ravings of a religious fanatic. The fact the patient had made a remarkable recovery from his allergic reaction was not of much import. Anyone who had been laid out for days, suffering the most extreme symptoms, would naturally get a lift out of the fact the pain had ceased. The disease had simply taken a back seat, so to speak, during that phase of crisis.

'But how do you know, sir?' Sante was baffled. 'How do you know that you are cured?'

Franzetti turned to him with a smile of bonhomie. 'When you've been as sick as I have, you can feel the disease working inside you. It was eating me up bit by bit. Well today, the Madonna – the one holding the olive branch – came before my very eyes. She raised her hand over my body and I saw the disease lift off like a black oil slick. Straight away I felt light, as if a ton of sludge had been sucked out of my system.'

Everyone stood around speechless.

*

Franzetti did not waste any time leaving the *Casa di Cura*, a move that suited Dr Troina also, for he wanted to hush up the whole matter and minimise any disruption to his establishment. A couple of phone calls found him a suite at the Hotel Trinacria, a resort by the sea not far from Milazzo. Sante offered to drive him there.

Franzetti hadn't just been cured of a dreadful disease, he was reborn. He was the chosen recipient of a miracle.

When he was told the young man he had just met was Sara-Jane's newly-discovered sibling, he showed no surprise. The world was full of yet-to-be discovered miracles. This young man, Sante – and what sublime evocation in that name! – sitting next to Sara-Jane, had an Australian father. A few days ago he would have been cynical about such a coincidence. Now he was willing to accept it, because life had become far more varied, far richer than he could have imagined. And yet, in all that complexity there was a core of stillness, an essence. If you managed to reach it, to hold on to it for an instant, life presented itself in all its luminous clarity.

Franzetti took in the tortuous landscape slipping by. Every stone, every tree, every gully seemed to have been there forever and spoke to him in deep tones from way out in the past. His head leant back on the headrest, utterly content. In this position he caught the profile of the young man. The world was full of miracles, and here was another one, staring at him.

'Why do they call you Sante?' He needed something to say. Of course he knew why.

'I don't know.' Sante smiled. 'I think because my mother, she's very religious.'

Everything was clear, everything fitted.

'You gotta a job?'

'Only a weekend job in Tindari. There are no jobs in San Sisto.'

'I'm gonna be sticking around for a couple of weeks. I'll need a driver, someone who can speak English. You interested?'

'Yes, of course.'

18

The day he was meant to collect the kid was a Saturday morning much like this one, heavy and muggy: the day after one of those nights when hadn't got home until the small hours. A bugger of a headache had made him lie in.

Around midday, he phoned to say he had been called to work that morning and would pick up the kid on the way home. It was the kind of day when the easterlies, coming from the desert, stirred your blood and the penis has a fever. It was, in other words, a day that drove him to make a move. Or rather, she did, the dago girl. When she came to open the door, he knew this was it. It was all over her face, an invitation written in faint lines of desire around her lips.

'Sheryl's gone to work and I've just put the child down to sleep.' She gave him an insolent look, and her fleshy bottom lip quivered. 'You'll have to come back later.'

'Nope, I'll take her now. She can sleep at my place.'

'I don't want to wake her. She'll be grumpy all day.' She was acting like she was the mother. She stood there, holding the door ajar, her eyes still and dense, looking through him.

'I'll wait then,' he said, brushing past her. 'Got some coffee?'

'If you like,' she said, like she was doing it out of a sense of hospitality.

But he saw, from the way she trailed her skinny arse, that she had an agenda. Inside, there was a smell of furniture polish. A potpourri of dried flowers sat on the windowsill and the kitchen smelt of frequent use. This was the house of two women: sterile, clean, and ripe for a male.

Through the partition he watched her in the tiny

kitchen. She kept avoiding his eyes as the kettle boiled to a hiss.

'It'll have to be instant.' Her voice sounded breathless, her movements self-conscious.

'Instant is how I like it,' he said, and made a pitch for her eyes.

She managed to evade his stare, went and got the Nescafe down from the overhead cupboard, poured a heaped spoon into the mug. She looked anxious. She opened and shut drawers with a bang, clanged the cutlery, clattered the crockery ...

'Do you take milk?'

'Nah, I like it black.'

'Sugar?'

'Yeah, lots.'

She came into the living room through the arched doorway, with the coffee in a mug lightly chipped at the rim. Her hand was shaking. 'Sorry, ' she said, 'we don't have any good cups.'

She was pretty lavish with her apologies. Sorries at every corner, hiding desire, fermenting in the air. He had been in that situation before, when things suddenly converge and you know, you just know, their time has come. At that point you have no control over events. What was about to happen was already earmarked, and there was nothing he could do about it. They both knew it.

She put the mug down on the cane table and as she retrieved her hand her finger caught the handle, the mug spun and tumbled over, spilling the contents. Hot coffee ran down the edge and on Russell's trouser leg.

'Sorry,' she said, 'I'll get a sponge.'

'No need.'

As she turned, he caught her arm. It was a stick inside his hand. Her forearm was covered in short dark down.

Normally, hairs on a woman's arm put him off, but in the close heaviness of the room that arm flashing into the band of light, flagged a signal, and his rod sprang into action. Some strange energy inside him had taken over, and the small glitch became yet another cog in the wheel of desire, spinning ever faster. She shuddered as her body twisted and their eyes clashed into each other. His steely blue ones full of the hunter's sharpness; hers dark and deep and wanting. The line was crossed.

'Let me go.'

Her words said no, but the rest of her body said yes, positively pleading for it. He had been in the police force long enough to know that point between fear, desire and subjugation. He kept his cool. To her squirming he countered with stillness, although under his arms perspiration ran in rivers. He pulled with a sudden jerk and sat her on his lap. His other hand went to her mouth.

'It's OK.' The throaty sound of his own voice was rousing him to a pitch. 'Don't be scared.'

He knew she had wanted it all along. With women, the more repressed they looked, the more hungry for it they were. He undid the metal button of his jeans, unzipped slowly over the hump of his sex, and let the uniform trousers fall to his feet.

At the sight of it she stopped struggling, as if mesmerised, her eyes glazed. He always knew there was something of a snake charmer about his tool, he thought amused, and hoped she didn't go fainting on him.

Sara was beyond the fainting. She looked as if she were a leering spectator in a sex act. Now it was all easy. He sat down on the edge of the sofa without taking his eyes off her, and spun her around.

'Take your pants down.'

She didn't respond.

So he felt under her skirt, put a stubby finger inside the elastic and slipped the garment to her feet. She stood there breathless, but clearly enjoying what was being done to her. He pressed down on her shoulder and got her to bend on her knees. Through her arched legs he slipped his knees between her skinny legs, parted them wide and her crotch dropped slowly onto his erect head. She shuddered and stiffened. He paused, allowing her to breathe, then pressed down on her shoulder again and again, each time reaching in a little deeper, slowly, enjoying the warm wetness over his penis. The sensation was so pleasurable he risked ejaculating before he entered her fully. Then suddenly he pressed right down and at the same time he thrust upward. He was barely through and everything happened: a rapture, a spasm, a flooding. In the rush he let go of her mouth.

The girl gave a piercing squeal, pig-like.

'This is what you wanted, isn't? Isn't?'

'Yes.' Her voice was hardly audible. 'Yes…' And then she gasped. Her eyes reeled and darted, as if they had seen a ghost.

He looked up and there in the doorway was the kid. Luckily, she was too young to realise what was going on.

*

He was tempted to let the mobile ring out, but then it might be an emergency from the station.

'Hello.' He snarled.

'Danny here …'

Oh fuck, not on a Saturday morning, a wet Saturday morning at that.

'You coming up to Gingin this morning?'

'Not today.'

'I need to see you. Something's come up.'

'I gotta busy day.'

'It's urgent … never mind, it'll have to wait till I see you at the park this arvo.'

'I wasn't planning on going today.'

'Russ, we gotta a horse racing today, remember.'

'Right then. I'll see you there.'

Now what was that all about? No doubt he was in some sort of shit. Danny O'Rourke was nothing but trouble.

*

Danny O'Rourke was the world's biggest whinger. And yet you couldn't say he hadn't had his chances in life. His mother had married old Vic Franzetti, a wealthy man, when Danny was just a kid. When the old man died, his son, Clem, got the business, but he left his second wife the family home, plus an annuity that would have set her up for life, had she not been saddled with Danny O'Rourke for a son. Danny sponged off his mother forever, but while the step-father was still living and controlled the purse strings, he protected her from the excesses of her son's demands. With old Franzetti gone, there was no stopping Danny.

It wasn't just his lifestyle she had to fund, but also his dodgy business ventures, his risky share market dealings and, most destructive of all, his gambling. Danny O'Rourke didn't miss a trick when it came to self-destructive vices. The old woman had no chance. Danny started to run up debts and the mother kept bailing him out by mortgaging the family home. In a few years, the house was gone and she was forced to move into a retirement village. As far as

Russell knew, she was still living there. As for Danny, he was given a job helping to look after his stepbrother's horses at his Gingin stables. It was probably his first legitimate job ever. To everyone's surprise, he took to it like the proverbial duck to water. Recently, he persuaded Russell to buy into a couple of horses with him.

By the time he got to the racecourse it was almost midday, and he found Danny already at the bar, in his leather jacket, dark tie on white shirt. Danny was a snappy dresser. Broke he might be, but he always had money to buy good stuff.

'Had lunch yet?' Danny was in an expansive mood. 'Let's go and get some decent tucker. It's on me.' He took the stairs to the restaurant, rather than the food hall.

Well, thought Russell, at least this time his problem wasn't money, although with Danny you could never tell.

'That daughter of yours...' Danny talked as he strode on. 'Is she still working as a journalist?'

Sergeant Russell, used to being the one to ask the questions, didn't like being interrogated about his private life.

'Why do you want to know?'

'Russ, I'm in a spot of bother.'

So, what's new? Russell thought.

Somebody was trying to get money from him, money he didn't have, by threatening to release evidence of his involvement with an Asian money-laundering scam. All untrue, of course, he was scrupulously trying to keep his nose clean, to impress old Clem.

'I'm his nearest relative, after the tragedy.' Danny looked contrite.

The tragedy was of course the death of Franzetti's wife and son, a couple of years ago, when their car ran off the road, killing both members of the family. The verdict? The son had been drinking, after their horse won the Perth Cup.

Everybody knew Danny stood to gain millions if Franzetti left even part of his considerable estate to his stepbrother. On the strength of that, Danny borrowed big. At least that was the story going round the racetrack, and knowing Danny as well as he did, it was a plausible one, as was the possibility he was involved in some money-laundering scheme.

'If the story got out, even though it's all bullshit, it wouldn't look good with big brother, especially now that we're making progress towards a family reconciliation. The guys are threatening to take the story to the media. Big brother wouldn't be too impressed.'

'Who are we dealing with here?'

'The Yasic brothers.'

Ah, say no more, thought Russell. There was a time, not long ago, that the Yasic brothers and Danny were thick as thieves, in a manner of speaking. He had a file as long as his arm on them. Russell's hunch was they must have fallen out, and now it was payback time.

'It's an injustice.'

'Yeah.'

'What's your leverage with them? Can you help?'

'I could. It's not gonna be straightforward though.'

'I'm prepared to cover the expenses.'

'How much?' Russell did not miss a beat.

'A thousand.'

'Wouldn't even cover the paperwork, mate.'

'Your call then.' Danny exhaled.

'Try three.'

'Shit, who do you think I am Clem Franzetti?'

'You could be one day. I tell you what – I don't start moving my pieces till I get two thousand in my hand, in cash. The rest can come later.'

Even before he was finished, Russell knew he could have raised the stakes even higher. Never mind. By the time he paid the 'incidentals' he figured he'd be left with a couple of thousand himself. Not a bad day's work, even if it got him out of bed.

The night before she left, the Marzano family travelled to Milazzo for a farewell dinner for Sara-Jane. It was a special night out and nobody in San Sisto knew how to turn on the style quite like the Marzanos.

Don Alfio looked urbane and patriarchal in a navy jacket – which did not quite manage to camouflage his waist-line – white shirt, and red tie and matching silk handkerchief in his breast pocket. The jacket was coordinated with new-wool trousers made by Lo Bianco, one of Palermo's most exclusive tailors, whose pressed cuffs sat on his brown Bruno Magli shoes, his favourite for an occasion such as this.

But the one that surprised Sara-Jane was Sara La Rocca. She wore a cream three-quarter length evening dress, gathered in a V neckline and tucked at her tiny waist. It was set off by a tangerine scarf tied around her long neck, matching high-heeled shoes that took her height almost to that of Sara-Jane's. The most striking transformation was achieved by her hair, which she normally wore gathered at the back of her head. Now let free, it sprang into a frizzy mass, opening out peacock-like around her ermine face. Her bottom lip was lightly touched in peach. Her eyes, large and hypnotic, were black pools hiding a mystery.

Sara-Jane was mesmerized by the power of this woman, and yet there were intimations of fragility too, revealed in glimpses, in lightening profiles, in flashes of her eyes. This was the woman Don Alfio loved, thought Sara-Jane.

She felt conspicuous in her short black dress that might have been fashionable at any time. But then, she could have worn almost anything and still make a splash. Her height and long blonde hair would have gained her the breathless attention of everyone, not least Don Alfio, who sizzled with pride at the prospect of stepping out onto the tiny stage of San Sisto that was its piazza, with two beautiful women.

The moves of San Sisto's first citizen and his family always aroused curiosity among the townspeople. Now, as they emerged from the *portone* in their finery, and with the added presence of their glamorous *parente* from Australia, all eyes were upon them.

None was more aware of this than Mayor Marzano, whose success was partly due to his being in tune with the collective consciousness of the San Sisto citizenry. As the three of them waited outside the entrance for Sante to pull up with the Alfa, Don Alfio knew the family was being watched, whispered about, admired. From Ciro's bar, to the shoe shop and the *alimentari*, not to speak of the balconies overlooking the piazza, eyes admired and minds wondered. What exactly was the relationship between the Marzanos and the beautiful foreigner? Initial speculation that she might be Sante's girl was dismissed. He was too young for her. Besides, look at the body language, it was not that of lovers.

Community wisdom, or lack of it, is a powerful thing. It can be wildly off the mark or uncannily accurate, either way it spreads like telepathy. Once the community wisdom decided they were not lovers, a new rumour took hold: that they were in fact brother and sister, a result of yet another dalliance by the young Don Alfio with an Australian tourist he had met in Taormina some quarter of a century ago, during his wild oats sowing days. Now the young woman had come to seek out her natural father and Donna Sara, magnanimous as ever, had come to accept the situation and welcomed the fruit of her husband's misdemeanour into her house. Consequently Don Alfio, who was biologically unable to sire children, was now the acknowledged father of at least two, and suspected of countless others. The irony of this amused Don Alfio greatly.

Of course he was not required to admit to his indiscretions. It would have been inelegant and boastful to do so, and disrespectful to his wife. But to acknowledge some kind of formal relationship, and for the sake of consistency – in view of the fact that Sante had begun to refer to Sara-Jane as 'my sister' – Don Alfio felt justified in describing her as 'my niece'.

As the car took off with a screech, stirred by Sante's youthful exuberance, Cosimo Spanò, the hairdresser with a roomful of his own artwork adjoining his barbershop, who stood outside waiting for customers, touched his beret and bowed his head. Don Alfio bowed, waved back and felt happy.

Sara-Jane sensed, without being attuned to the details of the situation, that in their eyes she had been adopted into the Marzano family. By nature a very private person, she would have normally run away from such scrutiny. But here it seemed fine, for it was a shared scrutiny. And of course, this was not her country; tomorrow she was leaving and there would be no repercussions.

Little did she expect, when she decided to make this trip to Sicily, that she would to end up playing happy families. She chastised herself for such irony. Despite herself, Sara-Jane had to admit she was enjoying the cosiness of the situation.

Come to think of it, there were many things she did not mind here; the same things would have aggravated her in Perth. Here she did not feel responsible. Responsibility fell on the wide shoulders of Don Alfio, who carried it all with aplomb. He liked the attention. He was an exhibitionist. He loved the whole ritual. His enthusiasm was contagious and even Sara La Rocca's usual bearing of penance improved to one of calm acceptance.

*

The Ristorante al Castello is situated at the foot of the town's best known landmark: the thirteenth century castle. You reach it by a steep, cobblestone street, lit by subtle, amber-coloured street lamps which add to the medieval atmosphere. The full armour greeting you at the entrance of the restaurant, the ancient walls of pumice stone, blackened by time and paraffin oil, attest to its pedigree. Despite electric lighting and the occasional sound of car horns from the city streets, the stones spoke that evening of medieval jousts, crusades and religious passion. The conversation, conducted mostly in Italian in deference to Don Alfio, fell on Franzetti's 'cure'.

'I think he is going senile.' Sara-Jane wanted to make it known that not all Australians were fanatical nuts.

'He seems strong and healthy to me, I have to say,' said Don Alfio.

'Dr Troina is convinced it is all in his imagination,' added Sante.

Don Alfio, who lost no opportunity to show he was a rational, modern man had to agree. 'Of course it is.'

'I would not be so dismissive, Alfio.'

An eerie silence followed. It wasn't so much what Sara La Rocca had said, but her voice, low-pitched and a little masculine, sounded sententious in the close confines of the car. She had the air, thought Sara-Jane, of someone upon whom life has been force-fed. Gloom coiled around her like smoke filaments. How could Don Alfio, so full of joy of living, be so devoted to a killjoy like her? Must be opposites attracting each other.

'Of course, miracles have been known to happen,' Sara La Rocca went on. 'Perhaps more often than we acknowledge.'

'Mamma,' Sante craned his head. 'This is the third millennium, I believe the age of miracles is finished.'

'On the contrary, we have never been more in need of them.'

'Anyway,' said her son, 'I too benefit from good fortune. Mr Franzetti has paid me a week in advance.'

They all welcomed the news, but Sara La Rocca was not impressed. 'He is too generous.'

'Generous? Clem Franzetti? That's a contradiction.' Sara-Jane had to laugh.

Sante's mother looked at Sara-Jane but addressed the question to her son. 'Then why is he so generous to you, Sante?'

'I don't know Mamma, I suppose he likes me. He...' The young man hesitated.

'What?' His mother was becoming impatient.

'He has offered me a job in Australia.'

'Sante, that's fantastic!' Sara-Jane placed her hand over Sante's arm and left it there for a moment. 'You must come, you must.'

Sante's mother gave the younger woman an icy glance. *Now see what ideas you have put into his head?* Words were superfluous to Sara La Rocca. She had a way of communicating emotions, mostly negative ones, without words. Her eyes sat upon you and clung there like claws, stripping you raw.

Her next question sounded cynical. 'To do what?'

'He did not say.'

'Maybe he wants to make a faith healer out of you,' Don Alfio was always eager to bring humour into the conversation.

'Sante will be thinking of his studies for now.' Sara La Rocca's tone chilled the cheerful atmosphere around the table. 'It's the most important thing.'

Sante was silent. He scanned the table, his eyes pleading to be rescued.

The sight of two men intimidated by a wisp of a woman would have amused Sara-Jane, except she herself was now caught in the emotional web spun around the group. She wanted to say something in support of Sante but felt she could not. It must come from him, she told herself, it was not her place to interfere. But an internal voice came over louder than the other.

He is your brother, it is your place to defend him. She looked across at Sara La Rocca and her words, when they came out, were more in the tone of a plea than a stout defence. 'Surely he can defer university for a year.'

The Italian woman addressed her son, as if it was he who had spoken. 'That is out of the question, your studies are your future and must come first.'

Sara-Jane wondered what it was about this place. She had now been in Sicily nine days and already was beginning to mistrust the physical closeness, which at first she found quaint, heart-warming even. All that kissing, hugging, holding each other by the arm ... was it true warmth or did it hide chronic insecurity? Wasn't this woman, after all, guilty of practising emotional bullying on the very people she purported to love?

It seemed to her that these mountain villages, with their dark alleyways, with their traditions and restrictive social mores, provided fertile ground for breeding emotions on an epic scale. In these houses memories, bitterness, rivalries and vengefulness lived forever. From the first day they met, Sara-Jane knew the older woman did not like her. She now assumed it was because she viewed her as the natural daughter of a man who had defiled her. That provided an ample platform on which to stand the column of hatred. Ironically, Sara-Jane had no love for her father. Nor did she hate him. She felt something which in a way was worse: indifference. Sara La Rocca might do herself a favour by watering down her rock-hard, time-hardened intensity with a dash of indifference.

As if by some signal to which Sara-Jane was not privy, all heads turned to the entrance, where a stocky man walked in, followed by three others, all older, all wearing dark suits. It was like the entrance of the male members of a wedding party. Don Alfio winced, Sara La Rocca's face strained, Sante sat up on his chair as the man headed straight for the Marzano table, followed by his retinue, marching in a single file.

The man took his hat off to Don Alfio, who sprang to his feet and shook his hand. He then bowed to Donna Sara, who responded with a curt acknowledgement. He shook hands with Sante, then turned to Sara-Jane and gave a long respectful bow without looking directly at her. It was at this point that Sara-Jane recognized the man as Mimmo Urzì, on whom she and Sante had inadvertently intruded two days before at the Marzano house.

A similar procedure was followed by his retinue before the maitre d' led them to their table. Sara La Rocca was fuming. She turned to the younger woman and spoke in English. 'I feel stalked. That man makes my blood run cold.'

Sante proceeded to explain the business of the olive grove to Sara-Jane, who showed slight interest. What was of more interest to her was that for the first time that evening the older woman had addressed her. Perhaps, she mused, having a worse enemy in the same room made Sara-Jane less of an adversary.

Mimmo Urzì, meanwhile, kept looking across at their

table. The other men addressed him from time to time, but the stout man hardly acknowledged them, his whole mind was tuned to the Marzano table.

'Alfio, we really must go.'

But Don Alfio did not seem to be too much in a hurry. A smile sat upon his face as if some amusing thought was tickling it.

'He is trying to intimidate us,' said his wife.

Don Alfio placed his warm chubby hand upon hers. 'I don't think so, *cara*, on the contrary, I think the fearless Mimmo is trying to endear himself to us.'

'What are you saying, Alfio?'

'I think Mimmo has caught the oldest and most affecting bug known to man.'

Don Alfio looked at Sara-Jane and smiled like a child who has a secret and is dying to reveal it. 'I am convinced that *la nostra cara signorina* has an admirer.'

'Alfio, you are talking nonsense.' His wife shook her head.

Sante chuckled. '*Chi? Mimmo? Madonna mia! Meno male che parti domani, Sara.*'

Sara-Jane, whose limited Italian sometimes caused her to miss the sense, was now lost in this quick repartee. She had a general sense that the conversation concerned her, by the way they all looked at her.

Sante translated. 'Father say that Mimmo is in love with you.'

Sara-Jane cringed, but the idea tickled her ego and she fell in with the general cheerfulness around the table. 'It's a good thing I'm leaving tomorrow then.'

Sante took her hand and held it. 'Sara-Jane, that is what I just said.'

The two parties settled to their fare as the evening sailed on under the watchful eye of the knight. Shadows from the flares lapped at the black volcanic stones of the wall. At one point Sara-Jane happened to look across in the direction of Mimmo's table, which made the latter go stiff on his chair and bow. The four suits did likewise in synchronized motion.

The Marzano table could barely contain itself. The trick was to make it look like a smile when laughter was pressing to erupt.

Laughter exploded once they were in the car. All the way home the jokes about Sara-Jane and the mobster provided the hilarity, and even Sara La Rocca, mellowed by the wine, was caught in the general mood.

She turned to Sara-Jane. 'Well, you can't say that your stay in Sicily has been uneventful.'

*

Before she left, Don Alfio called Sara-Jane into his study. He sat behind a beautifully grained oak desk. Above him, a map of Sicily, beneath a carved crucifix, was framed in shiny brown lacquer. Sara wondered what the purpose of all this formality was, and why Don Alfio needed to sit behind a desk to speak to her. Especially he, who seemed to her one of those rare individuals who considered power and its props a hindrance to the fulfilment of a genuinely humanist agenda.

'I wanted to tell you how much we enjoyed having you here.'

'Thank you, I enjoyed it too.' A flush of pleasure overcame her. 'I felt very much at home.'

'Well, this is your home in Italy. After all, you have a brother here, so I hope you will come back.'

'I probably will, but there is no reason why you can't

come to Australia.'

'Ah Australia: so pristine, so spacious, so ordered, so peaceful. Like Sante I have dreamt about it all my life. I am afraid to come for fear of being disappointed. Reality always disappoints, so in this case I want to preserve my vision of your country. Fortunately Sante is too young to suffer from such complications. He is determined to travel to Australia.'

'He is certainly of an age when he should start to venture out a bit.'

'And that is as it should be. Sante has been far too sheltered, too much of his mother's boy, like so many of our young people. I prefer the Anglo-Saxon way.'

'Of course his mother will take some convincing.'

'Ah Sara.' His eyes filled with tenderness as he spoke about her. 'You must not judge her harshly. Life experiences have made her more vulnerable, more insecure than is good for her.'

'Or Sante.'

'Or Sante,' Don Alfio assented. 'But after all she is only trying to protect him. Sara is a victim of her past. Perhaps in Australia the past does not have quite the same import as it does here.'

'Yes.' Sara agreed. 'Wanting to live in the present and planning for the future is our national obsession.'

'In Italy, it's quite the contrary – we revere the past. We capture it in our works of art, we preserve it in our myths, we incorporate it in whatever we do. We display it in our devotion to family and ancestors. It's our way of courting immortality, our gift to the world. It's our tragedy.'

It occurred to Sara that nobody she knew talked like that in Australia. And she wasn't sure if she felt disappointed or relieved.

Don Alfio went on. 'The future is in those new

progressive countries of the world. Sicily is the place for dreaming, for wallowing in the self-indulgent pleasure of decline, for a life folding sensuously into itself. You on the other hand …' He went up to Sara-Jane and took both her hands into his. 'You have brought us your vigour, a glimpse of possibilities. You have stirred our imagination. Thank you.'

Sara-Jane turned to go.

'Wait, you cannot leave without allowing me a *brindisi*.' Don Alfio took down a decanter containing a colourless liquid. 'Have you had this before? It's called Strega. How do you say that in English? Ah, *witch*. You have bewitched us.' He filled two liqueur glasses.

Sara took one and they touched glasses.

'To the future then.'

As she drank down the Strega, a warm sensation spread through her body.

*

The two Saras and Sante took a train to Reggio Calabria to catch a plane to Rome. Sara-Jane was surprised the older Sara had decided to come too. *Perhaps she's afraid I'll take him with me, she thought cynically.*

Sante sat next to her, his bare thin arm touching hers in the kind of physical closeness their new sibling status allowed him. At first she had found his tactility difficult to get used to. He often touched her to make a point or get her attention; held her arm as they walked, stood very near her when he spoke. It was invasive. A week on, she was beginning to get used to it – his touch on the back of her hand, her arm, the open and unabashed affection in his gaze … it all seemed to go with the territory.

It certainly did not come from his mother. Sara-Jane

could not imagine her in physical intimacy with anyone. Try as she might, she could not see her making love, strolling around the steep streets of San Sisto *a bracetto* with another woman, like she had seen many do, or embrace her son.

Sante, of course, touched her constantly. His mother was amenable but passive. Forever a receptor of his affection, her coldness was encased in steel.

Now the young woman's eyes were fixed on the fast flowing landscape of steep villages rushing down to hug the sea, but her inner eye was fixed upon her. What did this woman want from her?

She waited for Sante to leave the compartment. Did he obey his mother's tacit bidding, to leave them alone? 'I suppose you think I'm being over-possessive with my son.'

'Possessive? No … protective, I think.'

'But you disapprove all the same.'

'Well, as you say, he is young and very innocent.'

'You're being kind. I am of course aware that I may be doing more harm than good by watching over him the way I do. I can't help it. It's stronger than me …' Was she admitting to some inner turmoil, some weakness?

Sara Jane held her breath, 'I'm sorry too if I've been a little … formal with you, it takes me a while to get used to new people, but I assure you it's nothing personal.' Did it wound like a confession? This was the home of Catholicism after all.

'You see, your mother was an extraordinary girl, extraordinary. Yes, yes I know she could be unpredictable, impulsive. They talk about Italians being impulsive, but she was exceptional, your mother. I know she could appear to be thoughtless, that her actions might have been selfish at times, but when she gave she did so totally.'

Sara-Jane went still with surprise. Was this the icy Sara

La Rocca – who could chill you with a glance, or without one – talking passionately about Sheryl? Her mother, for God's sake! That was not the Sheryl Giffen she knew: the weak, irascible, irresponsible, unstable woman who first abandoned her and then led her on a terrifying slide of ever-changing homes and stepfathers.

The older woman leaned forward and now, carried away by the gush of her own intensity, grabbed Sara-Jane's arm, squeezing it hard. She hesitated at the edge of a personal abyss. 'The problem was we became very close, your mother and I, closer than was good for us … for me at any rate. In the end it was the violence that ended it.'

She returned to her corner of the seat. As if recovering from some internal tremor, she turned abruptly and changed course, 'I know my son will come to Australia soon, I won't be able to delay him for ever, and now that I have met you, I feel better about it. When he does come, please promise me you will watch him closely.'

20

Dr Troina looked at the X-rays on the screen and could not believe his eyes. Where there had been an oval dark stain, like an oil slick, it was now clear. The cancer had simply vanished. Not even a spot, nothing. He could feel the onset of depression. He would be the laughing stock of the medical community. Already he had to put up with derision from the sceptics who thought his olive leaf cure was a placebo, despite a string of successes the clinic had carefully documented.

Now this … The doctor searched for a mollifying euphemism, settled on 'mishap', to provide fuel for the doubters. He could just see the headlines: *The Madonna Bests Science at Dr Troina's Clinic*.

He would have to face the arched eyebrows of his colleagues, the malicious little smiles, the furtive nudges. And then, worst of all, his clinic would be overrun by religious nuts.

A feeling of impending doom surrounded Dr Troina, like a shark circling its prey. To insulate himself, he refused to read newspapers, and kept away from news bulletins. Then, a couple of days later, he went to work and found, at the gate of his own clinic, some dozen or so pilgrims waiting to go in: a couple with a four year-old lying on an inflatable rubber bed, a young paraplegic with what looked like his wife or sister, pushing him in a wheel chair; and a group of four women, one in a religious habit. Camera-clutching paparazzi started to click frantically as the physician's car reached the gate. The worst had eventuated; the story of the miraculous cure of the Australian had got out to the regional TV station.

Dr Troina wound down the car window and yelled. 'There is no miracle statue at my clinic. Go home!' He ordered that the gates be locked.

Alas, he had not counted on the power of hope in desperate people. Within the hour someone arrived with a long extension ladder. A couple of men swung it over the iron gate, which they scaled and unlocked from the inside. The crowd rushed in and posted themselves in front of the Madonna, with hands clasped and eyes fixed upon their object of veneration. The miracle had taken hold of popular imagination and nothing Dr Troina said would make any difference.

The *dottore* barricaded himself upstairs and called the *carabinieri*, complaining that his clinic was being occupied by marauders and what would they do about it, ah? The carabinieri arrived, with siren blaring, on their blue Alfa Romeo, looking every bit that they meant business in their well-cut uniforms. They were met by a most impressive sight. The crowd had swelled, with people pressing at the gate and stretching well down the road. This was more than any two carabinieri could handle.

'*Ma che succede*?' They looked round in puzzlement.

'Ah, another miracle!' A woman seemed rapt in devotion. 'The son of the pastry cook from Librizzi has been given back his speech by the Virgin Mary.'

The story of Giannino was known, even to the policemen. It had appeared in the *Giornale di Sicilia*. A nasty fall had deprived him of speech. Now, at the very first glimpse of the holy statue he turned to his mother, who he had not addressed for over three years, and said, in a voice as clear as a church bell, '*Mamma é belissima la Madonna.*'

The mother's cry of joy must have reverberated all over the countryside, for in no time people arrived in their hundreds. Even the mountains were no barrier to the news, thanks to that other miracle of modern technology: the cellular telephone. From all around they arrived: Milazzo, Barcellona, Librizzi, Santa Lucia del Mele and Castroreale.

There was little the carabinieri could do to disperse the crowd. They let it be known that so long as people kept out of the clinic, they could stay in the front garden, a compromise that was readily accepted by the crowd.

They were not interested in anything inside Dr Troina's establishment. The statue of Our Lady stood in the foyer, guarding over the congregation from its plaster alcove, looking miraculous in her eternally smooth skin, chiselled nose, pencil-lipped mouth, celestial blue eyes, holding forth an olive branch to the infirm and the desperate in a gesture of eternal hope.

Looking through the green shutters Dr Troina scanned the mob which had taken over his manicured gardens. There they were, radiating in a semi-circle from the foyer. How he regretted not disposing of the statue when he purchased the estate. There they were with chairs and inflated mattresses, food baskets, blankets, coolers, wheelchairs, magazines, umbrellas, rosary beads, and goodness knew what else. It reminded him of a scene from one of those TV news reports on the *Telegiornale*, which showed boatloads of newly-disembarked refugees, scattered along the shore of Lampedusa, as if they had never seen a piece of terra firma before.

The doctor shivered in his perfectly tailored suit, surf-white shirt with the splayed collar, blue silk tie and Schiavoni shoes. He stuck his thumbs – which only that morning had been manicured, while he getting his weekly trim – inside the waist of his trousers.

He looked out at that motley crowd and felt the full weight of mob hysteria upon him. He crossed arms over chest, his left hand seeking the comforting warmth under his arm, and gave a deep sigh, fearing his depression might be a preamble to an incipient migraine.

He was tempted to pray to the Madonna himself, to grant him a miracle – seeing the Good Lady was so generous in dispensing them – to make the unruly mob and their squalid accoutrements vanish.

After checking there was no dust on the windowsill – you couldn't even trust the cleaners these days – he rested his elbows on the sill and leant forward to consider the source of his despondency. With his handsome face slotted between the palms of his hands, and his butt jutting away from the windowsill, Dr Troina did not strike a decorous pose. But, such was his mood that he didn't care.

It was at this inopportune moment that a flustered nurse burst into the room. '*Dottore*, are you not well? ' She exclaimed in alarm, thinking he was having one of his fits of self-doubt. Her breathless voice irritated him.

'What now?'

'A visitor for you, Dottore.'

'*Ma insomma!*' He exploded, thinking it was some hack from the *Gazzetta del Sud*. 'Did I not say I do not wish to be disturbed?'

'But…'

'But nothing. I'm not in … *oooh!...*' He dropped his hands down in front of him, a gesture that denoted he had reached the limits of his patience. 'How many times do I have to give you instructions, *Signorina*?'

When he called her *Signorina* in that tone, she knew it was time to retreat.

Just before her quivering figure disappeared, an idea struck Dr Troina. '*Un momento!*' He called out to her, putting up a hand as if he were stopping a whole line of traffic. 'Get me the Australian patient on the phone.'

If he could persuade the old man to speak to the press

and publicly deny he had been cured, things might just get back to normal.

'But Dottore, it is he who wishes to speak with you.'

'You mean Mr Franzetti? Why did you not say so? Why...' Dr Troina summarily decapitated the secretary with his eyes. 'Where is he?'

'Downstairs.'

'Well, bring him in. What are you waiting for?'

In the time it took the nurse to fetch Clem Franzetti, Dr Troina made a remarkable repossession of mood. 'Ah, Mr Clem!' His voice was suddenly very cheerful. 'I am very eager to speak with you ...'

'Listen here –' Clem interrupted, using his deal-making voice. 'I'm not gonna beat around the bush. That statue of yours – what will it take for you to part with it?'

The use of idioms confused Dr Troina. 'I don't understand, you want to take the statue apart in the bush?'

'No, no! I want to buy it off you. How much?'

Dr Troina found the suggestion mildly offensive, although at first he did not understand why. The very notion of transacting a religious icon seemed unedifying. 'You want to *buy* the statue?'

'That's what I said.'

Dr Troina's agile mind recovered quickly, and he began to perceive an opportunity. An idea flew in through the window of his imagination. He was a proud man, but not above seizing upon a financial opportunity. Despite, or rather because of, the old man's gruff voice and no-nonsense approach, it was evident he really wanted the statue and was keen to do a deal in a hurry. Although he could not imagine what use the old man might have for it. Who knew what logic possessed such a strange foreigner?

For him, it was a wonderful opportunity to get rid of a nuisance and acquire extra funds. 'You know, sir, that is a much valuable work of art.'

But Franzetti wasn't going to fall for that. 'Nonsense.'

Such directness offended Dr Troina's sense of decorous haggling, and he pouted his displeasure.

'Look.' Franzetti was about to make himself clear. 'I want that statue, but I don't intend to be taken to the cleaners.'

Dr Troina screwed his nose and his eyes blinked as he tried to make sense of this bit of conversation. 'I do not understand, sir, what cleaners?'

'Never mind, it doesn't matter. How much?'

The businessman in Dr Troina made a quick dash for Franzetti's eyes and tried to assess the degree of his desire to own the statue. By the glazed look in the older man's eyes, he gauged the desire to be very strong, perhaps to the point of obsession. In which case, he figured, the only limit was Franzetti's ability to pay. On the other hand, he was an unpredictable man, and if the figure was set too high the old man could very well withdraw the offer in disgust.

He must not offend him by going so high as to risk bruising his ego. On the other hand, he knew he was a man of means. This sort of prevarication, he knew, was bad for the deal, but he still couldn't come up with a figure.

Franzetti shifted weight from one leg to the other. Finally, he lost patience. 'Tell you what, doctor...' He made it quite clear he was in no mood for lengthily haggling, 'I'm willing to offer a hundred thousand. Take it or leave it.'

Dr Troina was confused. Was he offering lire or euros? The first was offensive, the other preposterous. Surely it could not be the latter? Or perhaps it was. Such a possibility made his ears ache, cramp-like. He had a flash of inspiration. 'One hundred thousand euros? I don't think so.' He looked closely at the Australian's face. Much to Dr Troina's relief, his opponent did not bat an eyelid.

'Well, what's your price then?'

Dr Troina took a moment to catch his breath and rein in his galloping heart. 'Mr Franzetti we are discussing a most valuable piece of art. I would not consider less than two hundred and fifty thousand euros.'

The reply bounced back like boxing bag and just about knocked out Dr Troina.

'OK then, done. But you'll need to do something about that mob outside, so we can remove it.'

Dr Troina's first reaction, upon recovering, was that he should have asked for half a million. Too late, the mad foreigner was already proffering his hand. He took it, but the doctor did not feel a thing, numbed by the sheer magnitude of what had happened. He was already thinking of what he would be able to do with that sum; the improvements he would make to the new wing. Best of all, he would be able to get rid of that statue, and with it, the mob of fanatical bedouins.

In one masterful stroke, Dr Troina's problems would be solved and then some. He could not believe his luck. But of course, until he had statue removed and the money in the bank, he could not rest. His experience of life's vagaries made him wary. This was too good to be true, and things might go wrong. Still, he would surely be foolish if he did not seize the opportunity.

What a pity he hadn't asked for half a million!

*

'Spirited Away' read the headline in the *Giornale di Sicilia* the next day. During the night, the Madonna of the Olives had vanished, leaving no trace of the mode or reason for its disappearance. The most extraordinary thing was that none of the pilgrims, who had braved the autumnal night and had slept in the garden surrounding the holy relic, noticed any suspicious activity, yet incredibly, the statue vanished without trace.

There was only one mortal who could work such a miracle … and Clem Franzetti's money, of course. Because Mimmo Urzì's services did not come cheap, especially when those services needed to be promptly rendered. Much of Mimmo's success lay in the fact that he relied on canny instinct and the belief that the solution to intractable problems came down to calling on the right people.

For this particular job, he employed the same team that had lifted important records on a rival, from the municipal chambers, in broad daylight.

The trick was to distract the pilgrims away from the statue. Through a PA system on the back of a truck they announced that a luminous image of the Madonna had appeared on the roof of the house of Natalino Tripi, the Calabrese accused of murdering his wife, but acquitted for insufficient evidence.

For a few moments the pilgrims deliberated as to whether to remain here, before this solid effigy, or fly to its version in pure light some three kilometres down the road. Perhaps they were swayed by the prospect of witnessing a moving spectacle. One or two began to move, others followed in a trickle, then there was a surge and a general evacuation ensued. Some went for their cars, but soon the road was jammed. The crowd then ran down the slope lit by a full moon, rushing headlong to Natalino's house.

They arrived panting, only to realize that some joker had duped them. Their return, slowed down by fatigue and the fact it was uphill all the way, took a lot longer. Long enough to lift the icon from its place. It was a simple operation, seeing the statue had been fixed down by a single bolt to its plaster stand. The only person left behind, Zu Carmine, ninety-four and totally deaf, had slept right through the operation.

21

Sara-Jane woke as the plane descended over Perth, and at first did not recognise her own city. It looked like a model laid out flat, with straight bisecting roads, toy cars perfectly aligned, in pursuit of each other. The afternoon sun sprayed white light over endless suburbs that stretched along the wide coastal plain between hills and sea. The plane hovered for some moments, as if undecided, then dipped. She felt her heart sink. What was it?

She caught a taxi to her flat in South Perth. The traffic flowed, the roads were well maintained, the houses distinct and mostly new; the roadside was spotless, the lawns manicured. The taxi driver, a Serbian with shaved pink head, the tattoo of a sea maiden on his arm, and an attitude sharpened by thirty years of soapboxing inside a car, complained how the taxi industry was being taken over by new migrants from Asia and the Middle East. Then the conversation inevitably settled on the weather and how the shops had already put up the prices for Christmas. Yes, undoubtedly she was home.

It was good to be back in Australia: so clean, so well-managed. It was good to get back to order and routine, to go home at the end of the day and look back on what she had achieved in the previous twenty-four hours. Here she could tape measure her existence by the projects she had advanced, problems she had solved, goals she had reached.

In Sicily, you were held back by traditions, by rituals, by a complex network of links, of controls and dependence. In Sicily you hoped for your luck to change, for a miracle to come to your rescue. In Australia, you tried to make your own miracles, you got on with it, cleared your way through the jungle of life. In Australia you coped because, not being able to do so was your fault (or at least it was a sign of weakness) and bad luck was a result of bad management.

In the mountains of Sicily your existence was cumulative. Each day was added on to all the other days of your past, and to that of your ancestors. You existed in the shadow of a past sculptured in time-marked buildings, of mould-splattered rooftops, of trees that seemed to have been there forever. Sicily was a mind-set, a continuum, a refuge for stay-putters whose common wisdom was built on ancient proverbs.

In Australia the cliché ruled, OK. Here your everyman reinvented himself: sea-changed, upgraded, carried no baggage, took each day as it came and even tried to change it.

She reached the front door of her apartment, smelled the cloying profusion of lavender in the flower-box, and was overcome by an insidious sense of desolation. Once inside, she put down her suitcase and paced around it. She didn't want to unpack. She'd better knock this nonsense on the head, before the rot set in.

On Monday it would be alright, she would be back at work; problems would smoke this mood out of her. Work and its challenges would come to the rescue. Meanwhile, she had two nights and a day to get through. One side of her wanted to call Don Alfio, to speak to Sante, to listen to Sara. Sara! Absurd. Having allowed others to enter her emotional chamber, she was now discontented.

Of course she could call Bob, but it wasn't a Bob that she wanted. What she wanted was the comfort of closeness. What an embarrassing admission! To need someone's company seemed to her like a sign of real weakness. Better to want sex. That was acceptable. Like wanting a shower, or a massage for sore muscles. But this … this fretting for other faces and other places … it rendered you weak, irresolute. It eroded your self-confidence, diminished you. Not good. In Sicily she had picked up a debilitating contagion: nostalgia, with its symptoms of dissatisfaction, dreams and desire for other places.

She reminded herself that sometimes, when she had treaded those steep hills, a kind of panic overcame her, like a fear of being imprisoned inside, ostracised from the modern world, from change, from getting on in life. It was important for Sara-Jane to be of the times. Her nightmare was to wake up one day and find herself left behind and made irrelevant by a fast moving world: an anachronism floating in a sea of memories.

She had to admit though; it was such a pleasure to feel connected to the other side, to the Marzano family. Her visit revealed that the world was both more complex and more accessible than she had imagined, that reality was made up of myriads of glimpses, that one constantly touched others and was touched by them; that each contact could be both a risk and a rich experience. The present was in fact an unreal state of being, the 'now' was elusive, transitional, delicately poised between past and future, birth and death, memory and projection, space and imagination, self and other, body and spirit. What a turnaround! It made living precarious but exhilarating. It meant each moment lived could be a personal act of creation.

Of course Sara-Jane could not put any of this in a feature article that promised to serve up the 'Real Sicily' to the reader. She wrote about the mountain villages, the colour of the sea, the breathtaking landscape, the food, the quaint customs, the churches. She worked on it all weekend, losing herself in the task. As she approached the end, though, she began to feel overcome by disaffection. Having consigned the experience to the page she was struck by the inadequacy of the result. Nothing new in that: she never had any illusions about her travel articles. They were dishes served up to feed the dreams of the reader.

This time the formula seemed even less satisfactory. To write it truly she would have to write-in Sara's eyes; Don Alfio's easy acceptance of his own failures; Nonna's delusions; the murmur of the wind through the poplars; the sound of tired cicadas on an warm autumn afternoon.

She would have to write-in the head of a green-backed lizard appearing from a gash in a dry stone wall and sit there, still as eternity, observing the world from the edge. To write it truly she would have to write-in Sante standing in the midst of ancient ruins, with his youthful face bathed in orange light, speaking of destiny.

With a single touch on her keyboard, she deleted everything and started again. The new words leapt onto the shiny white surface of the computer screen like revelations,

'You cannot visit the Mediterranean and expect to return unchanged…'

*

Bob cornered her in the corridor, waving a draft of her article in his hand, as if it were the incriminating confession of a crime committed. 'You can't be thinking of publishing this.'

'Why not?'

He stopped and started to read. "You cannot visit the Mediterranean and expect to return unchanged. For the first- time traveller to Sicily, or Egypt, or Greece, or the Holy Land … it's like touching base with history, with the past, your very soul. A visit to the Mediterranean is a pilgrimage, a journey of self-discovery. It's the Western equivalent of the Haj."

She knew exactly what he meant. And because she felt caught out, she became defensive. 'What's wrong with it?'

'Well, you know our readers, they're interested in real things.'

'Real things, what does that mean exactly?'

'You know: what there is to see, what to do, where to stay, what it *costs*. They're not interested in spiritual birthing. We leave this stuff to New Age publications.'

Well, he was right, although she would not give him the satisfaction of agreeing with him. His was the voice of rational, no-nonsense Australia. Any attempt to speak to the soul became pretentious. Seeing it with Bob's eyes, she had to admit the article was an embarrassment. She hated Bob for it, but not as much as she hated herself for allowing her defences to come down.

22

Everything fits, everything slots into shape in the tapestry of life. This phrase repeated itself in Franzetti's mind like a mantra, as his Airbus bound for Down Under crossed Europe's sky into Asia's. He started dozing off, feeling cosy and at peace in the knowledge that the Madonna of the Olives was somewhere in the entrails of the plane. Not the most edifying of places, to be sure, but she would understand.

His life had been a jigsaw with parts missing. Now, in this fortuitous journey to the birthplace of his beloved mother, he had found the bits to complete the puzzle. How it all fitted! His illness, the discovery of the Madonna, his cure … every incident led to this. Tragedy had its role to play. Even the death of his loved ones, God rest their souls, was a necessary link, part of God's larger plan. So it was futile to fret. God was just, God was wise. All His acts, no matter how unjust they might seem, are for the ultimate good.

His recovery wasn't just physical. The real healing had occurred in his spirit. He had awakened to find a path in the landscape of his remaining years. In that strip of white light he clearly saw his destiny, the legacy he would leave for those who came after him. He was bringing to his spiritually sterile country, a precious icon.

In the somnolence of the pressurised air he began to formulate a plan, which had been taking shape in his mind ever since the day of his miraculous healing. He didn't have to think too hard. The next stage in this spiritual odyssey was there before the invisible eye of the mind, as lucid as if it were already executed. Everything slotted; it was a question of recognising the signs, of reading the pattern.

And what about the other piece, Sante, who had positioned himself into his life, at precisely the right moment! Could there be a more eloquent sign? Sante – the name rang inside his head over the hum of the jet engine – was perhaps the concluding piece in the puzzle. Franzetti fell asleep, grateful for the plenitude of his blessings.

The quarantine officer was being difficult. Afraid of introducing bugs into the country, he was. His manner changed when he realized who Clem Franzetti was, but he insisted the wooden 'object' would have to be quarantined. Old World contamination of the New World must be avoided. Well, perhaps it was for the best. It would give him time to prepare adequately for her arrival. What looked like a bureaucratic impediment seemed like yet another sign. And the Virgin Mary would forgive him for leaving her temporarily in the hands of the local bureaucracy.

He was surprised to see Danny at the airport, wearing his trademark leather jacket. Now there was a challenge for the Madonna. Danny badly needed a miracle, just to keep himself out of trouble. It required a huge effort on his part, to remain on speaking terms with his stepbrother. Christian charity had little to do with it, he had exhausted all of that long ago. What stopped him from offloading Danny was a promise he had made long ago to his father that, no matter what, he would look after his stepbrother.

Even so, the sight of him, with that permanent scowl on his face, put Clem in a bad mood. 'What are you doing here, Danny?'

'Come to see you Clem, you're looking good, brother.'

Clem hated being addressed as 'brother'. And not just because they were not real brothers, or that there was a 25-year gap between them. It was just that it sounded so phoney. And he had to suffer his lengthy handshake.

'Thanks, never felt better.' He thought he perceived a

wince of disappointment. Danny always brought out the cynical worst in him.

'I got great news for you. Stardust's had another win.'

'I know. Russell's kept me up to date.'

'He's running favourite for the Roma Cup.'

'Congratulations. I must get going.'

'Listen I gotta talk to you, Clem.'

'Make it snappy.'

'Not here. I'll catch you up at the farm. When are you gonna be there?'

Clem had a fair idea what Danny wanted. Whatever the details, it had to do with the dollar sign. He decided to be vague. 'I'm not sure about my moves. Just go and grab me one of them trolleys, will you?'

*

It was a couple of days before Danny landed on the doorstep of Clem's country house with a business proposition. He was going into the racing business in a big way. No, he wasn't after borrowing money; he had already secured backing from some of the main players in the racing industry. What he needed was a long lease on the property, so they could build proper stables, a training track … add value to the property.

From the veranda of the old house Clem's eyes were fixed on a large boulder rising from the ground, just down from the irrigation dam. He was thinking what to do about it; the rock spoilt the symmetry of his grove, and that would not do. Only perfection would suit the Madonna.

'So what do you reckon?' Danny was persisted.

'We'll have to dig up that rock.'

'What do you mean? '

'It'll be in the way.'

'No need, Clem. We're putting the track at the lower end where it's level. We'll save on site costs.'

'What track?'

'A training track for the horses – like I been telling ya.'

An aperture appeared in the focused intensity of the older man's thoughts, through which he looked at his step-brother, perhaps for the first time since his return from overseas. 'Danny, what are you talking about? I don't want any more horses. I'm planting an olive grove on the property.'

*

The old house, with its rusty corrugated iron roof and curling veranda hangers, was demolished. In its place he set out to build a new house of reconstituted limestone, in the style of a Spanish cloister, with a courtyard enclosed on three sides. At the open end of this courtyard Clem planned to build a fountain, in the centre of which the statue would rise, looking over the sweeping landscape of its domain: an olive grove.

Meanwhile, the land was prepared for the planting. Fortunately, there weren't many native trees on the property, since much of the land was used for pasture or to grow irrigated clover for stock feed. The few trees left from the original coastal scrub were quickly uprooted. What took a while were the boulders, which were scattered around the property. But just as Clem watched the explosives gang go to work on the biggest rock, inspiration struck once again. He rushed headlong down the slope calling to the men to stop.

The enormous boulder, which Clem called *My Ayer's Rock*, rose five metres from the ground and covered an area of some forty square metres. Perfect. Clearly it had been placed there, millions of years ago, for this very purpose. Everything fitted. He sent the explosives team away and called in the masons.

*

Three months later, the Madonna of the Olives stood in its man-made grotto. Not, as first envisaged, in the centre of the courtyard. Such an exalted position was not for the humble Madonna – rather, her position blended with the landscape as it undulated down the slope to the Great Northern Highway.

The entrance was fitted with an iron grill door, to keep out thieves and vandals. The last thing Franzetti wanted was for some heathen to come and steal the precious relic. Blue lights shone down from their concave recesses in the ceiling like heavenly stars. By day, sunlight filtered through tinted glass, and softly fanned the flawless cheeks of the Madonna.

This was Clem's legacy to his country, his path to spiritual redemption. But there was to be no grand opening, nor did he publicize his miraculous cure. No, the Madonna would find a way to reveal her presence in her own good time. For now, he relished the privileged intimacy of a space for private communion between him and Our Lady of the Olives. This was their secret. Not quite of course, there was Sante. He was sure that one day the young man would find his way here.

23

Sante is on his way to Rovaro in early summer, and the starlings are in a frenzy of expectation for the maturing wheat. As he nears the gate, he is assailed by the smell of old wood burning, then watches flames flaring out of the front door of the house, licking up the wall. A boy, six or seven years old, is sitting on the sill of the upper window, his mouth wide open as if he were screaming, but his mother is sleeping soundly under the olive tree outside, and does not hear.

Little Sante – yes, it's Sante himself! – then monkey-leaps onto the branch of a tree and hangs there, seesawing with his legs kicking in the air. Don Alfio materialises below him, holding out the folds of an apron-like garment and calls, 'Jump, Sante, jump!'

Sante woke, relieved it was only a dream. What he didn't know was that the actual event had taken place at Rovaro. In the damp old house, Nonna La Rocca had finally released her grip on the tug-of-war of life and delivered herself unto death. She had not eaten for a week, easing herself gently into the other world, to join her husband.

*

Don Alfio had to admit, both his parents-in-law had shown commendable grace in their dying. *Contadini* they might have been, but in their peasant stoic acceptance of death they had been dignified. Unusual, for Sicilians are not good at dying. So focused are they on themselves and their affairs, that death, when it arrives, is seen as an injustice, a personal affront.

Whatever the great writer Lampedusa might say, surmised Don Alfio during the funeral Mass in the Chiesa Madre, Sicilians don't think they are perfect, they just toy with notions of immortality. In the pursuit of that goal, Sicilians are good at mourning, and prolong it as far as form allows. That's why, in San Sisto, so many front doors were marked by *lutto*. The Marzanos had only recently taken down their notice of mourning following Mr La Rocca's death. They would need to attach a new one.

A timid and private person in life, in death, Nonna La Rocca was given a farewell fit for a mayor's mother-in-law. The hearse, drawn by two black San Fratellan mares, was covered over with wreaths of arum lilies and carnations. It left the Chiesa Madre and wound its way along the Via Tre Novembre to the town cemetery, followed by a convoy of mourners.

Out of respect for the Mayor, almost each family in the town was represented. Most of the shopkeepers on the Via Roma closed their businesses for a couple of hours. Along the way, women came out on their balconies or doorsteps, crossed themselves and genuflected at the passing of the hearse, while the men took off their hats and bowed. With Nonna resting in the crypt next to her husband at last, the Marzanos made their way back to the car, flanked by the citizenry of San Sisto.

Like Sara-Jane, Sante had been closer to his grandfather. Whenever he spent time at Rovaro he followed Nonnu, as he went about ploughing in the weeds, mending the fence, pruning the vines. When he passed away Sante missed him terribly, but the death of his grandmother was the end of an era. Now he felt rudderless, desolate, hollowed out. Sante held his mother, who looked a picture of dignified grieving, her cheeks damp from newly shed tears. With his right hand slipped under her left arm, he felt the dampness of her perspiration through the sheer material of her black dress.

The funeral cortège filed out of the *camposanto* gates, flanked by winged angels presenting their backs to the world, their eyes watching over the dead: surely another metaphor for Sicily.

Sante found himself looking at the world he had known all his life, from the outside, as if one part of him was gone already. Pools of tears flooded his eyes and streamed down his cheeks. The people of San Sisto saw, and thought what a wonderful young man the Mayor's son was. So *sentimentale, affettuoso*. And weren't the Marzanos lucky to have him! He was surely bound to be the next Mayor of San Sisto when his father decided he had had enough. Sante's tongue caught the tears on the corner of his mouth. As his brain registered their hot briny taste, he mentally composed an email to Clem Franzetti.

24

There were plenty of messages on the machine, but they could wait. She was famished, and she had had better days at work. She turned on the oven and took a pizza base out of the freezer. Over the stiff surface she spread tomato slices, canned chopped olives, button mushrooms, also from a can, and mozzarella. She put the pizza in the oven and turned on the answering machine.

A message from a rowing team captain, someone called Tim or Tom , probably a New Zealander, wanted to be called back. Her dentist reminded her that her six-monthly check-up was now due. Was she interested in selling her house? No thanks, it wasn't hers to sell, but the woman was going to call back anyway.

And then, out of the blue. 'Ciao Sara, I'm Sante, your brother. I have a big surprise for you. I will telephone you again later.'

She knew she should have waited for him to call back. Knowing how protective his mother was, she ought to exercise restraint. She mustn't give her the idea she was chasing Sante. And yet, while her head was reasoning this out, her finger was pressing the Marzano number.

The voice on the other end surprised her. '*Pronto!*'

' Don Alfio ... ?'

'Oh, *carissima*. It's delightful to speak with you again. Are you well?'

What a pleasure to hear his voice, the cadence of his Italian. 'Yes, I'm returning Sante's call. He rang here today, but I was at work.'

'I see, he must want to tell you about his journey.'

'Journey?'

'Yes, he is coming to Australia. Sara has relented at

last.'

'She has?'

'Yes, we have persuaded her to let him come for a working holiday. Franzetti has offered him a job on his farm.'

Sara-Jane was trying to get her head around that. Sante working on a farm? And where would he stay?

The distant Sicilian voice was still talking. 'But, don't say I told you. He'll want to surprise you. What about you, *cara*? When are you coming back?'

'I'm not sure.'

'We miss you already. You must come back soon. You must.'

'Well, we'll see … oh, shit …'

'What?'

A smell of burnt pastry reached her from the kitchen as smoke coiled out of the oven. Her dinner was burnt to charcoal, but that was nothing. Sante was coming. She would have to speak to Russell, her father; his father, their father. She needed a drink.

*

Russell's voice thundered over the mobile line, and for a second she was stumped for words.

'Who is it?'

'Sara-Jane here.'

'Who?'

She wasn't going to elaborate.

'Oh, hi! I wasn't thinking. I'm at Belmont Park, there's a lot of noise around here … how are you?'

'I've been overseas. Well, I've been back a while now …

I was in Sicily.'

'Where?'

'Italy.'

'Oh yeah. Good.'

Nothing registered with him, as expected. It would have surprised Sara-Jane if he knew of the connection with Sara La Rocca, or that he remembered her at all. This thought brought a flush of anger to her face. She wanted to say, 'I've met her, the woman you raped'. But that wouldn't help matters at all, so she spoke smoothly. 'How about coffee this week?'

'How come? Is there a problem?'

You could say that. 'Well … I just thought it'd be a good idea to catch up …'

'Yeah, Ok … Good idea…'

They made a date, over some strained breathing. He suspected something. He was a police detective after all. Well, let him stew a bit.

She realised she hadn't asked after his partner, whose name she had forgotten. A pretty common name: Susan or something, no … Christine … Chris, that was it.

*

She hadn't seen him for nearly a year, although she had spoken to him on the phone a couple of times. Now, as he walked into her apartment, he filled a good portion of the door's width. He had put on weight … even more weight! He looked tired, but not unwell, and his bulk gave him a deceptive air of good health. But Sara-Jane knew otherwise. She knew he had a few health issues. Come to think of it, the last time she saw him was at the hospital, where he had gone in for prostrate tests and refused an operation.

He was only forty-four and didn't fancy the consequences of an operation at his age, especially as his condition could persist for another twenty years before it came to anything serious. Of course, he had to look after himself; a big ask for him, although he did give up smoking, which might have accounted for the weight increase. You lose some, you gain some.

He was in uniform, a self-protective device. *I'm Detective Sergeant Toohey, don't mess about with me, don't you dare come too close.* And of course, there was no question of physical contact, not even a handshake. Normally, she wouldn't have even noticed; it was only now, having been to a place where physical contact was a social norm, if not an obsession, that this personal fortress stood out all the more.

'How ya been?' He slumped down on a chair without waiting for her to ask, and rested his clasped right hand on his hip. With the other he held his overhanging stomach. 'So, how you been?' He scrutinised her with his detective look, as if to inquire, what are you hiding? What have you got me here for? 'You made some coffee?'

Sara-Jane fairly jumped, glad to get away from his inquisitive stare. She felt his eyes on her through the archway into the kitchen.

He called through the space. 'Haven't you got any instant?'

'Yea – ah. Why? Don't you like it freshly made?'

'It's OK. I'm used to drinking instant.'

Oh yes, she understood; there was a spot of inverted snobbery about him. It was his way of saying, 'Now, don't go putting on any airs with me. I am who I am and I'm not gonna budge'.

She could have left it at that, one of the first rules of a successful transaction: give in on the small things, save your ammunition for the important ones. Yet, for some reason, she felt that this time she needed to insist on this small thing. She stood there, pot in hand, looking for a pretext.

'Besides, I haven't got much time. I'm running flat out today.' His words were brusque.

Inadvertently, he gave her a pretext. 'It's alright, the coffee is already made.'

He sat back and waited in silence until she came back with a tray and set it down on the table. He leaned forward, she thought to take his cup. Instead, he pulled a trouser leg up and it gathered towards the crotch, exposing faded black socks with perished elastic. With elbows on knees, he fitted his left fist into his right hand, and looked straight at her. 'You got somethin' to tell me then?'

At this point, quite unexpectedly, Sara-Jane's heart started to race, her palms went clammy. The enormity of what she was about to tell him struck her. How on earth had she got herself into this situation? It wasn't nerves, it was fear.

She was afraid of this man she had invited into her apartment, this man she hardly knew, despite the fact she was infected with his genes. The tinkling of a teaspoon in the saucer alerted her to the fact her hands were trembling. It was her fault for inviting him into her world in the first place.

But this, she realised, was not her thought. This was a guilt thought, a Sicily thought, an Sara La Rocca thought.

An absurd notion crossed her mind. Perhaps she was experiencing a sense of what Sara La Rocca had experienced a generation ago: the fear of this man's animal energy. This thought stirred her fighting spirit. It was just stupid. She could do better. This was another test, one of many she would experience in the course of her life. She'd better stand up to it.

She positioned her hands to counter his, resting her right elbow in her left palm so her right hand was thrust forward, not far from his hands. This physical proximity made him retreat, just ever so slightly. But it was enough to give her the advantage.

' I told you I'd gone to Sicily.'

'Yeah, you said…' his look expressed his real thought, which was, 'What's that got to do with me?' But he said, 'how was it?'

'I met Mum's friend, Sara La Rocca.'

His butt shifted on the chair, which gave a muffled squeak.

'She still keeps her maiden name, even though she's married. They do that over there, women, they keep their maiden name. And we thought we were ahead of them in the women's advancement stakes …'

He locked the fingers of both hands, caught his knee in his interlocking fingers and pulled towards his body as if to rein-in his bolting impatience. It was a position that spoke of smugness.

It angered Sara-Jane. 'Actually, what I really wanted to tell you is that there is a child … well, he's a young man now, eighteen years old.'

'Oh, yeah?' His hands stayed on his knee, only they pulled harder, and the greater tension applied raised his leg off the floor so his foot dangled free, and trembled in the air.

She also noticed his Adam's apple quiver in the fat of the neck. But he wasn't going to make it easy on her. As a detective, he must have learnt a few things from the victims of his interrogations. Now he was on the receiving end and he knew when not to speak. His gamesmanship unnerved her.

She grabbed the sugar bowl forcefully, releasing some of her tension down her arm and onto the object. She put it down slowly, deliberately placing it in the exact same place it was before. 'He's your son.'

Blood retreated from his cheeks momentarily. An aeroplane flew over on its way somewhere, its rumble overwhelming the space inside the room.

'What?'

'I said he's …'

'Rubbish.' He squirmed on his bottom; his gaze flitted around the walls of room, as if looking for a crevice to escape into. He picked up the cup to drink, but there was no more coffee left.

She didn't offer to refill it for him.

'Rubbish,' he repeated. 'I never knew the girl.'

It was strange to hear Sara La Rocca referred to as a girl,

'I hardly ever spoke to her.'

Deny everything, it was the first rule of defence, and he knew all about that.

So, there was no point arguing with him. 'He's coming to Australia,' she went on. 'He'll probably want to meet you.'

His eyelids, which had kept their droop all this time, now shot up and retreated beneath the brow line. His eyes looked menacing. 'I told you, I had nothing to do with this woman.'

'Oh, she's not coming, don't worry.'

'I'm not worried. This has nothing to do with me. I gotta go.' He leapt to his feet, stood hovering over her with his arms crossed over his chest, as if to say: See, I'm bigger than you.

Sara-Jane wasn't intimidated. Rather, she was appalled by his utter cowardice. He was pitiful with his heaving bulk, a wimp trapped inside cumbersome armour of mock toughness and denial. She did not get up, even though she was now forced to look up at him. She resisted the temptation of standing, of trying to reduce the difference in eye level between them. She would concede every centimetre of height he wanted, it wasn't important. The important thing was inner courage, and she realised this man had less of it than he pretended, much less than she had imagined.

She looked at him contemptuously; she held his stare and spoke quietly, the words echoing inside her head. 'You know what ...?' She sought an appellation: Russell... Sergeant Toohey... Dad... Father. None fitted. She had no name for him. 'Coward' suited him well, but she wasn't going to give him the satisfaction of resorting to insults. Name-calling was the refuge of the powerless, and yet ...

'I pity you,' she said finally.

He unclasped his arms and let them dangle by his sides.

Anger crunched his face between chin and forehead. 'So you pity me, da ya?' His head did a little dance of mockery on his neck. 'Well, don't bother. At least I know what I'm about. I'm comfortable on the seat of me pants. I can live with who I am. I don't need to go traipsing around the world lookin' fer shit. If you're into guilt trips, that's your business, just don't come dumpin' the shit on my doorstep. I don't need it. If mistakes were made when we were kids – and I'm not sayin' there's truth in this whatsoever – what's the point of diggin' it all up now? Things have moved on. Sounds to me like this woman's got an axe to grind. They come to the station every day, ageing women, with stuff they claim happened generations ago. The question is, why do they wait all this time? I'll tell you why, life's passed them by and they need to blame someone for the fact they're past it, and nobody wants 'm any more.' He walked to the door, held the latch in his fingers and pulled the door open.

A blaze of sunshine shadowed his frame, which filled the whole space. His head turned to her, but she could not see his face. A shadow spoke to her. 'As far as I'm concerned, she's dreamin' it all up. My advice to her is to move on, like everybody else. '

'Oh don't worry, she has. She's happily married.'

'Well then, what's the problem? We've all moved on, and I'd better move on to the station before I get moved out of my job.'

Sara-Jane slammed the door behind him. She heard his heavy feet thudding down the stairs.

Fuckin' jerk! Dickhead! Loser! She was so angry she imagined him missing a step, tumbling down on the landing. She watched his stomach wobble, his face twist in agony and blood trickle out of his mouth. Before she had time to rein in her vengeful imagination, she heard the car door slam and he was gone.

25

It was a rare experience for Sara-Jane to be caught between two contradictory impulses. Her natural propensity for independence, for immunizing herself against transports of emotions, for protecting her privacy – was now jostling with this ... indulgence, this tension that distracted her mind. The tug of war manifested itself in anxious waiting for Sante. Just when she should have been planning next week's edition of *Escapes*, her head was full of Sante. What was happening?

Provided there were no delays, or worse – God, how she hated this fretfulness in her! – he would walk through the door in less than half an hour, the same door through which only days before the man whose genes they shared had exited. Such a juxtaposition made her flinch. How could that man be father to Sante?

To kill some more time she decided to go and scrub down the shower and mop the floor. Nothing like physical activity to work through anxieties

She really wanted to see him again, no doubt about that ... he was her brother, but she did not want him to be a burden to her, to invade her space, to cramp her style, to get in the way of her career. She was a busy woman. As for cooking, he could forget that. She hardly ever cooked for herself.

And how would she greet him? Shake his hand? A bit formal. Kiss him on both cheeks *all'italiana*? That was OK over there, part of the social landscape, easy, like a stroll in the piazza. Here, the very prospect of Sante entering her house, making contact ... it felt odd. And another thing, over there the country had fitted itself around her like a garment made to measure, but how would Australia fit

Sante Marzano? Most certainly a lot better, if it weren't for Russell Toohey's hulking presence.

When the doorbell rang she jumped. She paced herself to answer the door. In that blurred frame against the sun, her heart faltered as she realized the man with the suitcase was not Sante.

'Would you like it inside?'

The voice was too strange and the accent too familiar to be Sante's. A moment's adjustment to the blinding light revealed the taxi driver. She squeezed past him and then saw Sante, struggling up the steps with another suitcase and a shoulder bag. Instinctively she ran down and reached for his bag. But before she could relieve him of his load, Sante had dropped the suitcase and thrown his arms around her. The bag swung and slipped down to his forearm as he hugged her.

Sara-Jane found she was squeezed inside his arms. She took in the scents of San Sisto on his skin and felt, once again, the permanence of a world encased in stone-layered time.

'Sara-Jane, at last!' He released her, held her at arm's length, and looked her up and down. 'I cannot believe I'm in Australia with you.' He had had a haircut. Gone were the strands of hair parted at the forehead, he now sported a trim college-boy haircut. It made his head seem larger and his forehead more pronounced. The effect was a stronger, more masculine Sante.

Sara-Jane felt she should like the look, and yet it unsettled her. 'You're loaded,' she said abruptly. 'Are you sure you didn't bring the kitchen sink with you?'

'What?'

'Never mind.'

Inside it seemed to be very dark all of a sudden. She pulled the vertical blinds to one side. Slats of sunshine patterned the carpet of the living room and reached Sante's feet where he stood in his fashionable runners, black denims and tobacco-coloured shirt. Sara-Jane looked around and felt she was seeing her apartment with new eyes: the semi-sheen, off-white walls, the low ceilings, the corner of the living room sectioned off by the desk, which she used as office space ... it was, she had to admit, of spartan austerity. The spaces, illuminated by the new presence, revealed themselves to be filled with the shadows of her insecurities. She had wanted to see Sante, now his presence felt like an intrusion. The apartment, which for years had been her refuge, now looked dingy, sterile, claustrophobic.

She pointed to the bed. 'It's the best I can do, there's not much space.'

'It is perfect, Sara-Jane.' Sante looked out of the kitchen window. Through a clump of trees in the park, a slice of blue water peered beneath the skyscrapers of the city. 'You have a fantastic view here. Is that the sea?'

'No, the Swan river.'

'A river! It is so big, so blue.' He could hardly contain himself. 'I think I will love Australia'.

And Australia will love you, she wanted to say but resisted. This was a new situation for her and very delicate. It required caution and restraint; she did not want things to get out of control. She showed him around the apartment, where to put his clothes, the bathroom they would have to share – although she hinted he might use the washing facilities in the laundry – how to use the microwave and the washing machine. He followed her around with that 'can't believe I'm here' smile plastered all over his face. Nothing dampened his enthusiasm, and when she brought the cold drinks on a tray with snacks, he suggested they should go out 'on the balcony'.

No, she thought, better not. The nosy neighbours: the

single mother next door with the autistic child and the two New Zealanders who never went out by day, would be looking through the blinds. Sara-Jane had no time for neighbours. 'I haven't got much time.' She looked at her watch. 'I need to get back to work.'

*

Sante sensed his sister's anxieties. People were a spectrum, he thought. They change according to how the light falls upon them in a particular space. He found it difficult to reconcile this woman with the luminous creature he had set eyes upon in the archaeological landscape of Tindari, and who had charmed the population of San Sisto. On her home turf, Sara-Jane came across as highly strung, laden with responsibilities of work and ordered by the time-piece she carried on her right wrist, which dominated her life. Would he change too, now that he had come to the land of his conception? More to the point, would he have the courage to square up to the man whose violence made his birth possible?

Meanwhile, Sara-Jane continued to attempt to de-stress through talk that fluttered from one innocuous subject to the other. Did he have a good flight? Was Don Alfio going on a diet like he said he would? Was Mimmo behaving himself?

'Ah, his comportment is the best. He ask about you many times, when you come back to Italy.'

'Not while he's around anyway.' They both laughed at her suggestion. 'At least he's not pestering you guys about wanting to buy your land.'

'No, but now that Nonna is gone, maybe mother will sell.'

'How is Sara? I'm surprised she's let you go.'

Sante must have interpreted her comment as a criticism of his mother, for he went serious. 'Mother is not so bad, really.'

Sara-Jane moved on to practical matters. 'Franzetti wants you to start on Monday. There's a bus to Gingin twice a day. The earlier one doesn't get there until nine-forty. You'll need to negotiate with him for a late start on Monday, otherwise you would have to leave here on Saturday afternoon, something I am sure you don't want to do. I think he'll be flexible. He's very keen to have you there.' Sara-Jane felt as if she were rehearsing a script. 'I've got to get going. I'll be back before seven. I'm afraid it has to be take-away tonight.' And because she didn't want him to think he was unwelcome, she added, 'I'm really glad you decided to come, Sante.'

Instinctively Sante reached for her hand, but reconsidered. He followed her down the steps and when she looked back at him from inside the car she caught the bottom outline of his chin and gave a start: it was Russell's chin.

26

At the gate Sante looked up at the long drive and thought he had the wrong place. Even though he had expected newly-planted trees, his mind's imprint of an olive grove was of time-gnarled trunks and anarchic fronds, clinging to patches of earth up steep terrain. He knew this would be different, but somehow he had not been prepared for this easy landscape of orange earth, punctured with identical shrubs, in precise rows, separated by a network of irrigation pipes. It looked surreal, like a model plan of plastic bushes exhibited on a table.

At the far end of the drive appeared a newly-built house, its gleaming silver roof disappearing over the hump of a stone outcrop, set against a vast blue sky. Next to the drive, and separated from it by a wire fence, a parallel track of rammed earth led to a rectangular shed with a corrugated iron roof, surrounded by paddocks. Sante stood there wondering how to open the gate, when he heard a ping, then the gate whirred away from the metal upright and slowly swung open. A four-wheel drive trailing a horse float came up from behind, slowed down, turned in and stopped, waiting for the gate to fully open. A man with a chubby face coming down to a feminine pinball of a chin put his head through the side window and called to him in a peremptory voice, as if Sante were an intruder in his property. 'Yes mate.'

He stroked the animal's head. 'You have a beautiful horse.'

'Who're you after?'

'I'm coming to work for Mr Franzetti.'

Danny gave the visitor a suspicious glance; saw his white pianist's hands with pink knuckles, the soft eyes, the expensive check shirt, the cargo shorts, the Nike runners and settled on a derisive smirk. 'Oh yeah! And what exactly you gonna do for him?'

Sante didn't understand, but recognised the tone, so he smiled. 'Sorry.'

'How come Brother's hiring you, then?'

'I work here only for some *munse*.'

'Work? What work?' Again, that suspicious look. 'Where you from?'

'I come from Sicily.'

'Ah, say no more, Mafia country, hey?' Danny gave him the wink-nudge routine.

Sante wasn't sure about the gesture, but felt the antagonism.

'I know who you are.' Danny nodded. 'You're the foreign kid everyone's been talkin' about, with that funny name … Sandy or something…'

'Sante.'

'Santy! What kind of name is that?'

'No,' the young man insisted, 'my name is Sante.'

'Whatever.' Danny stopped chuckling, and a shadow passed over his eyes. 'I wonder what big brother wants from you. I wonder…' The man wore a black leather jacket, even though it was going to be a hot day, with frayed cuffs at the wrist. His eyes were sharp and quick, and looked not at you, but the space around you. The blue of his eyes matched his shirt but there was no kindness in them. He looked a disillusioned man.

'I must go.' Sante turned away.

'Hang on a minute.' Danny turned off the engine and got out of the car. The horse pounded the floor inside the float. 'I'm not finished yet…' But before he had time to proceed, he looked up and saw Clem limping down the drive, leaning on a walking stick. Danny's face altered to fawning submissiveness. 'Morning, Brother.'

Clem ignored him and spoke to Sante. 'Ah, here you are, at last.'

Sante proffered his hand, but Clem took him in his arms. 'Welcome, my boy, I've been waiting.' The old man's face glowed. Uncustomary light danced around his eyes; for this was the moment he had been waiting for.

'Come, come Santy.'

Sante picked up his suitcase and followed.

The old man looked around. 'Where is your car?'

'I don't have a car. I came by bus.'

'No car! We'll have to do something about that, won't we?' He led Sante up the track to the house. 'Take no notice of Danny,' said Franzetti. 'He's a fool. Come, I'll show you your room.'

Danny watched them amble up to the house: the old man, taller and unsteady, strode with a slight tilt of his frame, and from time to time leaned on the young man's shoulder to steady himself.

Danny revved up the engine and took off in a cloud of dust. The horse pawed in the shuddering float. Danny was worried. What was that all about? Too pallsy-wallsy for his liking. He liked it even less when, later in the morning, he saw the foreign kid drive away through the gate in the convertible that had belonged to Franzetti's son. 'Hm!'

*

Sante smelled the mulch freshly laid out around the base of each shrub.

'So, how are things at the clinic? How's mad Doctor Troina? Still going is he?'

'I think so. And you? Are you well, Mr Franzetti?'

'Me? Never felt better…'

He looked thinner, though, particularly around the neck where flaps of skin fell to the jutting bones. Deep circles had appeared around the sockets, although the eyes themselves shone, brilliant with passion. A filament of cotton from the corner of his turned up collar touched the stubble of his chin.

Sante glanced at his walking stick. 'You have an accident?'

'A bit of bother with the hip. It's nothing.'

The guest room was at the opposite end of the old man's quarters. It was much larger than the young man's bedroom back home. The paint was fresh, the door was glossy cream, the same colour as the metal door frame. His bedroom window looked over the farm dam, with its walls of clay and dark brown water. Once they had inspected the house, the old man presented him with a set of keys, each marked with white adhesive tape.

Mr Franzetti did not come out of his bedroom again for the afternoon. Sante went and sat on the veranda, shaded by a magnificent wisteria coiled around the frame of a wooden pergola, a remnant of the old structure.

Across the highway, the terrain fell away to the coastal plain and the ocean, some twenty kilometres away, in a patchwork of stunted scrub and farmland. In that direction, beyond the Indian Ocean was Sicily.

From here it seemed a cosmos away, unreal; liable to dissolve in the vortex of memory. What work was assigned to him? He was given no instructions. Everything in this farm seemed in place, under control, newly laid out, completed.

He decided to take a walk down the slope, between the rows of olive shrubs. Sante took the tip of a branch in his hand, rubbed the lime-green leaves and took in the scent. It had delicacy and vigour, but lacked time-seasoned texture. A solitary silver-eye came to rest on a branch, disappeared into the foliage, in a vain search for food. It would be a few years before these shrubs would bear fruit.

He reached the brick-paved path that smelled of newly-baked clay and wound down some two hundred metres from the house, veered left and swung around a rocky outcrop, falling sharply to a small courtyard, on the lower side. Sante knew that Franzetti had built a private chapel. Sara-Jane had told him so, but he wasn't prepared for the kind of irrational fear that overcame him on reaching the entrance. The face of the rock was panelled by an iron gate painted black; the bars glared against the lowering sun and looking like monster with a menacing frown.

The gate suddenly vibrated and lifted off the floor with a subdued screech, disappearing into the rock face above. At the same time, a shadow advanced next to his,

'It's sensitive to the remote in my pocket.'

Sante turned and saw the face of Clem Franzetti, wearing a smile that was meant to be ingratiating but made him look a little sinister. Sante started to move, but Franzetti, who was half a head taller, grabbed him firmly, pressing down on his shoulder with his hand. 'Come, I'll show you something.'

The chapel was tiny, with a polished wooden floor and one single jarrah pew. From the ceiling, which was cupola-shaped and lined with curved wooden batts, golden lights formed a halo above the head of a statue. At first Sante did not recognise the Madonna of the Olives that had stood at the entrance of Dr Troina's clinic. In the confines of the chapel, the Madonna should have seemed larger, instead it looked forlorn as if, overwhelmed by that gleaming opulence, it had shrunk back into itself. A thought played inside his head, over and over: the Madonna did not belong there.

'What do you think?' Clem sounded proud. 'Magnificent isn't she? You can come here any time you want. I'll get you a remote. One thing – this is just between us – I don't want anyone else to have access to it. People here don't understand.'

Sante stepped back. He recognized in the old man the burden of fanaticism. 'Mr Franzetti…'

'Clem, call me Clem, Sante. This is not Italy, we don't go for formalities here.' Franzetti struck a match and proceeded to light a candle, then took it out of its holder and brought it across to the young man, holding it close to his face as if to better study his features. 'You look different. He scrutinized him up close. 'What have you done to yourself?'

Sante didn't know what to say.

'I know.' The old man sounded like he had solved the key to a riddle. 'You have cut your hair.' His face became serious, his voice churlish. 'You shouldn't have done that. You shouldn't have.'

As Sante was considering what to do, the old man's intensity dissipated, the flame-lit eye relaxed. He handed him the candle with what could have been a smile. 'Come Sante – help me light all the candles.'

Sante did as he was bidden, while the old man followed him, as if to make sure he was doing it properly, then stood in the middle to admire the fully lit-up grotto. Clem Franzetti was transported into a surreal world far away.

Sante felt the urge to bring him back. 'Mr Franzetti…'

The old man was not responding.

'Sir…'

Sante touched him on the elbow.

'Yes, what?'

'What is my work on this farm?'

Franzetti turned to him but his look was vacant. 'What work?' The old man seemed perplexed. 'What is the matter, Sante?'

'I don't understand…'

The old man studied him again, for what seemed an uncomfortably long time then, in a low voice, almost a whisper, he spoke. 'Of course you understand, Sante, it's in your blood.' He turned to the Madonna. 'He'll be alright, won't he?'

Sante considered the face of this sad man, with his sunken eyes and eyebrows that looked like worn out paint brushes. He saw a kind of energy, a fighting spirit, lasting into old age, which his own gentle, accepting grandfather never had. The young man was unsure whether to pity or admire him, but the old man ended the brief exchange with an abrupt exit from the grotto, as if something pressing was calling him back to the house. Strangely though, he forgot to lock the gate.

That night, the first he spent at the farm, Sante lay awake for a long time. When he finally went to sleep, he dreamed he was hanging by his feet, on the end of a hammock-like contraption of rope and wood, held over a huge vat of olive oil by Clem Franzetti. The more he wriggled to free himself, the more the rope lengthened, as if it had become elastic, and his body was lowered further into the vat. Soon his hair touched the oily surface. Just as he thought he would drown, head-down, he woke up screaming.

A light truck arrived at the gate in the morning. A sign on either side of the cabin door announced: Conway's Stone Work and Retaining Walls. Sante went down to open the gate. A lean man with freckly skin and wizened features put his head out and watched silently from inside the truck as the gate swung open, then drove up to the top of the block. Sante followed him up on foot.

'Hello, my name is Sante.'

'I'm Ken.' The man replied without looking at him, or attempting to shake hands. 'I'm gonna a put a fence right down the middle of this block.'

'But there is fence here already.'

'I'll have to take that out. He wants a high stone wall.'

'Why?'

'Search me. Privacy I suppose.'

'It will be a big job.'

'I reckon. I'll be here a couple of months.'

Well, perhaps he could help this man put up a wall.

27

Ken was a taciturn man and a tireless, though paced, worker. He wore knee-length canvas shorts, army hat to protect him from the implacable autumn sun, and cotton shirt done up to the throat. His movements were slow and mechanical, his face remained expressionless as he prepared the trenches and manoeuvred each block into position. Each Monday, a truck arrived laden with blocks of limestone strapped in braces of steel, and deposited them along the drive near the fence-line.

By the end of the week, the blocks were lain, the joints neatly filled with matching cement. He stopped only for two brief breaks of twenty minutes each, to drink tea, which he carried in a thermos flask. He filled the flask's cap and drank his tea slowly, spitting out the first mouthful to wash out the dust, then sipped silently, sucking through stained teeth, looking ahead as if expecting something to appear out of the mid-distance. Despite the fact he wore gloves, his hands were leathery. Whenever he removed the gloves, the fingers were crinkled and damp.

Sante quietly slipped into the role of mason's labourer, mixing mortar, carrying blocks, shifting equipment. The wall slowly extended from the back fence, downhill towards the highway. Ken only spoke in reply to a question or to give instructions, and then in cryptic style, ending each sentence with 'Sandy'.

'Just chuck it on the back of the truck, Sandy.' or 'Give's a hand with this, Sandy.'

The Sicilian boy gave up trying to correct Ken. He knew from his experience with Franzetti that there was no point insisting his name be pronounced correctly.

But 'Sandy' made him feel different: like some

indefinite amalgam that could at any moment change shape and consistency.

Ken seemed devoid of curiosity. He wasn't interested in Sante's family, or where he came from, even though it must have been clear to him he was a foreigner. Likewise, he did not welcome questions about himself or family background.

At first Sante thought the frequent repetition of his name indicated a desire for friendship, for wanting to do away with formalities and be on familiar terms. In time he understood this wasn't so. The familiarity was limited and specific within the boundaries of a working rapport, of the activity in hand. It was accompanied by a guarded stance that warned to steer well clear of his physical and emotional space. Paradoxically, first name terms produced a barrier rather than an opening a door.

By contrast, the Italian 'Lei' form tended to establish a social hierarchy, or at least a formality, within which one could negotiate a relationship, exchange opinions, information about family, experiences, the world.

In the midst of all that sky and orange earth, the claustrophobic space between Sante and Ken was a cultural void, in which conversation sank, desultory and impersonal. It revolved around the job in hand. The solid world of physical objects was the conduit through which Ken's conversation passed, and it gauged his relationship to the world. It was a relationship minimised to a simple request, a transaction, a practical description. The only time his talk wandered beyond the single sentence was when he explained the workings of a piece of machinery, or an activity they were about to undertake.

'See that piece of four-be-two; when I lift up the water tank off the floor, jam it under. No, not all the way, it's gotta jut out off the edge.'

It was difficult to know what was going on inside Ken's head, but Sante sensed a similarity between Ken and the inscrutable scrubland alongside the main road on the way to the farm. It was a kind of autism, a lack of connectedness. And yet there was no denying there was a dignity about him, not unlike the peasant farmer back in Sicily – also a disappearing breed – although the latter was more reactive, fearful of destiny, ever ready to blaspheme against God and all the saints, and blame them for his misfortunes. This worker was more restrained. What was common between them was a sense they lived their life in the absolute, without compromises.

At exactly four in the afternoon, Ken stopped his machinery, loaded his bobcat onto the back of the truck, and went home. Not directly home. He first called in at the liquor store and bought himself half a dozen stubbies of Mid-strength. He drank them in front of the box, watching the news on every station, starting on Channel 10 at five, and finishing at 7.30pm on Channel 2.

*

Growth comes in tiny, imperceptible advances and, at times, people find themselves standing on a new step of insight. For Sante, it arrived with the afternoon breeze which cleaved up the slope and brought the smell of the ocean to the interior.

This country was his too. This land that knew him even before his Sicily seeped into him through the walls of his mother's defiled womb. This land was part of his being. If he pursued it – not too vigorously though, because of the risk of rejection – if he persevered, then, in time, something magical might come of it.

Because it all came down to the land. Sante suspected he would have to look to the land and the people it produced. Franzetti's feverish passion, Ken's dignified autism, Danny's poisoned acorns. Most important of all, Sara-Jane: so strong yet so fragile, so driven, so independent. These were the fruits of this land. This new land would challenge and free him.

There was, of course, another fruit: a worm-infected fruit. There was no denying he had come to Australia also to seek his father, even after he learned of the sordid circumstances of his conception. His visit would not be complete without at least a glimpse of this man whose genes he carried.

And was Sante ready to confront the rancid side of his bloodline? He considered this and concluded he must face up to this devil, for to acknowledge it was to control it.

He was shovelling sand into the cement mixer when, glancing over the fence, he saw two men standing still, watching a horse inside the paddock. The shorter one struck a match, ducked down and buried his face in his cupped hands to light a cigarette. It seemed like a lewd gesture. He realised it was Danny. The other man was altogether larger. He walked through the gate of the paddock, just about filling it, and extended his hand. The horse came to him, and he ran his other hand along the belly of the animal, ruffled the mane on its long neck, pressed his own head against the animal's, and kept it there in an affectionate hug. The scene struck Sante as touching.

Before he had time to think further, his attention was distracted by the arrival of Sara-Jane, who came to discuss a project with Mr Franzetti.

She stopped and shouted to him over the rumble of the mixer. 'Hello! You've decided to get down to some real work at last.'

Sante killed the motor and bounded over to her. It was so good to see his sister. They had only been apart two weeks but it seemed ages.

He wiped his mouth on the sleeve of his shirt and gave her a peck on the cheek through the car window. He took in the full power of her perfume. For a moment it dispelled the smell of his own sweat.

'Look at you! You look like a typical brickie's labourer.'

'I enjoy it. This is good for me.'

'Is it? If your mother saw you, I don't think she'd be impressed.'

'What about my sister? What does *she* think?'

Sara-Jane smiled. 'Well, it's keeping you out of mischief, isn't it? Are you coming to town this weekend?' Outside the confines of the apartment she seemed more relaxed, warmer.

'Are you missing me?'

Sara-Jane gave him a playful look as she pretended to consider the question. 'I am just sick of eating take-away food.'

Sante's attention moved down the slope.

'Who is that man?' He pointed towards the paddock.

Sara-Jane looked through the window of her Honda at two figures in the paddock, on the other side of the half-built wall. One was cantering a horse inside the enclosed track, whip in hand, bridle in the other. The second man, taller and heavier, stood watching, leaning forward on the cross-bar of the wooden fence, his large belly pressed against the lower bar.

'That's Franzetti's relative,' said Sara-Jane, I can't remember his name.'

'Not Danny, the other one … the large man.'

Sara-Jane paused, squinted, as if the sun was getting in her eyes, even though she was on the shaded side of the car.

'I don't know. It's too far to see. One of Danny's mates, I should think.' She revved the engine. 'I'd better get going or Franzetti'll go aggro on me.'

Sante could not take his eyes off that stranger. As if aware of his gaze, the man suddenly turned and stared back. Normally, Sante would have raised his hand and waved, but the man's posture conveyed a message, even though it was too far to read his facial expression, of angry antagonism that made Sante quickly turn his gaze up the drive, to where his sister had just emerged from the car, carrying a briefcase. Before going into the house, she stopped on the doorstep, turned abruptly and looked back at him.

Across the fifty metres that separated them, he could tell her look was brief and intense, strangely similar to the one he had received from the corpulent man in the paddock, and the space between the three of them was turbulent with unexplained emotions.

The man came up every Saturday morning, took the horse out on the paddock – it was always the same chestnut mare – and spent a long time grooming it, brushing its coat, hosing the animal down in the sunshine. Sante wished the man would look up from time to time, and notice his presence or exchange a greeting. He was jealous of the attention the horse was receiving. And when the man drove off, after lunch, Sante felt the hollowness of his absence.

28

On the Friday Sara-Jane, who had gone to Northam on assignment, called at the farm again to collect him. She was looking forward to having him over for the weekend. The atmosphere in the apartment changed with his presence; his cheerfulness lightened the tensions of a work discipline she had cultivated over the years.

Something must have been churning in Sante's head, though, for when they stopped at the Midland railway crossing, out of the darkening blue he asked, 'You know that man that looks after the horses? Clem's brother ... step brother...'

'What about him?'

'I don't thin' he likes me.'

'From what I hear, Danny doesn't like too many people.' She sensed it was a preamble to the real question he wanted to ask. It wasn't long in coming.

'What about the big man. It is him?'

Sara-Jane held her breath.

'I know it is,' he continued. 'You don't have to say. ' There was an anxious silence. 'I want to talk with him.'

The train clanked up to the crossing, tooted long and persistently, displacing the rest of Sante's sentence. How fortuitous, thought Sara-Jane, and she proceeded to take advantage of the interruption by veering onto a different course.

'You're the colour of beetroot, Sante, are you putting on sunscreen?'

Sante knew this turn was merely a postponement, so he played along with it. 'Ken does not use sunscreen.'

'Never mind Ken. His skin's used to it, yours isn't. And you make sure you always wear a cap.'

Sante laughed.

'Sara-Jane, you talk just like my mother.'

*

Sara-Jane wished she could protect Sante from Russell's inevitable rejection. She knew all about rejection, by both parents. It wasn't pretty. But after preaching openness to his mother, she could hardly now behave in the same way. She would tell him tomorrow night over the dinner he cooked. Although that didn't seem right either. You never knew how he might react. She couldn't risk an emotional over-spill, while they were by themselves in the house. Better to take him down to Farrell's for coffee afterwards, and tell him in a public place. The presence of strangers would restrain him.

'What have you planned for tonight?' She asked the question in a nonchalant tone.

'Some students from the New Norcia Agricultural College have invited me out.'

'That's nice.' Even though she was a little disappointed, because this could have been their weekend, it was good that he had made friends with people his own age

Seeing Sante was going out, she decided she might as well put in a couple of hours at work, and catch up on things that needed doing. However Bob called to say the computers were down at the office and the technicians were working on the problem.

'Anyway this is Friday, what're your plans for the night?' Bob's invitation was fortuitous, for when Sante's friends came to the door to collect him, Sara was confronted by a couple of worrying types with rings in their eyebrows and tattoos on their chests. They drove off in a red Lancer. Had she stayed home, she would have fretted all night. At times like these, she decided, being a big sister was not a role she particularly relished.

They went to see *Lost in Translation*. It wasn't Bob's kind of movie. Bob wasn't into cinema. He might have sat through a good documentary but a made-up story … not his cup of tea at all. He spent most of the time shifting weight from one cheek of his bottom to the other. 'I prefer real-life action,' he said, and when he dropped her off, his eyes darted hopefully.

'I wouldn't mind a drink. Are you going to ask me in?' He tugged at the knot of his tie.

At another time, Sara-Jane might have found that kind of body language persuasive, now it left her cold. 'I'm tired,' she said, 'I'm having an early night.'

Once inside, she did not go to bed, but took out a book and did some reading. Although her eyes followed the lines, her mind did not take in the words, intent as it was on listening for a car to pull into the drive and bring Sante back. At around one in the morning, she went to bed and lay awake, waiting. She waited a long time because Sante did not come home.

29

When Sergeant Toohey entered, he did not see the figure; that is, his eye fell on something, a bundle slumped on the table, but he didn't want to look at that. What he saw were the four walls. The same four walls in which he had interrogated hundreds, now higher and starker; and the space had shrunk. He didn't want to be here. The space, designed to intimidate and trap suspected criminals, now was trapping him in no less a way. He just did not want to be here this morning. His ulcer, if ulcer it was, made him feel nauseated, a nausea which had not relented for some three days.

For a moment he thought it was a female: the face was buried in the crook of the right arm, the frame was slight. It was only when he looked at the forearm, exposed by the gathered up sleeve of an expensive woollen sweater and saw a down of fine hair all the way down to the wrist, that he realized it must be a male. He moved a step or two further, until he was breathing over him. That was when the person looked up.

The eyes, blue upon burnt skin in a frame of raven hair, washed with the salt of recent tears, looked up pleadingly. A flush of barely repressible contempt surged to Sergeant Toohey's face. He knew the type all too well; the son of some rich daddy and neurotic fretful mother. Brought up and molly-coddled in some two-storey, air-conditioned mansion in the western suburbs. A typical spoilt brat. It was all over him: the soft skin, the perfect teeth, the feminine lips.

Probably gay, thought Russell. Weak as piss, soft as cheese, someone who would do anything to avoid pain or discomfort. He was sure he would admit to anything, submit to anyone, to satisfy a craving or protect his precious little self from harm. He looked down at the sheet in front of him:

Marzano, Sante
Born 1984
Nationality: Italian

You can't get away from them, he thought. They crop up when you least expect it, and insinuate themselves into your life. He addressed the huddled figure. 'How long do you intend to stay in Australia?'

'I have a student visa for one year. It's on the passport.'

'I can see that. I asked you. You've been found in possession of illegal drugs. Are you aware of the penalties?'

Sante shrugged, an expression by which he meant he didn't know, but the detective interpreted it to be a dismissive *I couldn't care less.*

Sergeant Toohey flew into a rage. 'Don't you get smart with me, you little prick!' He shouted and thumped his fist on the table. A blotch of water spilt out of a glass and ran, worm-like, off the edge of the table and onto the young man's lap. He looked at it.

'Just answer the question.'

'OK, I don't know. I ... not sure.'

'Well I'll tell ya – possession of illicit drugs with intent to sell, that's six years minimum, in this country ...'

'I am not selling. The packet was put in my pocket. I did not know it was there.'

'Yeah, that's what they all say. You expect me to believe that bullshit?' He circled around the young man, his step heavy on the floor, his eyes menacing.

Sante sat there, cowering. New tears appeared in his

eyes.

Nothing aroused the older man's contempt more than emotional appeal. He would have preferred the skinny runt had shown some fighting spirit. He would have respected that. Instead all he got was this gutless Mommy's boy, with soft woman's skin and baby blue eyes. Geez, he hated the type, made him want to puke just to look at him.

Russell realized his reaction was far in excess of what the situation demanded, but he killed the thought at once. As a detective, he considered people's actions, studied their motives, analysed behaviours. When it came to his own attitudes, however, he never considered 'why' questions. Such questions were left to perish in the too-hard basket, under the weight of other similar questions destined never to be answered. It was Russell's way of dealing with a personality that seemed at times to be so convoluted, so tightly wound around itself, as to render him numb.

'Sir.' The young man started to plead, and pursed his bottom lip.

Russell noticed with disgust that his lips had more flesh than one of those magazine cover girls.

'Can I please call my sister? She will worry about me.'

'What you need is a lawyer, never mind your sister.' Russell Toohey left the room. Sweat was pouring out of him. Damp patches had appeared in the shirt under his armpits. He needed something to calm his nerves. He went to his office, got a Panadol packet out of his coat pocket, walked to the water dispenser in the corridor and filled a plastic cup. As he tilted his head back to drink he saw his daughter at the enquiry desk.

'What are you doing here?' Even as the words trooped automatically out of his mouth, the penny, which had been hanging precariously over the dark side of his consciousness, came down with a deafening ping. He'd better have another tablet.

*

Nothing was said between them on the way home. They did not turn to look at each other, for they were ashamed. To find themselves together in the presence of that putrefaction of a man, and realize they were made brother and sister by his violence, was more than they could adjust to. It was as if they had been divested of their garments and their shame was displayed to the world. Nothing so trifling as a fig leaf sufficed to cover it. They felt violated, singled out in the herd by a freakish destiny. Bad blood united them and shame stopped them from seeking comfort in one another.

A somnolence descended upon Sante and, as soon as he staggered into the apartment, he slumped on the couch and promptly fell asleep. His cheek rested on a Turkish green cushion, his mouth slack.

Let him stay that way, oblivious to pain, to a wasted world of posturing, of rancour and self-hate. Let him escape back to San Sisto, to sit on the balcony overlooking the piazza, shadowed by the baroque façade of the Chiesa Madre, with its statue of the Virgin Mary looking as if she were hiding a pregnancy beneath folds of elaborate marble garments. Let him retreat to that world, where such absurdities and contradictions are granted the gravitas of stone. Let Sante find solace in the jovial face of Don Alfio, sitting outside the Bar Ciro with his friends, beneath mustard coloured umbrellas advertising *Digestivo Averna*.

No such relief for Sara-Jane. Fortunately, she had her own way of staying on course. She remembered that on her desk was a job advertisement, seeking an anchor for a new travel show on Channel 10. Someone who had seen her being interviewed on TV about some tourist issue had suggested she might wish to apply. Of course she would. This was an opportunity to move on and out of a situation. Two moves in one. She took out her laptop and started to work on her CV. The task absorbed her totally. Thank God for work.

*

He woke up in the early evening, feeling puffy and moody. He looked out of the window, across the trees and the green lawn to the river that carried its waters to the sea. A boat was returning from the vineyards of the Swan Valley, with its cargo of well-wined merrymakers playing the last charades on a day that had been full of them. Life flowed on inexorably.

He saw Sara-Jane attacking the keyboard with absorbed intensity and, despite himself, made first contact by way of a whinge. 'You always work, Sara-Jane, always work, also on Sunday.'

His sister did not take her eyes off the screen. 'If I don't do it now, it won't get done. I've made sandwiches for you.'

But Sante was not hungry, even though he had not eaten for nearly twenty-four hours. He sat up on the couch, wrapped a rug around his shoulders and looked across at Sara-Jane.

'Are you OK?' She asked without looking up, making it clear it was a non-question which required a non-answer.

So he kept quiet, but he wasn't OK. He wanted to hug her and be hugged. It was, of course, the need of a child. Adults were not expected to have such urges, certainly not in this country. And really, he could see the advantage in such attitudes. Life was a daily test and you were meant to pass it all by yourself, so it was a practical and wise thing to toughen yourself and fortify your defences. But clearly it was also a question of pride. There was dignity in being independent and self-contained. Both his natural father and his sister were fitted with bulletproof armour. Perhaps he should consider working on some himself. Was he too weak? Did he not have the stomach for it? It was a sign of how this new environment was changing him that he thought this way at all.

Sara-Jane finally looked up from her intended career path, and fixed him with a stare. 'I told you he's a pig.'

Sante's shoulders rose and his neck sank between them, as if his sister had just landed a whiplash across his back. He knew he was expected to hate Russell for what he had done to his mother, for the way he treated his sister and him, for being the person he was. And yet, when he looked inside himself, he saw a man's tortured face, and felt no trace of hate, only sadness.

'Now you know why we didn't want you to meet him ...' She spoke softly, still seated at the keyboard. *We*: so much said in a simple pronoun. Sara-Jane and his mother in league to protect him. In Sicily such a stance was interpreted as a sign of care and affection. Here it seemed condescending, lacking in respect, or at least in faith. Or maybe he was at last growing up and acquiring an adult ego, fragile enough to need massaging. Was he glad or sad? Surely it had to be a good thing that he was seeing life from a new perspective.

'I am glad I met him, anyway,' he said.

Sara-Jane scrutinized him from where she sat. She looked puzzled and waited for him to elaborate.

But how could he make clear feelings which he himself

was struggling to comprehend? It was all he could do to add what he had already said. 'I wanted to know.'

Sara-Jane wanted more from him. She wanted blood and all she got was milksop. His passiveness, if passiveness it was, exasperated her and she gave in to acrimony. 'Even when he realised who you were, he just walked out. Not a hint of a sorry. Bastard!'

'He cannot, Sara, he is trapped. I feel sorry for him.'

Sara-Jane hated sanctimony. 'I suppose you are ready to forgive him.' She stretched her neck toward him, her irony fuelled by anger.

'It is my mother who must forgive him.'

'Well, not much of a chance of that happening in this life.' She shouldn't have said that, but then he deserved it for taking the high moral ground. Besides, it made him seem so old: a dried-up old man at eighteen. The simple fact was that she didn't want a saint for a brother. She wanted him to be normal, like other young men who reacted and got angry; who defended their space and had ambitions. 'What are you going to do with yourself, Sante?'

'How do you mean?'

'Just that – what career path are you going to choose?' Sara-Jane bit her bottom lip. She sounded like a schoolteacher.

'There are many things I want to do Sara, many, but I don't want to burden my journey carrying hate.' Surely Sante Marzano was heading for bloody sainthood.

Something was missing in him, he was incapable of hating. Too many other feelings got in the way, and distracted him. But then, perhaps it was simply an issue of self-preservation: hating just took too much effort. Maybe he just had a great need to love. Or was it self-love after all? Was he so monumentally conceited that he thought he could rise above ordinary humans and operate in the rarefied air of pure spirit?

Sara-Jane was beginning to see his goodness as a handicap, a conceit, a perversion. Unless he wised up to the ways of the real world, someone, or more likely a mob, would surely lynch him.

30

It hadn't been a great day at the races for Danny, his sure-things had turned out to be duds, so he vented frustration on the car horn, as a tractor chugged slowly up the drive and he was stuck behind it. He put his head through the window and yelled. 'Take your time, son, I got all day!'

Sante sidled the tractor.

Danny passed so close that Sante, in trying to avoid him, swung hard to his left and nearly slid off the side into the storm-water ditch.

Russell sat in the passenger seat. His arm, thick and sprinkled with freckles, hung out of the car. 'Watch it Danny, you just about hit him.'

Danny laughed, a nasty little laugh he had, that so irked him. 'Well, why doesn't he get out of the way, the little wanker.'

'He was – what's your rub with him?'

'We should have had our stables here, like we was promised, if it wasn't for him.'

'What do you mean?'

'I gotta hunch that the idea for planting the olives came from this little shit. What would Ole Brother know about olives?'

Russell spat out of the window, into the gravel dirt outside. 'Don't be stupid, Danny.'

'Well, you ask around and people will tell you. Old Clem's besotted with him. Something sick in that situation, I reckon. He sets him up in the house, lets him use his dead son's car. What does that tell you?'

'Tells me nothing.' Russell wiped sweat off his face with the rolled-up sleeve of his shirt. 'What's the point in leaving a car in the garage for years?'

Clem's summons to the house at first gladdened Danny. Big brother might have some good news for him, come to his senses at last, acknowledge him as his closest surviving relative and bequeath him his fortune. Danny's imagination served his strongest desires.

Clem was outside, perched three steps up a ladder, shears in hand. God knows how he managed to get up there, when he could hardly walk. He was busy pruning the massive honeysuckle, which had been spared in the demolition of the old cottage. Danny cleared his throat, but Clem did not turn around, and continued to reach for branches and cut away. On the back of his hand the veins were blue and thick and looked nicked in places. His skin was coarse and leathery. That sort of thing made Danny's blood curdle, another of the many discomfitures he had to put up with in order to keep Clem sweet. Not that there was anything sweet about Clem. And the fact he kept him waiting now didn't augur well.

Danny cleared his throat once again. 'Hi, Clem, you wanted to see me?'

Franzetti made no response. He took his time before he finally turned on the ladder and let his lame leg dangle by the rung. He still had remarkable balance. 'Are you any good at reading the signs, Danny? It says 30 Ks an hour at the gate.'

'I didn't do anything.'

'Yes you did. You nearly ran my man off the road. I saw it with my own eyes.'

'What do you expect me to do? He goes and parks himself in the middle of the track.'

'I expect you to behave like a grown man, Danny. Now you quit fooling around or I'm gonna have to ask you to take your horses somewhere else, get it?'

Danny O'Rourke's smiled. He got it alright. It couldn't be any clearer. It was a rare smile, because in Danny's world there was nothing to smile about. The world was rotten. The world had treated him badly. Danny O'Rourke knew he had no power, absolutely none. People could wipe their feet on him, just like big, mad Clem Franzetti was doing right now. Well, when you're down that low, when you've hit the bottom, you know there's only one move you can make, upwards. So you make your move a good one, one that will deliver the result you want. And in the end there's only one thing that counts: power.

You know what, Clemmy, thought Danny through his grin, *everybody cowers in the face of the ultimate power.* Everybody, including you – including that little runt down there, who's probably been kissing your arse more times than I've been broke. These thoughts produced Danny O'Rourke's smile.

'Yeah,' said Danny, 'I get it.'

Back at the stable, Russell was getting impatient. 'That took you a while. What did the old man want?'

'Nothing. He's just a cranky old bastard.' Danny spat on the ground and covered the glob by pushing a small mound of sawdust over it with his foot. He pressed it down.

31

Inflight's third did not satisfy Russell. That wasn't the way the race was supposed to have played out. Tommy was meant to keep him back with the pack and come home in the straight. Instead he was off like a shot, hit the front early and of course couldn't last the distance.

At the bar, he demanded answers. 'What was that all about?'

Danny played dumb. 'Whatch'you mean?'

'It was a lousy ride. You'd better have a talk to Tommy.'

'He reckons he couldn't hold him back.'

'Crap. What sort of jockey is he? I lost good dollars on that.'

'So did I.' Zlatan complained. 'I thought your horse was a cert.'

'Yeah, this was gonna be Inflight's race.'

'You can never be certain, Russ.'

The truth was, this was one race Danny couldn't afford to let him win. He needed money – quick – and Inflight wasn't going to get it for him.

'What're you doing to that horse, Danny?'

'Nothing. It's the rider that's crap.'

'If you want my opinion, Inflight's getting too old.' Zlatan had his own opinion. 'About time youse blokes upgraded.'

'You need big bucks for that.' Danny gave a shake of the head.

'Yeah…'

'What about old Franzetti?'

'Not a chance. Big Brother's got other interests these days: religion and young men. Bad combination.'

'What do you mean?' Zlatan's eyes widened.

'Seen the new kid he's got working on that farm?'

Russell ran the back of his finger on the frothy surface of the pint in front of him. 'Don't you start on him again, Danny.'

But Danny put his face to the froth of his beer and continued to address Zlatan. 'Tell you what, he's no farm-hand, if you ask me.'

'What 're you sayin'?'

Danny dropped his wrist inside the sleeve of his black leather jacket and cupped his hand. 'I'm saying he's one of them for sure.'

Russell turned a lethal eye on him. 'Bullshit!'

'No bullshit about it. I can tell that sort of thing a mile away. I seen how Big Brother's falling all over 'm, too. Tell you what, Zlat, I think there's some' queer about that set up.' Danny chuckled, amused by his own pun.

'And I think you're full of shit, Danny.'

'Ease off, Russell...'

'You're talking a lot of crap. I'm sick of it. I hate the way you go on, always slaggin' off people. People you don't even know.'

Something was bugging his mate this morning but Danny didn't dwell on it. He was too caught up in his own shit to bother with other people's. 'What's it to you, anyway, Russ?'

'Nothing. I'm just sayin'. You don't even know this kid.'

'Well I know one thing, I'm not about to let anyone cheat me out of what's mine.'

The threatening tone made Russell turn away from his beer and look at Danny, and he was surprised to find on that usually slack resentful face an intensity he had never noticed before. It made the big man nervous. 'What's eatin' you today, Danny?'

Danny drank down his beer. It was time to go and cash his win.

As he strode off, Zlatan turned to Russell. 'I'd keep an eye on Danny if I was you. He can be trouble.'

'Yeah, nothing else but. What's he done now?'

'Nothing, might be just … nothing. Me brother Branko and him have been thick as thieves lately. It worries me.'

'Well, that'd worry me too …'

'Me brother is mad as a rabid dog and Danny … well, you know Danny. When them two get together … could be trouble.'

'Yeah, I reckon …' Russell held his breath and winced.

'What's wrong?'

'Pain in the groin's been bugging me the last coupla weeks. Probly an infection of some sort.'

'Yeah, you'd better go and get it seen to.'

*

The thing about doing someone in was that, like everything else, practice made it easier. With Clem's loony kid he had hummed and ahed for months. His prevarication was not over whether to go through with it – he had made up his mind about it months before – but on how to get it done without getting caught. That was the thing.

The kid was a nutter, so he was no great loss to the world. Not that it was Danny's responsibility to look after the world, anyhow. The kid was on a downhill slide to self-destruction, and all that Danny did was provide him the means to do it quickly and put him out of his misery. The fact that the mother was caught in the updraught was unfortunate, but when you had a plan to carry out you didn't stop to consider collateral damage. George Bush couldn't afford to start worrying about how many would die in Iraq - he might as well have given up his job.

Now this new guy, the foreigner, this Johnny-come-lately who got the boss's ear and heart ... you could tell he had his mind set on big brother's millions. Danny's worst nightmare was coming true. Senile obsessive Clem might be contemplating the unthinkable, and adopt the kid. Clem Franzetti was getting more strange and unpredictable every day. What can you say about a seventy-four year old who started planting a bloody olive orchard, carved a church out of a rock, and spent hours underground looking at a statue? Weird or what! Danny wondered how much that whole project had cost already. Money down the drain. Danny's money. It was time to act, before it was all lost.

There was no doubt in Danny O'Rourke's mind that life had dealt him some pretty lousy cards. It wasn't the fact that, as far back as he could remember, he had to live under the shadow of someone, even if it was his own ambitious mother, old Vic Franzetti, and then Clem Franzetti. The galling thing was he knew he was a better man than any of them. Not just sharper – Clem was as thick as a brick – he was superior, with more ideas, more imagination than all of them put together, and yet rotten luck had been a bitch to him.

At every turn, just as he thought things would change, he found himself sidelined, cast-off, thwarted, put upon. Yeah, life was a lottery, or how could you explain the fact that a dimwit like Clem Franzetti, a lunatic with half his screws loose, was in a position to control people's lives?

If only he had a bit more luck, things might have turned out differently for Danny O'Rourke. Luck and people, they were the double bane of his life. People just didn't warm to him, despite the fact that, back in the days when she exerted that kind of power over his young life, his mother's dotage left no doubt in his mind that he was special. She made him believe, by words and by suggestion, that he could do no wrong, that great things were in store for him, that all he had to do was to locate the store and claim what was his.

He must have been about eight. His mother was dressing him to meet old Vic Franzetti for the first time. She had him all trussed up in a white shirt which he had outgrown.

Danny hated any constrictions around his neck and when his mother went to button up his shirt he had squealed about the stiff collar, which tore at the skin of his neck. 'I can't wear this, Mummy, it's too scratchy.'

'Don't be silly darling, you're going to meet a very important man.' She tried again. 'We can't have you looking scruffy, can we now?'

Such reasonableness only served to precipitate Danny's incipient tantrum. He threw himself down and started writhing on the floor, screaming.

His mother picked him up from behind and dragged him back to her. 'We're doing this for you, Danny, it's all for you.' She arm-locked his head and held him hard against her belly as she did up the top button. And when she released him he started pulling at the collar with his middle fingers trying to rip it loose, so she slapped his face several times until he stopped.

That night, after the ordeal, as she was helping him undress, she said, 'Now, that wasn't too bad was it, darling? See, you can do anything you want, so long as you set your mind to it.'

It hadn't turned out quite that way. Danny wanted to do big things, have an important job, make lots of money;

but somehow it hadn't come off for him. By his late-twenties he knew there was no store in society but a people-pyramid; and the only way to ease the crush was by clambering over bodies and leaving the masses below. Maybe that's what his mother meant. Her legacy to Danny was to make him believe he was above the ordinary. And the proof came two years ago, when he had shown to himself that when pushed, Danny O'Rourke was capable of deeds that ordinary individuals would balk at, because they lacked the imagination and the courage to carry them out.

For Danny there was no room for guilt or regret. His amorality was proof of superior breeding. He regarded himself above remorse. Let the middle-class struggle with it. He had better things to do with his life. So, whatever action he took to further his ambitions was beyond reproach, beyond moral judgement. What he had done – or rather organised, for it was Branko who had carried it out – did not cause him any soul-searching. Clem's idiot offspring was no loss to the world. As for his long-suffering wife, she was not much good to anyone, least of all herself. So his costly little arrangement with Branko, which had resulted in the car plunging into the Swan River, was worth the expense. Things had worked out, events were slotting into place, big brother Clem was coming round. Then he went overseas and came back a changed man.

Danny had no doubt all these changes: the new house, the olive trees, and that spooky shrine, were connected with that trip and the foreign kid. Clem had always been weird, anyway, but he came back from his trip positively wacko. And the kid was no fool either; he knew what he was doing, he knew how to play the game, despite looking as if butter wouldn't melt in his mouth. Before you knew it, he would diddle Danny of his rightful inheritance. Like hell he would. He didn't know what was coming to him. 'You gotta fight for your rights in this world, Danny,' his mother said, 'or else you get trampled upon.'

His mother talked a lot of shit too, like everybody, but some things she said made sense. Luckily, he had a trick or two up his sleeve, all the more lethal because nobody took him seriously; nobody imagined him to have any interest beyond the racecourse or the roulette table. Weird thing was, his perceived weakness turned out to be part of his armour. So it was in his interest to let everyone think he was weak; a contemptuous little shit, incapable of doing serious damage, of carrying out the perfect crime in order to get rid of a nuisance … or two.

32

Every Saturday morning, Sante looked out for the big Toyota with the roo bar, followed it with the margin of his eye as he groomed the chestnut mare, brushing her down, dousing her with the hose in the warm sunshine, taking her through her paces in the paddock. Across the distance man and animal looked … together.

Russell never acknowledged him, not a wave, not a glance. Was it possible he never, ever thought of his natural son, just on the other side of the half-built wall?

So close and yet so far. He had travelled halfway across the globe to connect with this land and this man, only to be thwarted by a waist-high wall of resistance. And his own sister wasn't being much help either.

'Look, Sante.' Sara-Jane gave him a look of impatience. 'He doesn't want to have anything to do with …' She diluted 'you' with 'all that stuff'. 'He's in denial and wants to stay that way. I'm afraid there's nothing you can do about it.'

'I know,' He looked disconsolate. 'I know that, but …'

Sara-Jane became exasperated with him. 'Don't let this thing take over your life.'

It already had. All obsessions are plugholes, *un foro di scarico*, to drain away the neuroses of living. Perhaps too, this fixation of his with that stranger-father, came from a need to be approved of, and conversely, from a refusal to accept rejection.

His motives were eminently self-serving. So really he needed to think less of his needs and more of those of others. Like those of his mother, who would be justifiably hurt by his persistence in linking up with the man who defiled her. And yet, viewed from this end of the world his mother's profile had changed too. She was no longer the infallible figure she had once seemed. Guilt and confusion made him mellow.

'Hey, look – ' Sante made a decision. 'Before I leave …'

Sara-Jane gave a start. 'Where are you going now?'

'Back to Italy. I only have four more weeks ...'

She had forgotten. Was it already time for him to go?

'Will you take a holiday with me?'

Sara-Jane had never taken a holiday in her life. She had travelled of course, as part of her job, but no holidays. Holidays were for bored, shiftless people, or retired old couples looking to fill time. 'A holiday? Where?'

'I don't know. I want to see more of Australia. Will you come too?' Sante was a child again, how could she deny those pleading eyes?

'Yes, let's take a holiday.' Already the heaviness inside was lifting, 'I'll take some time off work.'

*

The day of the accident, a misty Saturday morning, Sante was on the roof cleaning the gutters that drained into the rainwater tank, when he heard a call coming from the other side of the wall and saw someone gesticulating frantically. It was impossible to see who it was through the mist.

At first, he thought of Danny, because he could not imagine Russell calling out. He scuttled down the steps and ran across. Just over the other side of the wall, he found the big man bending over the mare that had slumped to the ground, its legs kicking the air. She must have tried to jump the wall and given the poor visibility, misjudged the height.

Russell had his shirt off and was using the sleeve to stop blood trickling from a gash in its right foreleg. He took Sante's hand into his bloodied one and pressed it onto the cloth. 'Hold it there, I'll be back in a minute.'

It occurred to Sante that the first-ever physical contact with his father was smeared with horse's blood. Sante knelt on the damp earth, his hand over the wound, pressing back the blood flow, feeling the animal's belly rise and fall.

Russell hurried back with a metal box marked First Aid. He sprung it open, took out disinfectant and bathed the wound, swabbing away dirt with a bud of cotton wool, starting from the outer periphery of the gash and working his way in to Sante's hand.

'Let's have a look.' His voice was calm, his expression dreamy.

Sante removed the cloth. The blood flow had slowed. Russell went to work on the wound with quick, gentle flicks of the hand. The horse stirred, kicking the sand with a front hoof, attempting to raise its head.

'Sit still.' Russell realized the antiseptic irritated the open wound, so he proceeded more gently. When he was done he raised his head. 'Are you any good at dressing?'

Sante didn't understand.

Russell took out a wad of gauze from the box and held it up. 'See this? Wrap it around the leg, while I hold it steady.'

'Me?' The younger man looked like a nursing aid who's been asked to perform surgery.

'Yeah, you do it and I'll try and settle her.'

As Sante carefully wound the bandage around the animal's leg, Russell gave directions. 'A bit firmer than that.' He rested its head on his lap, stroked it gently along the neck and spoke to the animal soothingly. 'Easy, easy girl. You'll be OK. Just ... hang in there ... the vet'll be here soon.'

The horse stopped kicking, giving Sante the chance to quickly wrap several layers of gauze over the wound. He then he secured it with a safety pin.

'That'll do for the time being.' Russell looked up across the belly of the horse. He wiped his cheek with the back of his hand. He grinned. 'You've got blood smeared all over your face. Janey'll think I hit ya.'

That trace of a smile on the big man's face gave Sante such a start his body gave a tremor and his elbow grazed Russell's naked forearm.

The older man instinctively retrieved his arm, unable to cope with even this little contact. Sante looked into those tired eyes and saw, with some surprise, that the anger was gone, leaving only confusion in its wake. At the end of a long, uncomfortable pause, punctuated by the panting of the horse, Russell spoke. 'Do you like horses?'

'Yes, very much.'

'You own one?'

'No, unfortunately.'

'You live in the city, I suppose.'

'A small town. We have land too, not big like this, a small land, with olive trees.'

Russell glanced across the wall. 'This must feel like home then.'

'No, it is different. It is different.'

The man gave him a blank look. He clearly didn't understand.

'Our trees are different,' said Sante.

'Years ago you didn't see one olive tree around here, now everyone's going mad planting them. Soon they'll glut the market. That's what happened to the wine industry.'

New country, different perspective. No, it wasn't that either. The boy might be connected to this man by blood, but a chasm divided them. It wasn't a question of what he had done, or that they had so little in common; it was simply that they were of a different nature, they thought differently. An ocean separated them, and he wasn't sure it could be crossed, or that he wanted to.

The same ocean divided him from Sara-Jane, and yet the moment she stood before the old house at Rovaro and said, 'I have seen this house before', at that instant the ocean had vanished and he understood the connection between them transcended space. No such moment would ever occur between him and this man. They were destined never to connect. Sad.

Crows staged an angry palaver on the gum tree, their croaking intensified in the mist. It sounded vaguely like a dirge or perhaps a threat from some unseen enemy. It stirred the horse. Its eyeballs spun in their sockets. It started to kick again, as if attempting to get up and take flight.

'Keep still.' Russell 's tone was firm. He pressed the head of the animal against his belly, and inclining his cheek to its nostrils. 'Won't be long now.'

But the horse butted and struggled to be released. Russell let go. Freed from the man's hold, the animal made one last attempt to get up, but the effort seemed to sap her energies. She grunted, fell back, gave out what sounded like a bovine bellow and fell back. The eyes remained open but they were blank.

Sante tried to read the older man's eyes but found the same empty stare as the animal's.

'So…' said Russell, as if concluding a discussion.

Over the drive came the putter of a motor, a silence, the slamming of a door and the outline of a figure advanced through the mist, calling, 'You there, Russell?'

Russell turned to his son and spoke softly, like the whisper of the saddest secret. 'So, that's it then.'

259

33

For a take-out job you could count on Branko. By nature a lazy man, he liked the woman to go on top, so he could just lie there and let her do all the work. It got to a point where the girls at Soho Nights Escorts complained that doing it with Branko was exhausting and wanted penalty rates. But that was another story.

The prospect of a new job never failed to bring out the best in Branko. All at once he was energized, his perceptions were sharpened. Energies which lay dormant for months, in the sensual indolence that dominated the routine of his life, suddenly stirred and a new Branko emerged.

One might speculate that Branko's problems could be channelled through work, artistic expression or, at worst, through addiction or vice. Unfortunately he was not endowed with talent, nor was he strapped with conspicuous vices. He was not a drinker; gambling required too much concentration and he had so much contempt for the druggies he supplied, that the notion of winding up like one of them was enough to put him off for life. It was true he spent whole afternoons – he liked to be in bed by eleven – in the velvety chambers of Soho Nights Escorts, but even that cloyed after a while, and all that perfume irritated his sinuses. So, it was fair to say the occasional contract job was his secret vice and a handy little earner it was too.

What absorbed him completely was not so much its execution as the preparation. He planned each job meticulously, leaving nothing to chance. Of course his was a risky business, a risk compounded by the fact that when dealing with people you could never trust them completely. In fact, Branko had little trust in people. So he tried to minimize the people-factor by working on his own, which was not always possible. His few failures – and there were some, no use denying it – had largely been the result of people letting him down.

Like the time he was contracted to take out the wife of a mining millionaire and got the mistress instead. All because the husband – who was due to fly out to Manila that morning – was rushed to the hospital by the wife, with a burst appendix, and the mistress had gone to the house to fetch some stuff for the office. How unlucky can you get!

No amount of planning can insure you against that kind of thing. As a result, the husband was left with a wife he didn't want and the tart he wanted to shack up with got a hole in the head. Of course the lucky thing about that kind of mistake was that there was little comeback for the client. He could hardly go to the law and complain his screw had been taken out instead of his wife, could he now? Branko apologized and offered to do the wife for free, fair is fair.

The silly bugger wouldn't hear of it and said he wasn't going to pay up, then started to get personal. 'It's you who should be compensating me for making a mess of it, you stupid numbskull.'

In the end Branko had to take him out. Which wasn't ideal, because he never got the money; but at least he covered his tracks, and in the profession everybody understood that Branko was not the kind you messed about with. Even his brother was impressed with the way he handled the situation, although on the surface he made a big song and dance about taking on a side-job without telling him.

His brother Zlatan would have to be the most scrupulous man he knew. If it was up to him, Branko'd be starving, he really would, because he was only prepared to do score-settling jobs within the business. These were rare enough in a place like Perth, and poorly paid. At most, an insider job, say, for a bikie gang, paid five thousand and they expected the extras, like getting rid of the body.

The privates, they'll pay four times that, even more, if they were desperate enough. The best one was old Duffy, the nifty dresser from South Africa, who used to hire him to take out a number of diamond-dealing rivals. What a gentleman he was! Ten thousand down-payment, and ten in cash within an hour of job completion. They're the sort of clients you want; they bring respect to the profession. Unfortunately Duffy got into bad company. A big-time dealer from the Middle East tried to hire Branko to do the dirty on Duffy. Of course Branko wouldn't have a bar of that, but the dapper Duffy got done all the same: his light plane crash-landed somewhere near Lake Argyle. In retrospect, Branko might as well have taken on the job; in his profession scruples were bad for business.

When Danny came to him with this job, he had to think a bit, something he didn't enjoy doing at the best of times. Danny still owed him from the last job when he did some work on the Mercedes – not the best of cars to do that kind of work on. But he did it, and what a beautiful job it turned out to be. Responded like a clock, went flying off the bridge at precisely the moment it was meant to. Of course Zlatan knew nothing about that particular job. He'd go off his head if he knew. Too risky. Yeah right, as if protection and drugs weren't risky! Anyway, you could limit the risk by going about your job professionally.

He hated doing it though. No, not the jobs. What he hated was deceiving his brother, but he had to. The kind of money Zlatan allowed him wouldn't even pay for his visits to the Soho Nights.

Anyway, he didn't trust Danny and he didn't like the idea of putting out a guy who worked on the property of his rich relative. Experience had taught him to try and steer clear of family feuds, though you couldn't avoid them altogether. A lot of private jobs involved a family member. So at first he said no, until Danny came up with $5,000 down payment, in cash. You couldn't say no to that kind of money. God knows where he got it, seeing as he was always broke. Anyhow, that was none of his business. Branko took the money and so there was no going back, he was committed to it; his professional integrity was at stake.

*

For two consecutive Saturdays he watched every move of his subject from the loft of the stable next door, sitting on a steel girder some six metres off the floor, in front of a louvered window, which looked over a half-completed wall, on the olive farm. Strange thing, while he was watching, his subject – a skinny-legged kid with dark hair – looked up and stared directly in his direction, as if he could see Branko sitting behind the high frosted glass louvers. It was impossible, because of the thickness of the glass and the layer of sooty dust on both sides of it. The first time Branko thought it was a coincidence, but when he kept doing it, it just about spooked him.

Branko had to remind himself the subject was just a skinny kid in a baggy T-shirt. What business could Danny possibly have with him? Lucky that Branko was not by nature an inquisitive man, so he didn't dwell on that too much. Besides, there were other things to distract him.

He sat up there on the dusty window ledge, which stayed dusty even though he gave the area a good sweep with a brush. It was still pretty unhygienic. The air was thick and damp like soup. Worst of all was the stink rising from the floor and wafting towards the roof; it just about scorched his nostrils. Those horses must have been constipated or something. Or maybe they fed them putrid broad beans. A most uncomfortable experience, anyhow. Luckily the worst was over. The night before, he slipped across the fence and into the farm shed, to work on the car. By the time Danny arrived at the stables to whisk him away to his own car back in Midland, everything was ready.

34

Franzetti withdrew into himself. He even stopped reading his own magazine. All that frenzied carrying on, the posturing, the melodrama, the false smiles ... all images of a confused and confusing world: insane, self-destructive. It was all a smokescreen to hide the profound state of unhappiness into which the world had dipped.

The past few months had given him a simple, yet profound, truth: the physical world was an obfuscation; a poor conceit for the real world of the spirit. The body did not matter. So the fact that his body was giving up on him was of no import. There was the Virgin Mary; that was real. And there was Sante. The Madonna of the Olives and Sante Marzano were bound together. The young man was not aware of his destiny, but for Clem Franzetti there was no doubt: one day soon, something in Sante would awaken and then the connection would be made clear to him. It was time to visit the grotto.

He trundled down the track as the sun stood poised atop a purple pyre of clouds and silver-eyes flitted from one branch to the other, dispersing sibylline whispers through the foliage. When he reached the courtyard before the gate he stood there contemplating the Madonna through the iron bars. There she was, safe from thieves and marauders, waiting for him, an expression of perennial gentleness upon her lovely face. He pressed the remote with his thumb and the gate rose. He limped in. Her presence filled him with joy every time.

A spirit was moving through the Madonna of the Olives. Clem Franzetti had noticed it for weeks now. The eyes had lost their sky-blue colour: in its place were two tiny black pools with a rippled surface. If you concentrated on one eye for long enough, you could see specks of white light gliding along the surface. Mesmerised by the vision, he lost all connection with time and entered the moment eternal.

What brought him back was a sudden tremor, although at first he could not tell whether the movement was in the Madonna or the surrounding space. Surely the Virgin Mary was not levitating before his eyes! Memory took him back to 1968 and the Meckering earthquake, when he was caught standing on a ladder against the external wall of his house, paint brush in hand, reaching for the gutter, and suddenly the brick walls swayed, the ground heaved and sank from under his feet. But this was no earthquake; this was something far too mysterious to be a natural phenomenon. He looked again into the Madonna's eyes and he felt faint with joy. The eyes were speaking to him with messages more intimate, more eloquent than words.

At last, Clemente Franzetti, the time has come. You are about to witness the final revelation, the moment to which your life has been leading: when matter burns and all that is left is the fire of the spirit.

The Madonna shivered and a flake fell from under her eye. Then tiny specs appeared at the exposed chip and ran down her cheek like tear drops. No, thought Clem, not another crying Madonna! The Holy Mother of his imaginings was glorious, happy, radiant. He took a few paces forward, stretched out his hand in a gesture of supplication. The tips of his trembling fingers touched the fold-covered knee, he pressed and his index sank into a hollow crevice.

Clem retrieved his hand, as if had been bitten by a snake and stood there too terrified to move. A gash had opened on the knee, it was teeming with tiny white ants which, caught by the light, went scampering for cover into the shell. He realized, with horror, that the shell was paper-thin, that the statue had been hollowed out from the inside by the voracious termites.

Instinctively, he braced himself to the Madonna at the bottom with both hands in a desperate attempt protect it from danger, or perhaps, in an equally vain attempt to shake off the offending crawlies.

More patches came way, exposing a fissure where the garment folded above the knee, from which a rill of sawdust poured out. Other flakes fell away to reveal a hidden world, quivering like sequins in the sun. Having recovered from shock, Clem flailed at the insects with his walking stick. Sawdust and insects flew off the statue, clouding the air of the grotto. A smouldering smell distracted Clem. He turned and saw that a candle had fallen, setting the drapes alight. As he considered this danger, the statue teetered, wavered and crumbled down on its own pile of sawdust. Thousands of termites fuelled the fire, and flames hissed menacingly. Clem watched, paralysed.

Sara-Jane felt light and heavy. Light with excitement that she had been offered a new job: producing her own TV travel show, and she couldn't wait to share her good news with Sante. She felt heavy at the prospect of another session in the editorial room with Bob.

At 4.30pm Sante left a message on Sara-Jane's mobile: Wondering what to eat tonight? Problem solved, your brother will cook for you. Secret dish!

Sara, who was heading for the editing room with Bob, texted him back: Thanks, my stomach's rumbling in anticipation. What will I do when you go back?

To which Sante promptly replied: Come to visit me.

Sara smiled into her hand.

Bob, who had gone ahead of her, as Sara's pace was slowed down by this communication, called back to her. 'Come on Sara, we haven't got all day.'

Sara-Jane ignored him. What was the point: in two weeks' time she would be gone, away from this work atmosphere that had become unbearable, and into the exciting world of television.

'Coming,' she said, and hurried to catch up, hoping this would not be another lengthy tug-of-war. A vain hope, for as soon as Bob set eyes on the first item, a piece on the marron farmers of Pemberton, he started finding fault. 'I thought we were going to feature the new Indian Ocean cruises.'

'We're leaving that one for a while, after the tsunami …'

'Nonsense, that's one more reason we should do it. Our advertisers expect us to push it.'

Only two weeks ago he had argued the opposite case,

but she let it pass. She just wanted to get home. 'Fine.' She was unconvinced. Tucking a stray strand of hair behind her right ear, she stood up. 'I'll come in tomorrow and work on it.'

'It can wait until Monday.'

'On Monday I won't be here.'

'Why? Where are you off to this time?' He knew very well where she was going. They'd had an argument about it, another one. Now he was pretending not to know, just to irritate her.

'I'm going to the Kimberleys with my brother. I told you that last week.'

'How am I supposed to remember that? How long for?'

'Just four days.'

'This is a busy time for us. You could have chosen a better time.'

Sara-Jane looked at her watch, in less than an hour Sante would be home.

*

Sante slipped the mobile in the side pocket of his shorts, slid the roller door closed and pressed the padlock shut. He headed for the car, thinking of the ingredients he would need for the pasta marinara he had promised Sara-Jane: prawns, mussels, parsley... What else? White wine, of course. As for garlic, Sara-Jane was bound to have it, although he had better get some, just in case. No need for chilies, though. He had some left over from the previous week's dish. There was no chance Sara-Jane would have used it, because she never cooked. That would be his worry about her, once he got back to Sicily: how poorly she ate.

He was accompanied to the car by the image of Sara-

Jane sitting down to dinner, taking in the scents, her nose twitching in anticipation, giving that emphatic 'Hmm! Hmm!' of pleasure when the first forkful passed her lips. That would be his reward.

As he backed the car away from the wall and turned towards the drive, he was arrested by a voice. At first he thought it might be a white cockatoo up on the gum trees that lined the side of the property, but then he saw Clem Franzetti running down the slope, treading on the damp spring weeds growing around the trees and almost stumbling. He stopped on a mound and waved the walking stick above his head, as if pointing to some apparition on the horizon, which only he could see.

Sante stretched his neck through the side window trying to hear over the idling of the engine. Too far to hear; but he saw the urgency in the frantic waving of Franzetti's arms. And then, further up the slope, he glimpsed smoke coiling over the grotto.

*

Armed with binoculars, Branko sat in his car the other side of the highway, saw the old man's wild agitation and swore aloud. He hated the unexpected interfering with his plans. It was like a bad omen. He regretted having set the timer to seven minutes from the start of the engine. There was a reason for it. Had the blast occurred when the engine was turned on, it might have set the store up in flames, creating a conflagration. There was no point in being destructive for its own sake. Branko hated messy things. It was better for the blast to occur well away from the farm.

Well anyway, all that was immaterial now. That crazy fruitcake had managed to sabotage his plan. Less than five minutes left on the timer, and the subject was taking the car in the wrong bloody direction. When he reached the grotto, he got out of the car and followed the old man into the cave. Branko could not watch what was about to occur. He slammed both hands over his face.

In the pandemonium that ensued, Branko found time to congratulate himself on the precision of his timing. He waited for the two men to come running out of the grotto, but no one did. Instead, a cloud of dust whooshed through the air like a tornado, blotting out the landscape all the way up to the house.

As the cloud lifted, he saw the blast had blown a gaping hole in the wall of the grotto, and the roof had collapsed. The two men must have been crushed under the rubble. This was not his day, nor theirs. However, as he drove away, Branko was gratified by the thought he was still entitled to the remainder of the money, most of which he had already allocated.

36

When Sara-Jane walked into her South Perth apartment just before six, expecting to be met by the wafting smells of cooking garlic and herbs, she found an empty house, with its all-too-familiar staleness. On the answering machine were several messages, but nothing from Sante.

She called his mobile. No answer. She texted him: 'Where's the food you promised me? Just you wait... I'll punish you with my cooking.'

Her jollity masked a deep anxiety. She resisted the temptation of calling around. In the fridge, she found some eggs and a bunch of rocket. She would make an omelette, just to do something, get busy.

As she got to the stove, the phone rang. It was the New Norcia Agricultural College. Sante had left his watch there when visiting a student in the boarding house the day before and hadn't come back for it.

Sara-Jane slammed down the phone. She didn't like the vibes she was getting. She liked the position in which she found herself even less. Long ago, she decided she would not be a wife, or mother, precisely because she wanted to avoid this kind of situation. Normally she could handle a crisis by self-talk.

OK, so what was the worst thing that could happen here? The worst had never seemed bad enough to panic over, because it concerned herself alone, and she felt she had some control over events. Now things were different, this was her brother, and what happened to him touched her profoundly. Her reality was no longer single. Her world had expanded, the whole was segmented and she was struggling to keep her eye on the pieces. What *was* the worst

272

that could happen? She didn't want to think.

By eight o'clock Sara-Jane could no longer stand the wait. An anaemic looking omelette sat on the plate, uneaten. She turned her attention to the telephone. As much as she disliked getting him involved, she had to call Russell. She could hear voices in the background, pub noise. No surprises there.

'Sara-Jane here. I thought you might be on duty.'

'I'm not. Why, what's wrong?'

'Nothing, I hope, I …' She realized how silly it would sound, but went on. 'Do you know of any road accidents reported in the last couple of hours, up Gingin way?'

'I can find out for you.' He sounded relatively approachable. Probably had a few already.

'What's wrong?' he repeated.

This time she noted a slight breathlessness in his voice.

'Sante's gone missing.'

'What do you mean? When?'

'He said he'd be here at six and he's still not arrived.'

'What time is it now? It's only… can't read my watch in this light…'

'Past eight o'clock.'

'Is that all? He might have got held up somewhere.'

'He would have called … besides … we're leaving for a holiday tomorrow afternoon. Look, can you check for me? I'm worried.' And she hung up. She was in no mood for arguing with him. But she did note that he too sounded concerned. In the simmer of her anxieties, this thought brought a bubble of pleasure.

*

A quick call to Central revealed nothing. There had been a couple of accidents, one on Great Northern Highway: a semi-trailer had run off the road and the driver escaped with minor injuries. Nothing on Marzano. While reporting this to Sara-Jane over the phone, Russell remembered the conversation with Zlatan, earlier in the day. It made him run to the car.

As he crested the hill to the house, Russell was met by the acrid smell of burning rubber. His heart began to race. *Easy, treat this like any other job*. But that didn't do the trick. His head spun. Following the scent trail, he veered right along the track where, over the darker silhouette of the big rock, loomed a half moon. He dipped his headlights and saw, next to the rock wall, the gutted remains of a car. He had seen enough wrecked cars to realize this was something else.

Russell got out, leaving the car lights on, and taking a torch with him. Sooty stones, shards of wood and bits of metal littered the courtyard. It must have been a mighty explosion.

The outline of the vehicle appeared like a smouldering mound upon a dusky background, over which sat a halo of blue smoke. Whose car was it? The question was merely a diversion from a thought worming itself into his head. He didn't want it. He must keep his cool, wear the detective cap. *Think, Russ, think*.

Navigating his way around various bits of debris, Russell reached the car and shone the torch. To his relief there was no sign of the driver. Water swirled around the soles of his boots. He followed the flow on the paved floor, skipping over puddles and skirting around litter he reached to where a stream of water was bubbling to the surface from under a pile of rubble. Russell guessed the source was a burst water pipe inside the grotto, whose entrance was blocked by debris from an imploded side wall. The light beam revealed a charred stack over which the iron gate had collapsed. The detective felt the immense darkness press upon him.

A night creature shrieked, and then, from within, a wheeze responded.

He clambered over rubble, feeling a gash on his knee as he slipped on a smooth damp surface; he shone the torch over the pile and there, trapped beneath the collapsed gate, was an elbow jutting out of the iron grid.

Russell proceeded to remove bits of stone, wooden bats and plaster; tossing them over his head into the dark, making intrusive sounds as they fell. He stopped. As if on cue, the body beneath stirred, the whimpering was unmistakable. Underneath a wooden beam lay the figure of a man, face-down, caught by the collapsing roof, not fleeing, but running in, his head just centimetres away from a ripple of silt washed down by the flow of water, which threatened to drown him. With the face blackened by damp soot it was difficult to distinguish the features, but he knew the shape of the head, the texture of the hair. He felt the unmistakable proximity to someone who loved him. The recognition overwhelmed him.

He took out his mobile and called. 'Send an ambulance and a rescue team!' He heard himself yell, his voice choking.

A gash had opened where the man's thigh was crushed against the side pillar at the entrance, pinning him to the ground. Just as well, because, had he been able to move, he would have upset the pile above, causing the weight to come crashing down on his head. The beam that trapped him also protected him. First thing: he had to remove the debris above and around the beam to loosen and free it. Normally, he would have waited for the rescue squad to arrive; this wasn't his job, he had no training in it, it wasn't his responsibility. But this situation was different, the usual platitudes that governed his actions no longer applied here. He had to act to save his son.

After spending a life running from what he had done, from himself, he had come to the end of an alley whose way was blocked by a mirror. There was no way out but for him to stand before it and look at himself. The prospect was both as terrifying and alluring as death. Staring him in the face was a pointless self-indulgent life trapped within the confines of ego, resentment and pride. Regret made him shiver and shook him out of his paralysis.

He sat the torch on the ledge of the cave, and got down to work, removing fragments of bats, plaster, sheets of wood whose varnish he could still smell beneath the pungency of cinders. Having cleared the top layer, he started digging away with his hands, not caring about cuts, until his hand struck something sharp, a metal edge and a gash appeared on the lower edge of his hand.

'Fuck it.' Russell winced.

No matter, the piece of metal, part of the guttering, came in handy for scraping away the dirt. He cleared a space around him. He had the strange sensation that with each item he removed, he was disinterring a new self: the self he could have been, that he wanted to be. His fingernails got caught in some piece of garment, touched the surface of damp skin, followed by the comforting feel of Sante's breath on the inside of his wrist. He lowered his head and gently placed an ear over his chest, listening to the thumping of his heart.

The boy would survive. Tears squeezed out and streamed down his cheeks. A tremor shook his body and a forty-four year weight seemed to fall off him. Oh, what a release! What joy! He wanted to embrace the whole world, just hold it right there. He wanted to hang on to that moment forever.

'Water.' It was Sante.

When Russell came back, water cup in one hand, torch in the other, car beams lit the drive from the highway. It wasn't the ambulance; the headlights of Sara-Jane's car spilled across the courtyard, lighting the way to where Russell was kneeling, cup raised before him as if he were about to drink a toast.

'Is he…?' Sara-Jane could not finish.

'He'll be fine.' Russell's voice had never sounded so calm, his words never so welcome. 'I thought you were the ambulance.'

The words drowned in a sea of relief that her brother was alive, and amazement at seeing Sante's head on Russell's lap.

When the ambulance did arrive it caught in its light beam an unlikely trio, comprised of Sante held in the arms of a burly man, with a young woman kneeling down over them, her shadow launched across the foreground. The figures formed some kind of synthesis, a symmetrical whole, almost … a family portrait caught by an Old Master.

*

Sara-Jane and Russell watched the back of the ambulance disappear down the highway.

'Do you think he'll be alright?'

'Yeah, of course.' Russell sounded confident. 'He'll be fine, he's young.' There was a hint of regret. Was he thinking of his wasted life?

'Are you coming to the hospital?'

Russell turned to her surprised. 'Me? I don't think he'll

want me there. I don't think so.'

'I think you're wrong there, Russell.'

Children always want their parents, she thought, even if it's only to blame them.

*

Sante Marzano had survived unscathed 'by the skin of his teeth', quipped the headline. In Sicily they might have said, 'through a miracle'. In Australia miracles were harder to come by, but Sara-Jane, a sceptic by nature, was now inclined to emulate Don Alfio and hedge her bets.

Russell came to the hospital, bulked up with beer-gut and machismo, and a lifetime's attitude fuelled by anger, born out of a long suppressed need for touching and loving, ever ready to transmute into violence. He was there to play the good brave police officer for the cameras, since the media had appropriated the story and needed a protagonist. And so, Russell Toohey, whose life was precariously balanced on the edge of the law, became, for a few seconds, its icon: a reluctant hero.

He found the role challenging. Out of habit his uniform flagged a warning. *Keep your distance, the rescue was part of my job. Nothing's changed.*

He shook hands with Sante in front of the camera, while the presenter gave her commentary on Russell Toohey's bravery. No mention of their blood connection. None of them wanted to be outed. To Sara-Jane, watching the story on the evening news that night, it seemed like fiction on reality television. The reality? Well, things do change, with or without our consent. The reality was far too complicated for public consumption. But isn't that always the case? She thought.

Russell presented Sante with flowers, perfectly arranged for TV footage. Folk in their living rooms would be gratified to be served a feel-good story with their evening meal. The real story was more subtle, elusive, hidden away in the midst of the anemones and the blood-coloured gerberas. The real story was told by an olive branch: silver, unassuming, overwhelmed by all that flamboyance of colour. It had been placed there by Russell. The urgency to put it there came out of knowing that he had less than six months to live.

*

Danny O'Rourke always knew he didn't have much luck in life, although he must have always hoped for it, or he would not have spent so much time at the casino or the race course. Now, on learning that mad old Franzetti had not left a will, he thought he spied luck's eyewink at him, from the corner of a golden frame. After all, he was the Old Man's closest relative.

Just when he started reckoning how many millions he would come into, and how he was going to spend them, the shock news hit him via the media. Franzetti's empire had debts so large that his creditors would be lucky to receive twenty cents in the dollar of what they were owed. In other words, Clem Franzetti was bankrupt. As a consequence, the olive grove would have to be sold, probably to a cooperative which planned to demolish the stables. A modern crusher would be built, to service the booming olive oil industry of the region.

Danny O'Rourke would have cried in self-pity if only

he knew how. This was a final confirmation that fortune was indeed a bitch. Just think: a lifetime of sucking up to someone, only to be screwed one more time, even when that person was dead. Yeah, the last laugh went to Old Clem Franzetti, as always.

37

Carissima,

   Manderò una copia di questo messaggio anche a tuo fratello perchè …

My dear,

   I'm sending a copy of this message to your brother, because what I have to say concerns both of you. I am delighted to hear that Sante has reconciled with his natural father, but very saddened to learn the gentleman is seriously ill. No matter what happened in the past, he is the link between the two of you. For that reason alone his life has been invaluable and this reconciliation will make your bond stronger. Actually, one only has to think of you and Sante to conclude that goodness must have resided in this man's heart. And because this is beginning to sound like a homily, I will change the subject.

   You might both be interested to learn that the whole of the region, from the hills of San Sisto to Milazzo and beyond, is abuzz with excitement because the rumour has spread that Mimmo is going to marry Federica Fresina. This is big news because Federica is the daughter of Tindaro Fresina, yes of the rival Cefalù clan. So, it seems like a marriage made in mafia heaven, for it is designed to make peace between the two factions. I take little notice of such rumours usually, though I admit to having a weakness for gossip, but this has the confirmation from the protagonist himself.

   Mimmo has confided in me (yes, thanks to you I have that sort of familiarity with Mimmo) that although his heart beats as strongly as ever for *Signorina* Sara-Jane, there are certain responsibilities that have fallen upon him, which he cannot avoid. He confesses he cannot love Federica in quite the same way as 'the Australian beauty' (understandable, given that Federica is decidedly plain, potentially mamma-sized and with a demeanour tending on the dour). Mimmo believes what she lacks in beauty she compensates for in character, and that kind of love tends to take on an amorphous growth. I am willing to give Mimmo the benefit of my hope.

All of that is a lengthy way of saying it is safe for you to come back to us, Sara-Jane. Indeed, I must reveal to you (Sante already knows) that it will be my birthday next October 21, and we are having a small celebration at Taormina. It gives me absolutely no joy to reveal to you that I am about to reach the deplorable age of fifty-three. So it's an occasion for both of you to come and commiserate with me. The years of life's enjoyment are fast disappearing, what a tragedy! However I promise not to be lugubrious. Indeed, I have come to the conclusion that it's all the more reason to make the most of what's left of them, hence my wish to celebrate with the people I love. So, Sante and Sara-Jane, I give you no choice: you must be in Taormina with us.

Vi attendo,
Vi abbraccio,
Alfio

38

Tourists milled around the bus parked on the flat-topped rise, overlooking the gorge. Peaks of ochre, grey and tile-red rose from a fresh water pool under a brittle sun. Around the water an oasis of tall gums tended skyward, triumphant over a planetary landscape. A screeching flock of black cockatoos in spear formation lanced through the sky. On reaching over the gorge they spread out at the flanks to form a semicircle, before coming to rest in the foliage of the tall gums. An elderly man, a Canadian in cargo shorts and peaked cap, with kangaroo and emu emblazoned on the front, took off his sandals and waded into the pool.

'What are you thinking about?' asked Sante.

'San Sisto.'

'Strange connection.'

Of course they were different worlds, poles apart, and yet there must have been an association. More and more she saw this world in relation to the other, and vice versa. For this reason alone her first trip to Sicily had been valuable. Seeing one place through the lens of the other revealed previously-unknown nooks to her; shades never seen.

'I too have been thinking about San Sisto.'

Sara-Jane held her breath. 'Do you think you'll go back for good?'

'No, I don't think so, Sicily for me will always be home, but Sicily is the past, I want to seek out my future here.' And yet, even before he had finished the phrase, he realised how facile it sounded.

In real life things were never that simple, life could not be contained in a neat aphorism of time and space, or segmented into definitions of colour. Any one moment of one's existence contained all the flow of time and all the colours of the spectrum, in ever-redefining hues. One's past, with its joys and hurts, is always in the present, as is the future with its dreams, hopes and fears. Sicily and Australia were in him, as he was part of them. He was a conduit through which time and space flowed freely, yet precisely, in the chaos of existence. In him Australia came before Sicily – for this was the country of his conception. Sicily was the setting of his earliest memories, but this remote galactic landscape spoke of times more ancient than the Mediterranean.

Sicily brought them together; it took a pool in the Kimberley to crystallize the significance of that event. This moment was always there, in Sara-Jane's consciousness, waiting to surface. Nothing is ever created anew; it's merely recovered and remodelled. Everything is already made, always present beneath the surface of time and space. She had now reached a milestone, a marker in her journey, one that needed to be dwelt upon, before it propelled both of them forward, to their own destinies.

The cameras of the tourists were out, fingers clicked away in a desperate effort to record the moment, to still time and frame it.

Sante smiled. 'We forgot our camera.'

'It doesn't matter.' Sara-Jane meant it. There was no need. A camera recorded the image, the impression, the illusion. They would take something far more important: experience, that wonderful conflation of place, time and feeling. Experiences were the signposts of memory. What they shared was absolute, permanent. Long after they had moved on, pursued their careers, perhaps married and had a family… each would remain the touchstone of the other. It would suffice for each to know that the other existed and would be thinking of them.

People on the bus had initially assumed they were a couple. A woman with a perfectly set hairdo remarked to her companion that it was unusual for siblings of their age to take a holiday together. So Sante tried to explain things: that they had only found each other recently, that they were compensating for lost time. But Sara-Jane told him there was no point. Did it matter what people thought? Her euphoria made her daring, mischievous. To live fully one must not be afraid to enter grey territory. Only in that indeterminate space could one experience the intoxication of true freedom. Above all, one had to never be afraid to love, to open up to hurt, if it came to that.

Sara-Jane held out her hand. 'Come Sante, I'll race you down.'

They ran hand in hand, leaping over stones and low bushes, raising an orange dust behind them. When they got to the edge of the pool, they knew what to do. They dived in, fully clothed, and sought each other in the newly-muddied water, exchanged an embrace, and emerged still clinging to each other.

People watched and interpreted, giving each other looks. So let them. For the moment they bubbled with anticipation, because they realized – knew without exchanging a word – that they had come separately to the same decision. In a few days they were going to Sicily… together.

Translations Glossary

Note: *Some of the phrases in the text are in Sicilian dialect, others in standard Italian*

Reference page
8a Sara, where are you?
8b Sara isn't here. She's gone. She's not here.
8c Where is that child? Where is she? She's vanished
8d Here I am!
9 Look Sarina, I'm going to show you a beautiful thing.
10 You're worse than a kid.
17 Dear Grand-parents, I'm Sara-Jane, do you remember me? In two weeks' time, that is from October the 10th, I will be coming to Sicily. It would be a great pleasure for me to visit you. Here is my address: Hotel Ruggeri, Station Avenue, 71, Milazzo
24 *Mother, give me one hundred lire*
   As I want to go to America.
   I will give you one hundred lire
   But to America you will never go.
83 *parente* = relative
83 Does your father not feel well?
104 That Australian business.
112a Can you hear me?
112b Come on, Ennia, I'm speaking to you, can you hear me?
114 Wind at Tindari
   Tindari, tranquil you are
   Among wide hills reclining over the waters
   Of the sweet isles of the god
   Today your memory assails me
   And you cleave in my heart...

132 To a good listener, few words suffice.

133 Come, come. Let me introduce Mimmo Urzi.

141a Do you know who this is?

141b Yes of course, this is Sheryl.

141c Sheryl? What does Nonna mean?

146 Hurry up, my child. I have to go and cook for your grandfather.

147 *Provalo* = try it.

149 Mum, what is she saying?

150 Good thing she's gone.

151 What a pity!

153 Oh my goodness!

155/6 Stop him for God's sake. He'll hurt himself.

158 Goodness, what a strange character. What's come over him?

177 Who, Mimmo? God forbid, it's a good thing you are leaving tomorrow, Sara.

184a *Ma che succede?* = What's going on?

184b Mum, the Madonna is very beautiful.

204 So sensitive, so affectionate.